The
IMMORTAL
REALM

Also by Frewin Jones

The Faerie Path
The Lost Queen
The Seventh Daughter
(also published as The Sorcerer King)
Warrior Princess

The
IMMORTAL
REALM

Book Four of The FAERIE PATH

FREWIN JONES

HARPER TEEN

An Imprint of HarperCollinsPublishers

HarperTeen is an imprint of HarperCollins Publishers.

The Immortal Realm
Copyright © 2009 by Working Partners Limited
Series created by Working Partners Limited

Library of Congress Cataloging-in-Publication Data
Jones, Frewin.
    The Immortal Realm / Frewin Jones. — 1st ed.
        p.   cm. — (The faerie path ; bk. 4)
    Summary: Princess Tania thinks she has finally found a way to unite the world of Faerie
with the modern world, but her beloved Immortal Realm is threatened when a grave illness
takes hold of the kingdom and she must find a way to save it.
    ISBN 978-0-06-087155-0 (trade bdg.)
    [1. Faeries—Fiction.   2. Princesses—Fiction.   3. Sick—Fiction.   4. Fantasy.]   I. Title.
PZ7.J71Im   2009   2008051831
[Fic]—dc22   CIP
                                                                                                AC

Typography by Al Cetta
09   10   11   12   13   CG/RRDB   10   9   8   7   6   5   4   3   2
❖
First Edition

For Chris Snowdon

Faeries tread the Faerie path
One sister lost, another bonds in wedded bliss
Yet shadows gather in the Faerie night
As deadly as a serpent's kiss

A half-breed princess torn by doubt
A love betrayed, a promise given to break or keep
As sickness stalks the timeless land
Immortal Realm is drowned in peril deep

Part One:

The Day After

Happy Ever

After

I

Princess Tania stood on the green hilltop, her face to the west and her eyes half closed against the setting sun. For the first time in weeks she felt at peace. She twined her fingers with those of her beloved Edric, and all her burdens washed away on the Faerie air that came in warm from the Western Ocean, sea-scented, pure, and clear.

She opened her eyes again, gazing at Edric, watching the way the breeze lifted his dark blond hair. He turned and smiled, and she lost herself for a few blissful moments in the warmth of his brown eyes.

"What are you thinking?" he asked.

"Nothing at all," Tania replied, squeezing his hand. "I'm just enjoying having you to myself for a while." She laughed softly, resting her head on his shoulder. "When was the last time we were alone together?"

"I don't remember. Not since you brought Clive and Mary through, that's for sure."

Tania nodded. "That's three weeks, then," she said.

Clive and Mary Palmer: Tania's Mortal parents, the mother and father of the human half of her nature. Oh, but she had caused them such anxiety and fear when all this had started.

First there had been the boating accident on the eve of her sixteenth birthday. Then had come her disappearance from hospital and her reappearance three days later, telling tall tales to hide the truth of what had happened to her. And the second time she had vanished, she had left her home in chaos: a Mercedes Benz crashed in the garden, the back door ripped off its hinges, broken windows, dead starlings strewn over the kitchen floor, and her own bedroom door hacked and split open by sword blows.

And then her sudden return with Edric in the middle of the night. The need to convince her parents to have faith in her despite all that had happened. The four of them in her bedroom, holding hands, her mother desperately anxious, her father about to explode with anger—then that simple side step that had taken them out of the Mortal World and into the Immortal Realm of Faerie.

Tania smiled at the memory. "All things considered, Mum and Dad have done really well," she said. "When I first got here, I thought this whole place was one big crazy dream."

"They had help adjusting," Edric said, slipping his arm around her shoulders. "You were all on your own . . . at the start, anyway."

"I guess." Tania fingered the pendant necklace that

Edric had given her: a token of true love—a teardrop of black onyx, warm and shiny and smooth to the touch.

The sounds of the festivities carried up to them from the valley that lay at their backs: laughter and music and happy, calling voices.

"We should go back soon, I suppose," Edric said. "We'll be missed."

"Not just yet."

Tania pressed herself against him, wrapping her arms around his back, breathing in his scent. She felt his hand stroking her long red hair. She tilted her head. His lips were soft on her forehead, then lightly kissing the closed lids of her green eyes, brushing along her cheek, moving gently to her mouth.

She came out of the kiss and opened her eyes. Turning in the sheltering circle of his arms, she gazed westward over the ocean. She knew that beyond the horizon the foul, sorcerous island of Lyonesse brooded in distant waters. It was almost impossible to believe that only three short weeks ago, she had fought and triumphed over the King of that dreadful land.

And now all she wanted was to be in Edric's arms and to drift away forever on the enchanted Faerie evening.

The sun hung low on the horizon, a golden globe that spilled its burnished light onto the ocean so that the waves seemed flecked with amber fire. At their feet the hill sloped down in rugged terraces to a cliff edge that fell away to tide-washed rocks of ancient granite.

On this momentous evening it seemed as if the sun had turned everything to gold. The air glowed with it, heavy and rich as honey; every grass blade was limned with flaxen light; every pebble along the shoreline seemed gilded.

Tania's heart was almost too full for her to speak. "I don't ever want this moment to end," she whispered. "This is so perfect."

She felt Edric's arms tighten around her. "I want to ask you something," he murmured, his lips close to her ear.

"Ask away," she said.

But before he could speak again, the call of bright horns came echoing up from the valley behind them.

"What's that?" she asked, breaking loose from Edric's embrace.

"It's the nuptial carillon," Edric said. "We need to get down there right away. It's time for Cordelia and Bryn to perform the final ritual of marriage."

"Okay, but what were you going to ask me?"

"It can wait."

Subduing her curiosity, Tania took his hand and together they ran back down the winding earthen path that had brought them up out of the long green valley of Leiderdale.

Tania's heart leaped at the vista that spread out below them.

The wide valley was filled with tents and pavilions of brightly colored silk and satin. The flags and banners of many Houses of Faerie fluttered in the breeze. Above the largest canopy floated the standards of the King and Queen of Faerie. Oberon's colors—the blazing yellow sun on a field of sapphire—and the pennant of his wife, Queen Titania—a white full moon on a background of deep blue.

All of the Faerie court had come here to the Earldom of Dinsel to celebrate the marriage of Princess Cordelia to Bryn Lightfoot. The Royal Palace had emptied and its lords and ladies had traveled to this western promontory to witness the joining of the fourth daughter of the Royal House of Aurealis to the handsome young man from the Earldom of Weir.

Bride and groom had first met only a few short weeks ago in the distant hills of Weir when Bryn had saved Cordelia, Tania, and Edric from the fierce unicorns of Caer Liel. Bryn Lightfoot lived alone on the moors; he had no family to attend the wedding and his only friends had been the beasts and birds of the hills and valleys of his wild homeland. Cordelia loved all animals and had the gift of speaking with them, and an instant rapport had blossomed between her and the wild young man who lived safely and alone among the dangerous northern unicorns.

The whole length of the valley of Leiderdale was hung with garlands of wildflowers, and the air brimmed with their scent while white and pink petals floated in the breeze before settling in the grass, thick as snowdrifts.

Tania and Edric leaped over stones and through long grass as they made their way down into Leiderdale. All the people had gathered in the center of the valley. The close-packed crowd had split into two, leaving a wide grassy aisle that led from the royal canopy all the way to the great gray, flat-topped stone known as the High Chantrelle.

The great Singing Stone of Leiderdale rose out of the grass, its eight sides so sharp and smooth that axes might have hewn them. Its platform rose to shoulder height and glittered with minerals.

The sun was out of sight now, and the long valley was falling into deep, sumptuous shadow. A few torches began mystically to ignite, their light spreading until points of rosy flame could be seen dancing along the entire expanse of Leiderdale.

A hush descended, a quietness threaded through with anticipation and suspense. Happy faces turned toward Tania and Edric as they made their way through the crowd, pressing on hand-in-hand until they came to the front of the congregation.

The tent flaps of the royal canopy were drawn back. The long-awaited moment had come. A flock of white doves burst from the opening, rising high into the sky and circling the tent. At the same moment huge flocks of birds sprang from the hilltops all around, filling the air with their chatter.

Tania gazed upward as the birds wheeled across the darkening sky. They raced over the heads of the watchers, darting from one hilltop to the other, splitting into arrowhead formations that reeled out like spinning threads.

"Do you think Cordelia organized all this?" Tania said breathlessly. "She never mentioned it to me."

"I don't think so," Edric replied. "The wild birds are here because they love her—as do all the animals of Faerie. The bond between the princess and all beasts is strong; they're celebrating her happiness."

The flocks parted and the sky emptied. The hilltops resounded to the hum of a hundred thousand wings. As quickly as it had begun, the sky-dance was over and the hillsides were black with the birds, silent now, still and watchful.

A lamb emerged from the tent. It turned its woolly head back and bleated once before continuing. In its wake came a procession of other animals: cats and dogs and wolves and martens and foxes and beavers and wild pigs. Small southern unicorns trotted along behind, their hides as blue as snow under the moon, their horns like silver. And with them came ponies and deer and a bear and a twelve-point stag so tall that it had to dip its majestic head to pass under the canopy's awning.

And then Cordelia and Bryn appeared, smiling as they walked slowly between two of the wild unicorns of Weir. The crowd erupted into cheering and applause.

"Happiness eternal to the princess and her groom!" came a shout. "May the stars shine forever upon your joyful union!"

More voices called out, wishing bliss on the smiling couple. "May the sun and moon bless you for all time!"

When Cordelia had first spoken of her intention to marry Bryn, Tania had been taken aback by the speed at which they were moving their relationship forward. Even when she had come to terms with it, she found the idea of all the pomp and ceremony of a Faerie wedding overwhelming.

But now her heart leaped at the sight of her Faerie sister smiling radiantly, dressed for once in something other than her beloved brown dress. Her wedding dress was a full-skirted gown of iridescent silk taffeta that moved with a shimmer of sky blue and gold, embroidered at the bodice with gold thread and studded with sapphires and tawny agates. The sleeves were long, lace-trimmed, and pointed, decorated at the cuff with fine needlework. Resting in her red-gold hair was a coronet of white yarrow blossom. A broad, flowing train glided along behind her, the delicate gauze floating over the grass as she paced solemnly at Bryn Lightfoot's side.

Her groom was dressed in a forest green tabard edged with gold and with three unicorns embroidered on the chest. Beneath it he wore a shirt of ivory silk. His leggings were of oakwood brown and his boots of supple leather. Around his unruly black hair he wore a garland of russet ivy, and as he walked the aisle of grass with his bride, his dark eyes shone with joy.

"Way to go, Cordie!" Tania shouted, lifting her voice above all the others, tears pricking behind her eyes as the procession passed where she and Edric were standing.

Cordelia turned her head, hearing Tania's voice in the throng; then, catching Tania's eye, she pulled a wry face as if to say, *Look at me in all this finery. What a sight I must be!*

"You look beautiful," Tania called.

King Oberon and Queen Titania stood under the shadow of the entrance to the tent, their faces glowing with happiness as they watched bride and groom walk toward the High Chantrelle. Their majesty was undeniable, the King in a white doublet and hose, his Queen in a satin gown that shone like new-fallen snow.

Tania turned, trying to find faces in the crowds. Ah! There. A little way along on the other side of the aisle she could see her sister Hopie with her husband, Lord Brython. And Earl Marshal Cornelius, brother to the King, was close by with his two tall stepsons and their mother, the beautiful Marchioness Lucina.

"Love Immortal while Faerie lasts," called Edric. He looked at Tania, his eyes shining. "Love for all time!"

She laughed for pure joy. "Love for all time!" she echoed.

She caught sight of her Mortal mother, dressed in a coral-colored Faerie gown, smiling and clapping as Cordelia and Bryn walked past. And just behind her mother, she saw her father, looking a little uncomfortable in his borrowed Faerie clothes. Even at a distance Tania could see that his face was flushed; he had not been well for a few days now. He passed it off as a mild summer cold, but all the same, Tania thought, it must be wretched to be the only ill person in a land where there was no sickness and no disease and where no one ever grew old and died. Poor Dad! As soon as the ceremony was over, she'd go and make a fuss over him.

Tania waved, trying to get her parents' attention, but there was too much noise and activity for them to notice her. Soon Cordelia and Bryn were almost at the end of the aisle. As they approached the High Chantrelle, the animals split into two lines, one circling the great gray stone from the left, the other from the right, so that by the time bride and groom came to the stone, it was ringed with waiting animals.

Five stone steps led to the wide, polished summit of the rock. Cordelia lifted the hem of her dress and picked her way carefully to the top. Bryn followed behind, gathering her train and then spreading it around her so that it foamed at her feet.

Tania and Edric made their way closer to the High Chantrelle, the people gladly opening a path for them as they moved through the tight-packed crowds.

Cordelia and Bryn turned to face west. They stood side-by-side looking back down the petal-strewn aisle to where Oberon and Titania were standing.

An absolute silence fell.

Tania held her breath. She had never witnessed a Faerie marriage before, but she knew that this was the final act, after which her sister and the unicorn friend would be truly bound in wedlock. It had taken three days so far, beginning with the Hand-Fasting Ceremony in the Hall of Light in the Royal Palace. Tania had found that sacrament difficult to watch; it had stirred too many bad memories. She, too, had once been betrothed and had come close to having her own Faerie wedding—with Lord Gabriel Drake of the House of Weir as her groom, a wicked man who had almost brought Faerie to ruin.

Many other ceremonials for Cordelia and Bryn had taken place over the following two days, and then everyone had boarded ships to take them to Dinsel for the final celebration. The Royal Family had sailed aboard the *Cloud Scudder*, the King's own galleon with its silver-white decks and spars and sails.

And now all that remained was the Song of Betrothal.

Cordelia's voice rang out strongly through the silence. "Alas, I cannot sing as well as my beloved sister Zara would have done," she called. "But to her sacred memory I dedicate all that takes place here, knowing this to be the region of Faerie that was most dear to her heart."

Tania bit her lip; the death of Zara was still too raw, too vivid in her mind's eye for her to think of it without much pain. Edric's fingers tightened around hers in a token of understanding. She was comforted, but even though she knew her valiant, carefree sister was at rest now in the Blessed Land of Avalon, she couldn't help but grieve for her.

Tania's thoughts faded as movements on the surrounding hilltops caught her attention. All along the rolling hills that cupped the valley of Leiderdale, animals were gathering. There were sheep and goats and cattle and oxen; there were deer and wolves and bears and wild boar; and in among them were smaller beasts, foxes and badgers and dogs and wild cats. All of them stood silhouetted against the sky, looking into the valley, paying reverence to the princess who loved and honored them so much.

The King's deep voice welled out. "Sing!"

And the Queen's voice rang out also. "Sing!"

And Cordelia and Bryn sang.

> *With eyes raised to the stars*
> *There is no fear of loss*
> *The light that shines afar*
> *Reveals the bridge to cross*
> *Where lovers meet at last*
> *And never more do part*
> *And seen through a soul of glass*
> *Your warm and beating heart.*
> *And I will guide you there*
> *Beyond this shallow land*

What lady is more fair
What lord to take your hand
As ever on we dance
Among high heaven's host
And I see at every glance
The one I love the most

As they sang, their voices echoed, growing in strength and cadence, rolling along the valley, splitting into descant and countermelody so that they sounded like a choir of heavenly voices.

And when the song ended, the reverberations of the phantom choir continued to rebound across the valley, gradually fading back to silence under a dusky, star-speckled sky.

Tania snatched a breath, realizing that she had hardly been breathing during the beautiful song.

The silence was broken suddenly by the voices of the animals on the hilltops. They all began at once to bleat and howl and roar and bellow and bark and bay, filling the oncoming night with a riot of noise. Cordelia lifted her arms to them, turning slowly on the High Chantrelle, saluting the animals as they called down to her.

Tania squeezed Edric's hand. "Wow!" she said.

The sound of the animals died away, and the beasts on the hilltops turned and departed into the night.

There was applause as Cordelia and Bryn stepped hand-in-hand down from the High Chantrelle as husband and wife. Cheering crowds instantly surrounded them.

"There's more to come," Edric told her. "Something amazing."

Tania looked at him. "More amazing than *that*?"

He nodded. "I was present for the wedding of Princess Hopie and Lord Brython," he said, his eyes shining. "Watch and wait!"

Tania did not have to wait long. She was aware that the crowds were quieting again and moving back to allow someone to pass through. Oberon and Titania climbed up to the High Chantrelle. They stood on the glittering summit, hand-in-hand, turning to the west as Cordelia and Bryn had done.

"Here it comes," Edric whispered in her ear.

The King and Queen began to sing, Oberon's voice a deep bass, resonant and powerful, while Titania's rose above it in a rich, full-throated contralto.

Blessed be the night!
Blessed be the puissance strong of the sinews of
*   the land!*
Blessed moon and stars!
We call upon the potent powers; we take them in
*   our hands*
Sentinels of the night, singing as stars do sing
The clash of cymbals, the beating of drums
Moon-mad men and merry maids
Leap like rivers into the skies!
This is to those of wonder's dove

This is a merry once
This comes on wings of raven sheen
This is the evening dance
Of those who wake in shadows

As they sang, a white light began to grow about them, a swirling, circling light that had flecks of every color in it. It spun around them, growing brighter and moving faster, the colored flecks stretching until they were rainbow rings that almost hid the King and Queen, sheathing them in a whirl of flashing brilliance. And then the column of light exploded up into the night, bathing the sky in washes of color that spread like fluttering curtains.

Tania tilted her head back, her eyes full of the streaming, swooping banners of rainbow light. She had never seen such colors before. The lights frolicked across the sky, weaving and pulsing, twining and threading together, from the deepest of throbbing violets through infinitely shaded blues and greens and yellows to vibrant reds.

And as the flying lights filled the sky, the Faerie folk began to dance, moving through a world that was bathed in shimmering color. Tania became caught up in the dance, laughing with happiness, holding hands with Edric.

She glimpsed one unmoving figure, standing apart on the hillside. Her Mortal father, his expression uneasy, his brows knitted as though the lights hurt his eyes. But she was swept away from him, her eyes full of rainbows, her hair streaming out.

After a timeless whirl of ecstasy, the dance came to an end. The lights faded, and Tania found herself gazing dizzily at the starry sky of a deep Faerie night.

Edric was right: There *had* been more to come. Something amazing!

Tania walked through the crowds, arm-in-arm with her Mortal mother. She had left Edric talking with Titus and Corin, the stepsons of the earl marshal—he had understood that she needed to be alone with her mother for a little while. The wedding celebrations were in full flow, the festivities taking place by the light of torches and blazing bonfires. The last glimmerings of Oberon and Titania's enchanted lights flickered on the hilltops, glossing everything with delicate hues.

The valley was a scene of boisterous and noisy merrymaking. Courtiers danced to the music of lute, rebec, and krumhorns while others applauded the antics of tumblers and jugglers. Still more were being entertained by troubadours, storytellers, and jesters, and some were gathered near the feast tents, enjoying meats roasted on the bone and new-baked bread, succulent sweetmeats and candied delicacies.

Cordelia and Bryn were dancing in a great circle of smiling onlookers. They held each other tightly, spinning across the grass as the music grew, and Cordelia's long gossamer train rose and swirled about them like a fluttering banner.

"Come, all shall be merry!" cried Cordelia, and the audience sprang forward to join in the dance.

Faerie children played everywhere, hovering and flying above the ground on their translucent wings. Tania envied them their freedom—she had memories of flying; they had come to her in dreams or visions, but they had still felt achingly real to her. She knew that when they reached the age of ten or twelve, these children's wings would wither away and be lost and they would be earthbound like their parents. But for now, as Tania watched them, they darted in and out among the adults, shouting and laughing and turning cartwheels in the air.

"So?" Tania asked her mother. "What do you think of all this so far? Any good?"

Her mother smiled. "It's overwhelming," she said.

"Isn't it, though?" She squeezed her mother's arm, trying to quell the anxiety that knotted in her stomach, knowing she needed to tell her mother something *huge*. "I'm so glad you and Dad were able to come here and experience it all." She gave her mother a sideways glance. It was still a little odd to see her mother's face above the frills and lacework of a Faerie gown, her slender features framed by short dark curls, her brown eyes intelligent and knowing. "Am I forgiven for keeping it secret at first?"

"What could you have said that we would have

believed?" her mother replied. "We would probably have thought you'd gone batty if you'd tried to tell us the truth." She paused and looked around. "I'm standing right here and I can still hardly believe it."

"Tell me about it," said Tania. She turned, taking her mother by both hands and looking into her face. "I've been putting this off ever since you came here," she began, wishing there was some way of avoiding this revelation. "But there's something I have to tell you."

Her mother gave her a sympathetic smile. "I already know, sweetheart," she said.

Tania frowned. "You already know what?"

"That you have to choose between our world and Faerie," said her mother. "And that you've chosen Faerie."

Tania stared at her in dismay.

Mrs. Palmer laughed softly. "What did you think Titania and I have been talking about these past weeks, the weather?" She gripped Tania's hands. "It's okay, sweetheart, really it is. Who wouldn't choose all this? Listen, your dad and I were fully expecting you to go away to university soon, anyway—and then you'd have wanted to set yourself up in a place of your own." She laughed. "You're just leaving home a little sooner than we anticipated, and you're going a bit farther away than we expected. I had been hoping for Oxford or Edinburgh. Oxford would have been nice; we could have driven up to see you quite easily." Her eyes sparkled. "I don't suppose driving to Faerie is an option."

Tania felt a huge burst of love for her mother. She

hugged her tightly. "Mum—you're totally amazing!"

"Aren't I, though?" Mrs. Palmer said. "And I'm looking on the positive side: At least you won't be arriving on our doorstep once a month with a great big sack of laundry like most kids do when they first leave home. At least, I hope you won't; I have no idea how to wash these Faerie clothes."

"I'll come home as often as I can," Tania said, ignoring the people who were coming and going all around them, not caring that her eyes were brimming with tears. "But what are we going to tell everyone? What am I going to tell Jade?" In the Mortal World, Jade Anderson was Tania's best friend. Before all this craziness had happened, Tania and Jade had always confided *everything* to each other.

"How do you stay best friends with someone when a whole huge part of your life has to be kept secret from them?" she wondered. "I can't tell her. There's no way she'd be able to keep something like this to herself. But if I *don't* tell her . . ."

Her mother patted her shoulder. "We'll think of something."

"You don't understand. Jade will know if I'm keeping stuff from her. She has a total radar for that kind of thing. She'll hate me if she thinks I'm shutting her out. And it's not just her, is it? What do we tell the people at school next term? They'll want to know why I've suddenly stopped turning up."

"We can tell everyone you're taking a year abroad," said her mother. "We'll say you've gone sheep farming in New Zealand or that you're getting work experience on an oil rig or doing scientific research in the Arctic." She looked into Tania's eyes. "Listen, you've had to cope with a whole lot of impossible stuff over the last couple of months. Don't try and figure everything out in one go—it'll drive you crazy. Take things one at a time." She smiled gently. "That's what your father and I are doing."

Tania frowned at the mention of her Mortal father. "Where is Dad? How's he doing?"

There was a burst of laughter and applause. They were passing a crowd gathered around a troop of acrobats. The tumblers had formed two tall pyramids, the uppermost performer of each pyramid balancing upside down on the heads of two others while their feet juggled gold and silver balls with liquid precision.

"I think he went to lie down in our tent," her mother replied, clapping with the crowd. "He's feeling a bit sorry for himself. You know what he's like when he's got one of his colds."

"But how is he doing in general?" Tania asked as they moved on through the festivities. "How's he coping with all this?"

Mrs. Palmer pursed her lips. "He's struggling a bit, but what do you expect? You've always been his little girl—and now it turns out you have another father in another world, and to top it all, your new father is an Immortal King. You've got to admit, that's a lot for any dad to assimilate. Most fathers freak out when their daughter brings her first boyfriend home—but in your case Edric wasn't the half of it!"

"I think maybe I should go and talk to him."

"He'd like that. Just don't get impatient with him if he doesn't seem to be warming to the whole princess thing."

Tania looked anxiously at her mother. "Why? Doesn't he like it here? What's he said?"

"Not so very much," her mother replied gently. "You know him: He likes things to be *just so*, and this is all a bit too unpredictable for him. But don't worry. He loves you to bits. He'll come to terms with it all in the end."

"Will you be okay on your own for a while?" Tania asked.

"Yes, I'll be fine. I wanted to go and visit the crèche tent, anyway." Her face clouded. "There was a baby—he seemed a bit hot and feverish when your dad and I were in there earlier this afternoon."

Tania smiled. "You worry too much, Mum. You know people don't get sick in Faerie. There's a reason why it's called the Immortal Realm."

"Yes, well, if you say so, sweetheart," her mother replied. "But even in Faerie, you'll find that babies need a good deal of care and attention."

They kissed a quick good-bye, and Tania watched as her mother weaved through the crowds toward the great white pavilion that was being used during the wedding as a nursery and play area for the smallest of the Faerie children.

Tania made her way to where rows of small tents

had been set up at the western end of the valley. According to what her mother had said, that's where she'd find her dad. Edric would be fine with the earl marshal's stepsons for the time being. Still, she did wonder what it was that Edric had been meaning to ask her earlier up on the hill.

Maybe he wants to take me on a grand tour of Faerie, she thought. *That would be really cool!* She had traveled the length of the land a few weeks ago, but her journey had been an urgent one and danger had dogged her footsteps. *It would be nice to wander without any pressure.*

And she also harbored the hope that memories of her Faerie childhood might return if she was shown places that she had visited in her life as a princess. She could remember nothing of the life she had led before that fateful night when she and her sister Rathina had made the mistake of experimenting with Tania's "gift" and she had walked between the worlds and become lost for five hundred years in the Mortal World.

Even among all the glories and delights of Faerie, she still felt achingly distanced from her royal mother and father and from her sisters—Some newfound Faerie memories would mean so much to her!

Tania pushed her head through the closed flaps of the small lilac-colored tent, which was oblong and just large enough to accommodate two bunk beds and a deep oak chest for clothing and other possessions. A lantern hung from the roof pole, filling the tent with soft yellow light.

"Room service, sir," she said. "Here at the Leiderdale

Hotel, if there's anything you need, you only have to ask." She stepped into the stuffy interior of the tent. "Just don't expect a minibar; they don't do alcohol in Faerie."

Tania's father was lying on one of the beds, propped on pillows, reading a book. He had kicked off his shoes, but apart from that he was fully clothed in the Faerie garments that she and her mother had chosen for him.

Although she would never have told him so, she thought his face looked a little comical poking out from the white linen Faerie shirt with its pleated neck ruffles and fine embroidered needlework. He was also wearing the traditional puffed and slashed breeches, olive green with a lining of lime silk, and an embroidered doublet, clasped down the front with buttons of green marbled stone.

"Hello there," he croaked, laying down his book and smiling. "Come to visit the sick and ailing?"

"That's just about it."

"There's no need. It's nothing, really."

"They'll put that on your gravestone!" Tania scolded him gently. "Here lies Clive Palmer: died of *nothing really*."

Tania sat on the edge of the bed and rested the back of her hand across his forehead.

"You don't look well, Dad," she said. She frowned at him. "Typical *you*, getting ill at the worst possible time. Remember that holiday in Greece?"

He nodded. "Sweltering outside and I was stuck in

bed with a head cold," he said, lifting her hand from his forehead and clasping it in both of his. "At least I got to see a Faerie wedding, eh?"

"Spectacular, wasn't it?"

"Remarkable," he said without enthusiasm.

Tania picked up on her dad's tone of voice. "I wish you seemed more comfortable with this," she said. "It's *real*, Dad; it's not going to go away. This is who I am. And this is where I belong. Can't you be happy for me?"

He sat up, coughing a little. "I'm a science teacher, Tania," he said. "My life and my work are based on certain solid principles, like the laws of physics, like the basic idea that if you add one and one together you end up with two every time. This world doesn't conform to any of the rules I use for making sense of the universe. For all I know this whole experience could be the result of a chemical imbalance in my brain." He coughed again. "I could be lying unconscious in a hospital bed. At least that would make more sense."

"You can't seriously think this isn't *real*."

"No, I can't," her father said heavily. "But I'd love it if I could."

Tania took his hands in both of hers. "Is it really that hard for you?"

There was a pause as her father seemed to gather his thoughts. He stared out through a gap in the opening of the tent. Tania followed his eyes, seeing a sliver of the valley alive with lights and with the reveling folk of Faerie. "How do you see things progressing here,

Tania?" he asked. "What exactly do you intend to do with your life?"

Tania laughed. "Are you kidding me? There are a million things to do here. I have a whole new family to get to know, for a start. And I'd like to travel—to find out all there is to know about this place."

"Before all this happened you were talking about taking a year after school to tour Europe and America," her father said. "And then if your grades were good enough, you were set on going to university." He looked closely at her. "You told me you were thinking of training as a journalist. Remember that?"

"Yes, of course I do." She remembered it, but it was like looking at things down the wrong end of a telescope. All her previous dreams, hopes, and ambitions seemed very small and far away. She couldn't bring herself to say that to her father. It would have been like telling him that all the things they had discussed together over the past few years were meaningless to her now.

"So?" he said quietly. "Do you intend to finish your education?"

She gazed at him, noticing his flushed cheeks and the sheen of sweat on his forehead. "I hadn't thought about it." She looked at the crumpled sheets of his bed. "Get up for a minute," she said. "You can't be comfortable like this. I'll straighten the covers for you."

"The new term starts in September," he said, heaving himself off the bed. "Why not come back home after the summer? Do your exams. Go to university;

get some qualifications under your belt. What harm can it do? And then if you still feel you belong here, well—you can make your final decision then." She moved around the narrow bed, tugging at the sheets, smoothing the blankets. She picked up his pillow and plumped it between her hands. His hot fingers touched her wrist. She turned to see his eyes burning into hers. "All this must have put your head in a spin, Tania. I'm concerned that you're not giving yourself the time to take a step back and think it through properly."

"You make it sound like I have a choice, Dad," she said slowly. "As if I get to pick whether to be Anita Palmer or Princess Tania. It's not like that at all. I love you and Mum, but the person I am with you two— she's only *half* of who I really am."

"And exactly who is this other half?" asked her father. "You told me yourself you don't remember anything about her."

"I might, given time." She placed the pillow back on the bed and gestured for him to lie down again. He sank onto the mattress, sighing as he settled himself.

"And in a world where people are Immortal," he said, puffing, "how exactly does a princess give herself a sense of purpose, Tania?" A hint of impatience came into his voice. "I know this place must seem wonderful to you at this moment, but eventually you're going to have to decide what you want to do with your life." He took hold of her hand, his skin hot and damp against hers. "You're in a fairy story right now, Tania, but what happens on the morning *after* happy ever after?"

Tania pulled her hand out of his. She didn't know what to say to him. Why couldn't he just go with the flow? Why did he have to analyze the joy out of everything? Why did this have to be so hard?

He began to cough, breaking the awkward silence.

She used the moment to change the subject. "We should have brought some lozenges through for you."

"Don't fuss. I'll be fine." His voice became brisk and teasing; it was clear he wanted to break the tension just as much as she did. "Now look here, young lady, you shouldn't be stuck in here, getting my germs all over you. Don't princesses have any duties or responsibilities in this world? Get out there and mingle."

"I don't want to leave you here on your own."

He picked up his book. "I'm never alone with a new physics textbook," he joked. "Besides, I'll just finish this chapter and then I'll come out. I promise. Your mum's threatened to teach me one of those peculiar dances."

"I'd like to see that."

Tania got up, leaning over quickly to kiss his hot forehead. "Feel better, all right?" she said. "That's an order."

"Women!" muttered her father, his nose already in the book.

"Men!" she retorted, pushing out into the starry night.

Tania made her way back into the heart of the valley. All around her, lanterns and torches and bonfires sent shadows dancing. Minstrels filled the night with sweet music; folk danced in rings and formal Faerie squares or formed long sinuous lines, hand over hand, that wound through the crowds following the rhythm of the pipe and drum.

Tania paused to watch a pair of jugglers, a man and a woman dressed in black and white diamond-patterned suits, who stood on a high dais and sang as they threw to each other balls that kept changing color: red and green—silver and black—orange and blue.

Tania was totally absorbed in the performance until a voice whispered close into her ear.

"I've been looking for you."

"Edric!" She threw her arms around his neck and kissed him. "I went to see my dad." She wrinkled her nose. "It was a bit awkward. He thinks all this has turned my head a bit. He's worried I'm going to waste my life. He suggested I should—"

He put a finger to her lips. She looked at him in surprise.

"I want to ask you something," he said, drawing her away from the densely packed crowd around the two jugglers.

"Is this the same something you wanted to ask me before?"

He nodded, his face wreathed in a smile. "Tania, will you make this perfect day complete for me? Will you marry me?"

"Will I *what*?" Tania blinked at him. Of all the things she had imagined he might ask, she had never dreamed of this.

Edric dropped to one knee, taking her hand in

his, and gazing up into her face. Tania was aware that a few people nearby had stopped and turned toward them.

"Princess Tania Aurealis, beloved seventh daughter of King Oberon and Queen Titania," he began in a loud voice, a trace of Faerie formality coming into his speech. "In front of all these people, under the eternal stars, with a heart filled with love and humility, I ask you from the very depths of my soul, will you consent to be my wife?"

Tania stared down at him. Speechless. Stunned. Time seemed to come to a shuddering halt. She was intensely aware of his face—of his eyes gazing up at her—and on the edges of sight, all the people who were standing around them.

She swallowed hard. Trying to regroup. To reboot her crashed brain.

"Get up, Edric." She heard her own voice as if it was coming from the far end of the universe. "Please—get up."

"Not until you consent to be my wife." The expectant eyes. The smiling mouth. The hands holding hers.

A panic began to rise in her. She tried to pull away from him. "Stop it, Edric," she said, glancing around at the watching people. "You're embarrassing me."

The light in his eyes flickered and his smile faded. "Tania?"

She was desperate to bring this to an end. "If you don't quit it, all these people will think you're being serious," she said, trying to joke her way out of the situation. "Get up and stop fooling about."

There was a subdued murmur of voices. Tania turned her head, forcing a smile. "Show's over, folks," she said brightly, but unable to prevent her voice from trembling. "Move along, please. Nothing to see here."

Edric got to his feet. The hurt and confusion in his eyes tore at her heart.

She gripped his hand. "Come with me," she said. "We need to be somewhere more private."

She moved quickly through the crowd, towing Edric along behind her, not daring to look into his face again—not till they were alone.

He brought her to a halt between two pavilions. She swallowed hard then turned to face him.

"Why did you do that?" she said fiercely.

He seemed confounded. "I want us to get married," he said. "I thought you would want the same."

"Edric, I'm *sixteen*. I don't want to get married. What were you thinking?"

"Do you not love me, then?"

"Yes, of course I love me. You know I do," Tania said. "But I can't *marry* you."

"I don't understand. Why would you reject me like this?"

"I'm not rejecting you," Tania said, exasperated. "I'm just giving you a reality check. I haven't ever *thought* about getting married. Seriously! The idea has never even crossed my mind."

"You never want to marry?"

"Of course I want to get married," Tania said. "One day—in a few years' time, I guess. Get married, have kids, the whole caboodle—but not now. Not this minute. It's crazy."

"Why crazy?" Edric persisted. "If you love me as much as I love you, you'd want to share your life with me."

Tania felt a moment of shock as she realized how wide a gulf of expectations there could be between a young man of Faerie and a sixteen-year-old London girl.

"I *am* sharing my life with you," she exclaimed. "What do you *think* I'm doing? But getting married—that's a forever kind of commitment, Edric." She blew out a hard breath as she realized the enormity of what she had said. "And in Faerie I guess forever really does mean for *ever*." She looked anxiously into his face. "I'm not ready to make that kind of promise, Edric. I'm sorry if I've hurt you. I never meant to." She moved in close, reaching up to touch his face. "We're together. Isn't that enough for now?"

He pulled back from her hand, his eyes pained and his voice bitter. "In this world, Tania, love without the covenant of commitment is a promise written on a cloud." He bowed sharply. "Let me know when you feel grown up enough to be my wife. I will be waiting." He turned and began to walk away.

She ran after him, catching hold of his arm. "Edric! Don't be so stupid!"

"I'm not being stupid." He wouldn't even look at her.

"I love you!"

"But not enough, it seems."

"Edric!"

He wrenched his arm free of her hands. "Let go of me!"

Before Tania could speak again, a high-pitched wail rang out across the night, sharp as a knife through the dark air.

"My baby!" shrieked the voice. "My baby is dead!"

III

Tania ran through the bewildered crowds that were gathering at the entrance to the crèche tent.

She remembered her mother's words. *I wanted to go and visit the crèche tent, anyway. There was a baby—he seemed a bit hot and feverish when your dad and I were in there earlier this afternoon.*

She plunged breathlessly into the large tent. The light within was subdued, a warm coral glow that came from many paper lanterns. There were cribs and cots set up between the tent poles, but most of the nurses and serving women were grouped around a single pallet.

Tania was aware that her mother was there, but all her attention was caught and held by the plaintive sight of the young golden-haired woman who sat on the low bed with a swaddled baby in her arms. The woman was no longer wailing, but tears poured down her cheeks as she rocked back and forth on the bed with the infant cradled in her arms.

None of the gathered Faerie women were speaking. A few were weeping and wringing their hands as they stood around the grieving mother.

Only one woman had dared to come closer. Tania's mother was kneeling at the woman's side, her hand on her shoulder.

"I'm so sorry, Mallory," she was saying. "I'm so very sorry."

Tania was aware that more people were coming into the tent, filling the place with the murmur of distressed voices.

"What happened?" Tania asked, coming onto her knees in front of the heartbroken Faerie woman.

Her mother looked at her with sunken eyes. "I don't know. The poor little mite was so hot; he was burning up. I tried to cool him with wet cloths, but nothing I did made any difference." Her voice cracked with emotion. "Why don't they have medicine in this country?"

"We have medicaments, Lady Mary," said a voice at Tania's back. "Let me see the child." Tania looked up. It was Hopie, her healer sister. If anyone could do something, it would be Hopie. Tania scrambled to her feet, gently ushering the others aside so that Hopie could get through.

The dark-haired princess sat beside the grieving mother. "Give the child to me," she murmured. "Come now, be not afeared. I will do him no harm. What is his name?"

"Gyvan," whispered the mother, reluctantly laying

the baby in Hopie's lap. She leaned close, her fingers clutching a tiny foot, as if she could not bear to be separated from him. He was dreadfully still. Hopie leaned over him, her deep blue eyes intense as she carefully unfolded the linen wraps.

"Gyvan," Hopie murmured as she ran her hands lightly over the infant's body. "A good, strong name." The child's filmy wings lay folded along his back like crumpled lace. Tania bit her lip till she tasted blood. The infant was so terribly still; there was no sign of breath being drawn. His eyes were closed, his cheeks bloodless, his lips blue. Tears welled in Tania's eyes as she looked at the little hands and feet, the fingers and toes so perfectly formed, each with its little crescent moon nail. How could something so exquisite not be alive?

"Hopie?" Tania looked up at the sound of the Queen's voice. Titania had arrived without her noticing. She rested her hand on Tania's shoulder as she leaned close. "Can you do anything?"

"The child has passed beyond my skills," Hopie said, her voice trembling. "Is Eden to hand? Mayhap she can use her arts to bind soul to body again." Tears ran down her cheeks. "For I can do nothing!"

"Fetch the Princess Eden!" Titania called. "Swiftly now!"

"I am here!" Eden made her way through the growing crowd. Tania stepped aside, looking into her oldest sister's solemn face, Eden's eyes a piercing blue tinged with sadness and hard-won wisdom, her hair an ash white fall like a cascade of frozen water.

Eden nodded in acknowledgment and touched Tania's arm as she passed. There was hope now! Eden was a student of the Mystic Arts. Only the King and Queen, and Eden's ancient husband, the Earl Valentyne wielded more power than she did.

Eden spread her hands out above the baby as it lay in Hopie's lap. She spoke strange words in a sinuous language that Tania did not know. A greenish glow emanated from her hands and emerald particles of light rained down on the infant.

"My lady, by your pity, heal my child. . . ." Mallory groaned, her shaking fingers caressing the unmoving limbs.

"My daughter will save Gyvan if she is able," whispered Titania. "All that can be done is being done."

Eden's face contracted in a grimace of pain. The green light grew darker and her hands shook. "Awake," she whispered between gritted teeth. "Abred shall not have thee. Reach out thy arms to me, little one."

Tania could see her sister trembling with tension. Eden bowed lower, her legs faltering. Tania knelt, putting her arms around Eden's waist, holding her up as the strain vibrated through her.

The corona of green light that bathed the baby darkened almost to black and then it vanished. Eden gave a low cry and went limp in Tania's arms, slipping sideways so that between them Tania and Titania only just saved her from falling.

"I could not awaken him." Eden gasped. "He sleeps

the endless sleep." She put her hands over her face. "I could not awaken him!"

"No! Gyvan—*no!*" Mallory cried, throwing herself forward over the child.

There were cries of consternation and horror from the women gathered around the pallet. A few drew away, as if they could not or dared not be close to the dead infant. Some stood with their hands to their faces, tears running between their fingers; others simply stared with blank disbelief, their eyes uncomprehending.

Another hand reached past Tania's shoulder, a long, withered hand with bone-slender fingers and mottled paper-thin skin. Tania looked up into the ancient face of Earl Valentyne. His deep-sunk eyes were half closed as he rested his hand on the baby's forehead.

There was a moment of silence, then the earl withdrew his hand. "He shall not wake again," he said, his voice as cracked as a winter wind. "Some great evil has done this." A grim light glowed in his eyes. "Mayhap the lady Lamia casts new spells on us from across the ocean?"

Tania stared up at him in alarm. Lamia was the Queen of Lyonesse. Less than a month ago, her strength enhanced by her Faerie mother and father, Tania had destroyed Lamia's husband, the Sorcerer King. It had been thought that the Hag-Queen Lamia would be helpless without him—but could the Sorcerer King's widow still have the power to inflict damage on Faerie?

Judging from the ripple of dismay that went through the crowd, the earl's question had struck a fearful note.

A voice rang out from the entrance to the tent. "If the Hag-Queen had a hand in this, I shall indeed wreak a dour revenge upon her!" The crowd parted as Oberon came to the bedside.

Tania gazed up at her Faerie father. Surely with all his powers he could put things right again. He *had* to!

The King rested a hand on Mallory's shoulder. The desolate mother picked the child out of Hopie's lap and held him up to him. Tania saw that the baby's shrunken wings were cracked and withered like autumn leaves.

"Your grace," Mallory said weeping. "Of your mercy, bring my child back to me."

"Nay, my lady, even I cannot bring the dead alive," he said softly. He looked for a moment at the dead infant, his face rigid with anger. When he spoke again, his voice was a threatening rumble like distant thunder. "Such a thing has not occurred in this land since the Great Awakening. That a child of Faerie should die!" He turned to the earl. "It must be confirmed whether Lyonesse lies at the heart of this dark deed. Come, my lord—I have need of your Arts."

Oberon swept from the tent with Earl Valentyne at his side.

Mallory groaned and swayed, her eyes swimming. Hopie drew mother and child to her, cradling them in her arms.

Titania turned to the crowd. "Leave us now," she said to them. "No further good can be done here. Let the festivities cease and if the minstrels have the heart to play, let it be a dirge of lamentation and grief, for a thing has happened here that has not happened for ten thousand years. Be gone now!"

"I will not leave my child in this forsaken place!" cried one woman, running to a nearby crib and snatching up her baby. Holding her daughter tight to her breast, the woman hurried to leave. Many other women and men snatched up their babies and children, their departure accompanied by the sound of newly awoken infants crying out in fear and alarm. The rest of the folk slowly filtered out of the tent until only a few people remained.

Mary Palmer put her hand on Titania's arm. "The baby had a fever," she said. "I would have paid it more attention, but . . . but it came on so quickly." She looked into the Queen's eyes and Tania was suddenly aware of how strong a bond had formed between her two mothers. "Has this really never happened before?"

"Never," said Titania.

One of the nurses threw herself forward, coming down on her knees in front of the Queen, her face filled with dread. "Save us, your grace," she cried. "Do not let our children die!"

"Get you up, Alma," said the Queen, lifting the woman to her feet. Titania looked at the other nurses. "Go to, good women," she said, her voice calm and clear. "Go now and make sure all is well with those of your charges who remain."

"By what signs will the sickness show itself, your grace?" asked one of the nurses.

Titania paused as though uncertain what to tell them. Tania looked at her for a moment then stepped in.

"Look for flushed cheeks," she said. "Put your hands flat on their foreheads. If they feel hot, let us know."

The nurses moved away, gliding from crib to crib, stooping low over the babies and children, their hands resting softly on foreheads.

Tania called one of them back. "We need to make sure there's no chance of it spreading," she said to the woman. "Guard the entrance to the tent. Keep everyone else out of here. Tell them how dangerous it could be for them!"

Titania's eyes narrowed as if with a sudden pain. "Is there not fear enough already in Faerie?" she said in a harsh undertone.

"Nothing compared to the fear they'll feel if this illness spreads any further," Tania replied.

She looked into her Faerie mother's emerald eyes— into the face that was a mirror of her own. *She's as terrified as everyone else,* Tania realized with a shock.

Mary Palmer rested her hand on Titania's arm. "What would usually happen now?" she asked.

Titania stared hollowly at her. "Usually? There is no *usually*, Mary. *Spirits of Love*, but do you not understand that yet?"

Mary Palmer nodded, her voice soft but firm. "Yes,

I understand. But even here people die sometimes, Titania. There must be the occasional fatal accident, surely? A fall from a horse or someone drowned in a river? Tania told me about the funeral rites you held after the battle. Do we need to prepare something like that? Or is this kind of death treated differently?"

"When a child is killed by mischance," Titania began, "the mother wraps the lost one in white satin and bears the burden to one of the boundaries of the world, to a high hilltop or to the seashore or to the banks of a river—to a place where the elements mingle and merge. There she must wait for the time between time, when it is neither day nor night. The child will be taken then."

"The seashore is but a brief distance from here," said Eden. "Mallory should take her child to the ocean and await the dawn."

"But that's *hours* away," said Tania. "Does she have to sit there all on her own with . . . with . . ." She couldn't bring herself to say *with her dead child*.

"Not alone, if she will allow the comfort of another," said Hopie. "A father, a brother, a sister, or a friend."

Mallory still held the child clasped in her arms. "My husband is in the north, in Caer Rivor at the court of Lady Mornamere," she said quietly. "I came south with our child to pay my last respects to my brother, who was slain in the battle of Salisoc Heath." She looked up at the others, her voice breaking. "I am alone here. Entirely alone."

Tania swallowed hard, a determination growing

in her. "I'll go with her, then," she said. She crouched in front of Mallory. "If you'll allow me to, that is," she asked.

Mallory lifted her face, her eyes filled with grief.

Tania touched her knee. "Will you let me go with you?" she whispered.

Mallory gave a single, silent nod of her head.

The valley of Leiderdale was eerily silent as Tania and Mallory came out of the tent. A great crowd stood waiting. The faces turned to them were filled with fear and shock and disbelief.

The people parted as Tania and Mallory stepped forward, shrinking away from the two of them as if they were contaminated with some unspeakable evil.

Among the watching faces Tania saw Edric. He had the same look on his face as all the others, but there was something else there, too—something that looked to Tania like suspicion. He looked away as soon as she met his glance.

Why suspicious? Suspicious of what?

Two people stepped out of the crowd. Cordelia and Bryn moved toward Tania and Mallory, their faces grief-stricken.

"That such a thing should happen on such a glad day burns my heart," Cordelia said, resting her hand on Mallory's shoulder. "I grieve for you, truly I do."

"All our thoughts go with you, lady," Bryn added.

Mallory paused and bowed her head but she did not reply.

Cordelia looked at Tania. "'Tis bravely done, sister," she said. "May you give the lady good comfort."

Tania nodded, walking at Mallory's side as the young Faerie mother bore her tragic burden in her arms, her dead child wrapped tight in white satin. They passed through the somber crowds and made their way up the hillside.

They came to the spot where Tania and Edric had stood just a few brief hours ago.

Night shadows mantled the land, but the Faerie starlight was bright enough for Tania to see a pathway that led down the cliffs. "I'll go first," she said. "Please be careful."

As she began to descend, she turned her head back so that she could keep Mallory in sight. It was tricky, especially in the half-light, and the occasional loose stone went rolling away under her foot.

Mallory gave a sharp cry as she almost lost her footing, her arms tightening around her swaddled child.

Tania stepped up toward her. "May I carry him for you?"

"No, my lady Princess," Mallory murmured, holding him closer.

"Call me Tania."

Mallory gave her a bleak look. "No, Tania, thank you. He will be taken from me soon enough; I would hold him in my arms a while longer."

"Of course," Tania said, her heart aching for the poor, brave woman.

At last they came down onto a narrow shingle beach

confined within the broken teeth of black surf-washed rocks. The waves came hissing in over the shingle, white foam boiling among the stones.

They sat together in the shingle, the tall cliffs at their backs and the restless sea in front of them.

The night went on forever. There was the pitiless darkness. There was the black cliff at their backs. There was the chill salt wind off the sea and the cold light of stars, far away and uncaring.

But above all there was Mallory's agony.

Sometimes the bereaved young mother was so silent and still that Tania felt the need to check that she was still breathing. At other times sobs wracked Mallory's body and Tania held her until the tears soaked through her gown. She would forlornly shift the dead child on her lap as if making sure he was comfortable, tucking the satin in around his small body, caressing his cheeks with her fingertips.

But slowly Tania saw that the tide was receding, the waves falling back to reveal a beach of rippled gray sand beyond the shingle banks.

"It is time," Mallory said softly.

Tania felt it, too. Although the sky was as dark as ever, she sensed that a change had come, as if a stifling veil had been drawn away to allow clean, fresh air into the world.

Mallory walked a little way down the beach then stooped and laid her satin-swaddled child in the sand.

Tania shivered as she saw the baby lying there, but it was not the cold that made her tremble, it was the thought that such a beautiful spirit, such a *new life*, should have been so mercilessly snuffed out.

Mallory stepped back, reaching her hand out to Tania.

Together, clasping hands, they stood in silence, looking down at the rounded satin bundle.

Tania could not have said when it started, but she was suddenly aware that the air was filled with the soft singing of a high-pitched voice.

Away across the sea to the west the long line of the horizon glowed with a pure white light.

The small voice sang an aching bittersweet melody that climbed and climbed until it reached a pitch that Tania could no longer hear. She was aware of a shimmering all around her, a tingling on her skin, as though the air still vibrated with the inaudible refrain.

Mallory let out a soft sigh.

Tania looked down.

The baby was gone, his satin coverings lying in flattened folds in the sand.

Dawn had arrived. Gyvan had been called to Avalon.

IV

Mallory looked into Tania's face. "Thank you," she said. "I could not have borne this night alone." She picked up the empty satin bundle, holding it to her face and breathing in the scent of it. "He is gone—gone to the Long Home of the fallen. Mayhap the Princess Zara will watch over him for me."

"She will," Tania said, her throat thick with emotion. "I know she will."

Mallory began to weep again, pressing her face into the folds of white satin. Tania touched her shoulder, waiting for the sobs to fade.

"Would you like to go back now?" she asked at last. "Or would you rather stay here for a while?"

"I will stay for a little while longer, but you must go."

Tania gave Mallory a final brief hug then made her way up the shingle to the cracked face of the cliff, looking for the path that had brought them down.

She began to climb. She felt strangely calm, as

though the dawn had washed her clean of the desolation that she had felt all through the long night. And, strangest of all, she didn't feel in the least bit tired. She ought to have been exhausted.

A cloaked figure was awaiting her on the cliff top.

It was Rathina, her beautiful, dark-haired sister, her red gown swathed in a cloak of midnight blue. "This was a night as long as aeons," Rathina said heavily. "How fares the sorrowful lady?"

Tania looked back down to the beach. Mallory was a small forlorn figure, sitting now in the shingle with the satin cloth bundled in her arms.

"I'm not sure," she said. She looked into Rathina's wide hazel eyes. "I thought we'd got rid of everything horrible when the Sorcerer King was killed."

"As did we all," Rathina replied. "It is fearful indeed to think that the Hag-Queen can sit in her foul castle and cast evil upon us over so many a wide league of ocean. And who shall she ensnare next with her witchery?" She held her cloak open. "But come, Tania, you look chilled to the bone."

Tania stepped into the warming shelter of her sister's arm. "Can Father do anything to stop her?" she asked.

"Let us hope so," Rathina replied. "Our mother and father are mighty in power, Tania. They must prevail, surely? Fie! 'Tis unthinkable that they will not!"

"I hope you're right."

They turned and walked arm-in-arm along the grassy hilltop, the light growing around them, washing the world with fresh color.

"Sister, are we friends again now?" Rathina asked quietly. "Am I forgiven my madness?"

Tania looked compassionately at her.

For sure there was a lot to forgive Rathina for. Stupefied by her unrequited love for the treacherous Gabriel Drake, she had unleashed the Sorcerer King of Lyonesse and set events in motion that had culminated in mayhem and warfare and the death of many innocent folk, including that of their own sister Zara. Some amends had been made when Rathina had cut Gabriel Drake down in the great battle, but it was still hard for people not to look at her with judgmental eyes.

Tania was one of the few who truly understood Rathina's agony. She also had gazed into Drake's hypnotic eyes, and she had felt the power of his mind tightening like a venomous snake around her will. And Tania also knew the self-loathing that was gnawing away at Rathina. To live with the knowledge of what she had done was terribly hard.

She squeezed Rathina's arm. "You are completely forgiven," she said. "By me, at least."

"But not by others?"

Tania gave a rueful smile. "Give them time."

Rathina sighed.

They came to the crest of the hill and walked on toward a final ridge, beyond which the land fell sharply away into the valley of Leiderdale.

"Do you not have news for me to lighten the burden of this sad day?" Rathina asked.

Tania frowned at her. "I'm sorry?"

"Voices whisper it abroad that Edric Chanticleer asked for your hand in marriage yestereve." She squeezed Tania's arm. "A bold knave to act so without seeking permission of the King and Queen—but mayhap the time he spent in the Mortal World addled his sense of propriety."

"People are *talking* about that?" Tania asked uneasily. "Oh, *great*! That's all I needed."

"It is good tidings, Tania."

"No, actually, it isn't."

"How so?"

"I turned him down." The sun climbed out of the ocean as they walked along, its light sending their shadows streaming away over the olive hills.

Rathina turned, her eyes narrowed against the bright dawn. "Sweet sister, I strive to understand your strange modes of speech," she said. "But I confess I do not know what you mean. What is 'turned him down'?"

"I said no."

Rathina stopped in her tracks and gasped. "You refused him? Why would you do such a thing, Tania? I thought him the love of your life."

"He *is*," Tania said. "Of course he is."

"And yet you would not wed him? What perversity of your nature is this, to love and yet to refute wedlock?"

"Not you, too!" Tania exclaimed, walking on so quickly that Rathina had difficulty keeping up with her. "I'm not *refuting* anything. I'm sure that in a few years time I'll be totally up for it, but right now getting married is the last thing on my mind. I'm too *young*, Rathina."

"But you were betrothed to . . . to *another*," Rathina said, her voice faltering over the name of Gabriel Drake. "You were to be wed on your sixteenth birthday."

"That wasn't *me*," Tania said. "Well, it *was* me, but not the me that I am now. I don't remember the girl who agreed to marry Drake. I hardly know anything about her." She touched her hand to her forehead. "Part of me in here is still a sixteen-year-old girl from West London. Where I grew up, people don't usually get married that young."

"Do Mortals not experience love in youth, then?" Rathina asked.

On a better day Tania could almost have laughed at that. "They experience plenty of love," she said. "People my age fall in and out of love all the time. If everyone married the first person they were crazy about, the divorce rate would skyrocket!"

"Tania! Use language properly, for pity's sake!"

"If teenagers married the first person they fell in love with, most relationships would be guaranteed to break down," Tania explained. "Don't people in Faerie fall out of love?"

Rathina gave her a long, slow look. "No, Tania, they do not."

"You're kidding me!"

"I speak nothing but the truth."

"Wow! That's incredible." Tania stared at her sister as a sudden awful thought struck her. "But that would mean . . ." She stopped. What she had been about to say was too dreadful even to consider. If the people of Faerie never stopped loving, then Rathina must surely still love Gabriel Drake—despite all the harm he had done to her and to Faerie and despite the fact that she had ended his life with a thrust of her sword.

Rathina's eyes burned with a deep agony. "Love never dies in Faerie, Tania," she said. "Never."

"Oh, *Rathina* . . ." Tania couldn't bear to think that her sister would be trapped in such misery for all eternity. "You'll fall in love again. I know you will. You must."

Rathina lifted her fingers to Tania's lips. "Hush, now." She turned, hiding her face from Tania, but her cracking voice betrayed her desolation. "We will not speak of it."

Below them, silent and sad, lay the valley of Leiderdale with its clusters of tents.

"Look now," Rathina said. "We are come to the brink of Leiderdale. Let us attend upon our mother and father in the Royal Pavilion. Mayhap it will be that the King has good tidings for us. Mayhap he has already conceived a method to throw back the ill-wishes of Lyonesse."

The Royal Pavilion was full of ivory light—more light than could be explained by the rising sun, invisible still beyond the western hills. The canvas walls of the great tent were hung with tapestries, the intricate needlework depicting beautiful Faerie landscapes: mountains, waterfalls, rivers, and rolling downs, flowered meadows, forests, and heather-clad heaths—peaceful scenes that seemed to Tania to be cruelly at odds with the somber gathering.

The floor was strewn with cushions set in a wide ring, and at the end of the pavilion farthest from the entrance, three low wooden chairs were set up. On two of these chairs sat King Oberon and Queen Titania. Earl Valentyne of Mynwy Clun sat in the third, a slender crystal stick gripped in one hand, his wife, the Princess Eden, standing at his side. Next to them were the King's brother, Earl Marshal Cornelius, with his wife, Marchioness Lucina, and his two stepsons.

All of Tania's sisters were there: Hopie with her tall, bearded husband, Lord Brython; slender, bookish Sancha; Cordelia with her new husband at her side; and Rathina, of course, seated close beside Tania.

"The news is both good and ill," Oberon began. "The earl and I have spent a burdensome night of endeavor upon the high hills, and we have discerned no trace of the sorceries of Lyonesse."

"Not Lyonesse, then?" said Sancha, her face pale and her dark eyes anxious between the eaves of her long chestnut hair. "But then, who?"

"Who indeed," came Valentyne's timeworn voice. "What other enemies have we? I know of none."

"Your pardon, my lords and ladies," Bryn said

awkwardly as he stood up. "Have you considered that the evil might come from Weir? We have it from Princess Tania's own lips that the Great Traitor Drake visited his father in Caer Liel in the days when the Sorcerer King was in the ascendancy—and that Lord Aldritch agreed to do nothing to aid the House of Aurealis in the coming battle. Might Weir have sent this deadly bane upon us as revenge for the death of his only son?"

"Lord Aldritch is no sorcerer," said Eden. "And even had he the Arts to do this, I do not believe that he would stoop to such devices."

"Weir is not a traitor," said the Queen, leaning forward in her chair. "I have spoken with him in a water-mirror; he repents his son's deeds and curses the day he first became embroiled in the Dark Arts."

"Indeed, all who dabble in that sinister brume are lost," Hopie agreed. "But we must not blame the father for the deeds of the son."

"Excuse me," Tania said, lifting her hand. "I remember so little about this world, but is it really *impossible* that the child simply got a fever and died of it?"

Earl Valentyne frowned deeply. The King and Queen shook their heads, and there were murmurs and furrowed brows from the others.

"Such a thing has not happened since the Great Awakening," said Earl Valentyne, his knuckles whitening as he gripped his stick. "Yes, I believe that it is impossible."

"That's the second time I've heard a reference to the Great Awakening," Tania said. "I know I'm supposed to understand what it means, but I don't. What is it?"

Eden stepped forward and rested her hand on Tania's head. "I shall show it to you," she said. "Open your mind and behold the nativity of our land."

For a few disorienting moments Tania felt as though she had been plunged into the heart of a whirlwind. Gasping for breath, she spun through oceans of gyrating air.

Then, quite suddenly, she found herself standing on a wooden quay overlooking a flat blue ocean. She turned and saw that she was among a great crowd of Faerie folk all gathered on the quayside and gazing out to sea. Behind the crowd stood long walls, and beyond them were towers and steeples of red brickwork decorated in cream-colored stone and pierced by a hundred shining windows.

The high battlements and great buildings stretched away into the distance, following the line of a wide river that wound its way deep into the land.

It's the Royal Palace! And I know exactly where I am. I'm on Fortrenn Quay at the estuary of the River Tamesis.

But everything seemed brighter and fresher than she remembered—as if the palace had only just been built, as though the long boards of the quay had only recently been put down, as if the sea was washing up against the land for the very first time, as if everything around her was brand-new.

There was something unreal about her surroundings. She felt dislocated from them, as if she was watching events through a thin veil. Although she was standing on the wooden boards of the quay, she had the sensation of floating; she could feel nothing under her feet.

"The white ship!" came a voice. "The white ship comes!"

Tania gazed out over the shining sea.

A shape on the very edge of sight: a swan riding the distant waves. No, not a swan. A ship: a galleon in full sail, a galleon that shone like the moon.

"The *Cloud Scudder*," Tania murmured.

She knew the Royal Galleon well, with its spars and masts and rigging of shining silver and with decks and rails of pearly white. She had been aboard the *Cloud Scudder* on a night when Zara had whistled up a fine wind to fill the sails and when Oberon and Eden had sung a song that had set them sailing into the sky to the enchanted island of Logris.

And more recently it had been the *Cloud Scudder* that had brought her and her sisters to Leiderdale for Cordelia's wedding.

But the *Cloud Scudder* looked different: newer, brighter than she remembered. As bright as if its keel had only just been laid and as if its sails were unfurling for the very first time.

The galleon moved with a stately grace but so quickly that it might have been driven by storm winds.

It was soon gliding alongside the quay, pouring its silver light on the upturned faces of the people who lined the waterside.

Tania noticed that the ship had no visible crew. There was no one on the decks, no sailors in the rigging, no hand at the wheel. And yet the phantom ship came gently to rest with hardly a bump against the quay, and a few moments later a long gangplank slid from the high bulwarks.

A man stood at the top end of the plank.

"*Oh . . . my . . . god . . .*" Tania gasped, her hand flying to her mouth as she stared at a figure that was both familiar and changed.

It was King Oberon—but it was not the full-grown man that Tania knew as her Faerie father. It was Oberon as a slender youth, beardless, and with golden hair that hung to his shoulders. The crown of Faerie rested on his temples, a simple white circlet of crystal studded with jewels of black amber.

My father, Tania thought. *From way before I was born. I get it now! I'm seeing things that must have taken place thousands upon thousands of years ago.*

As he began to walk down the gangplank, all the people save one dropped to their knees. Tania looked at the one man as he stepped forward to greet the King. Again there was something familiar about him: He was tall and broad-shouldered, his face long and thin with sunken cheeks and wise, dark eyes, his hair gray as mist.

It was Earl Valentyne—much younger than Tania

knew him, but still old, even so very far back in time.

"Greetings from your people, sire," said Valentyne, bowing his head as the King stepped onto the quay. "All is prepared for your coming. The Hall of Light awaits you on your coronation day!"

There was the vortex of reeling air again, and Tania found herself back in the Royal Pavilion, gazing around like someone shaken out of a deep sleep. She stared at the King, disoriented to see his familiar, mature face again so soon after witnessing him in his youth.

"Wow," she said. "What was *that*?"

"You have been shown the very beginnings of the Immortal Realm of Faerie," Eden said to her.

Tania blinked at her. "I don't understand. . . ."

"None remember the time before the Great Awakening," said the King. "None have any knowledge of the time before I came in the White Ship to Fortrenn Quay."

"Not even *you*?" Tania asked him.

"Not even I," said the King with a grave shake of his head. "Those times are lost. Forever lost."

"The Coronation of the King was our birthing," said Earl Valentyne. "And never since that ancient day has any man or woman or child of Faerie died of old age or of sickness." He paused, his long, thin hand coming to his chest, a frown gathering on his wrinkled brow.

Eden turned to him. "My lord?" she said. "What is the matter?"

The earl's hand fluttered in the air. "'Tis nothing," he said. "We have weighty matters to consider. The question before us is unchanged. What distemper is it that has entered our Realm and stolen a life from us?"

Tania looked at the ancient earl. Did he seem flushed? Perhaps it was anger at the evil that had come into Faerie . . . or was it something else?

A new voice rang out in the pavilion. "Your majesties, my lords and ladies. My pardon for this intrusion, but I may have the answer that you seek!" The voice belonged to Edric; he was standing just inside the closed tent flaps.

"You presume much on your friendship with Princess Tania, Master Chanticleer!" called the earl marshal, his face furious as he glared at Edric. Others, too, stared at Edric in dismay and outrage. "This council is for those of the House of Aurealis," Cornelius continued. "None other have permission to enter or to speak."

"Nonetheless I ask that you hear me," Edric insisted. "I do not believe we are being attacked by Lyonesse, nor by any other enemy. I believe I have with me the source of the blight." He opened the tent flap, letting in a blaze of early sunlight. Two shapes stepped into the long triangle of light.

Edric let the tent flap fall.

Tania gasped. "Mum? Dad?" Her mother's face was full of consternation. Her father looked even more unwell, but he also seemed worried and uneasy. Tania got to her feet, not understanding what was happening.

"Edric, what's this all about?"

Edric didn't even look at her.

"It's all right, Tania," said her mother. She looked across at the King and Queen. "I am so sorry," she said. "But I think Edric is right. I think it's our fault the child died."

Clive Palmer stepped forward, his face flushed and beaded with sweat. "In our world a virus can be the most dangerous thing human beings ever encounter. Titania—you lived there—you know what I'm talking about."

"I do," Titania said. "But I never thought such a thing could pass between the Realms."

"Virus is *disease*; do I understand that aright?" asked Hopie.

"You do," Clive Palmer said, bringing a handkerchief to his mouth as he coughed. "I have brought a virus into your world—and it must have killed that child." He bowed his head. "And I am more sorry for that than I can possibly say."

Tania saw the faces of her Faerie family turn toward her Mortal father, their expressions showing sudden fear and disgust.

"No!" Tania shouted, running toward her Mortal parents. "No! I don't believe it." She looked around the assembly, alarmed by their reactions. "It's just a stupid head cold, that's all," she said. "It can't kill anyone." She felt as if the breath was being squeezed out of her. "And where's the proof that people in Faerie can even catch human diseases?" She turned to her Mortal mother. "Mum! Tell them it isn't true." She rounded on Edric. "How could you do this?" she hissed. "Why are you trying to blame them?"

"I'm not trying to blame them," Edric said, turning to look at her. "But I think it's time for—what did you call it? A reality check. For the first time in thousands of years a Mortal has brought an illness through into Faerie. And a few weeks later a baby is dead from a fever. Connect the dots, Tania!"

Her father put his hand on her shoulder. "Tania, it's not Edric's fault. I did this. I should have known better than to come here when I wasn't feeling well."

"I do not understand," said Cordelia. "Are you saying that this 'virus' can be passed from person to person?"

"It can," Titania said, her face twisted in torment. "In the Mortal World many thousands can die of a disease carried by a single person. I curse myself for never once thinking that the folk of Faerie may suffer so!"

"Sun, moon, and stars!" Sancha gasped. "Are *all* at risk, then?"

"I'm afraid you might be," Mary Palmer said, her voice breaking. "I only hope the infection is limited to that one poor baby."

"Hopie?" Oberon's deep voice sounded for the first time. "You are master of herbs and medicines; do you have the skills to fight this virus?"

"It is possible that medicaments could be discovered, were I given enough time," said Hopie. "But the search may take months or years, and it may be that there is no cure in all of Faerie for such a malady."

"Then there's only one answer, and even that may be too late," said Clive Palmer, his breath wheezing as he spoke. "King Oberon, Queen Titania, my wife and I must leave your country immediately." He stopped, coughing into the handkerchief. "Excuse me!" he gasped. "We should go before we do any more harm."

"No!" Tania cried. "No! That's not right. We should all calm down and think this through properly! Just because Edric says it's all my parents' fault doesn't make it true!"

"Peace, daughter," said Oberon. "The well-being of Faerie rests on this decision."

Clive Palmer stepped toward the King. "You don't have a choice," he said. "Who knows what damage I've already done."

The earl marshal held out an imperious hand. "Come no closer to their majesties!" he cried. "I will not have them fall victim to your sickness."

Tania saw that others were also looking at her Mortal father with dread in their eyes.

"I'm sorry," Mr. Palmer said, backing off. "Forgive me." He looked at the Queen. "Tell them what a disease like this can do. *Tell them!*"

Titania stood up, her face ashen. "I have seen it before. I witnessed the Great Plague of London in centuries past. Without medicine such a disease could rage through our people like wildfire." She looked at Tania and her eyes were full of sorrow. "First it would take the more vulnerable of us—the infants and the elderly—but then if it were not checked, it could rampage through the entire population."

The Marchioness Lucina got up from a cushion and stood at her husband's side. "It grieves me to say so, for it presses hard upon all our hearts to do hurt to Princess Tania, but these Mortals speak the truth. They must be banished and never more be allowed into Faerie."

"*These Mortals?*" Tania shouted. "You're talking about my *parents!*"

"Tania, calm down," said Mary Palmer.

"No, I won't calm down! They're talking about you as if . . . as if—" She came to a choking halt. She had been going to say, *as if you're outsiders, as if you're different from them.* But the truth was they *were*; they were totally different. They were aliens from another world.

The King looked from face to face. "Is this the will of the entire council?" he asked. "Banishment for all time?"

"It is," came a quiet chorus of voices.

"Is there no other way?" asked Rathina. "Surely there must be?"

"I don't think there is," said Mary Palmer. She looked at the King. "Do it now—before we cause any more harm."

Oberon stood up from his chair and raised his arm, lightning flickering at his fingertips.

"No!" Tania screamed.

"Silence, daughter. The council has made its will

clear. Your Mortal parents must be sent from this place—never again to return to Faerie!" Oberon gestured toward them. Lightning crackled through the tent.

Tania threw herself in front of her parents, her arms spread wide. "You can't do that!" she shouted. "I'm *their* daughter, too!"

"Stand clear, Tania!" boomed Oberon.

But it was too late. Before Tania had time to react, the lightning struck her and she staggered back, caught in a blazing ball of white fire that dazzled her eyes and filled her ears with roaring flames.

V

Tania had the sense of hurtling through the air in a haze of white sparks. She could move but only slowly, as though under fathoms of water—and through the frosted halo that surrounded her she could see into a deep velvet blackness studded with huge stars. She was flying through the sky high above Faerie.

Moving with her were three other balls of white fire racing like comets through the darkness, trailing beards of flame.

The stars wheeled around and her stomach launched itself into her throat as the four fireballs plummeted and a great stretch of green land came racing up to meet them.

Tania found herself standing on a grassy hillside. Beside her, wide-eyed and gasping for breath, were her Mortal mother and father.

"You are safe," came a deep, gentle voice. "The

horse of air is swift and wild, but it does no harm."

Tania turned and saw Oberon standing with his back to a tall round tower of brown stone.

"Bonwn Tyr!" she murmured. She knew this tower well: It was the portal through which she could come and go from her bedroom in London.

The ways in and out of Faerie were called portals or doorways, but really they were neither. Faerie and the Mortal World were shadows of each other divided by an invisible membrane through which only a few people had the art or skill to pass. Princess Eden and some handful of similar lore-masters could do it, but they relied on long study of the Mystic Arts to allow them to open a portal between the worlds. For Tania, whose ability to walk between the worlds was a gift of her royal heritage, moving between the worlds needed but a simple, effortless side step.

Tania turned and gazed down the hill to the endless profusion of towers and courtyards of the Royal Palace, stretching away in either direction along the snaking course of the River Tamesis.

Tania's Mortal father seemed dazed from the journey, his face red and the sweat standing out on his forehead. He was leaning forward, his hands on his knees, panting for breath. A frown deepened on Oberon's face, and he stepped forward as if to help him.

Clive Palmer pulled himself upright and stretched out his hand. "No! Oberon, no. Don't touch me. It's too dangerous."

Oberon nodded. "So be it," he said.

"We're sorry for the harm we've done in your world," said Mary Palmer, moving to her husband's side.

Mr. Palmer held a handkerchief to his mouth, stifling a cough. "We must go. Tania, you have to take us through into London—and then you have to come back here again."

Tania nodded. "I'll visit you as often as I can," she said.

"I don't think that would be wise," said her mother. "At least not for the time being—not while your dad is still contagious."

"Then I'll stay in London with you," Tania said impulsively. "I'll help look after Dad." Angry tears burned behind her eyes. "Why did this have to happen? Everything was so perfect. And now everything is wrong and broken."

"Mistress Mary, Master Clive, my good wishes go with you on your journey," said Oberon. "I do not blame you for what has befallen us, for you were not aware of the danger you posed to my people." He turned to Tania. "Take your Mortal parents into their own world, my daughter. Then return to me. Your knowledge of Mortal sickness may be of help to Hopie as she seeks a cure." He strode to the tower and drew the door open.

I won't cry. I will not fall to pieces!

Silently Tania led her parents into the soft gloom of

the tower and up the spiral stairway to the upper floor. It was a simple room of bare stone walls and dusty floorboards. A single arched window cast a wedge of light across the room. Tania paused in the middle of the floor, holding out both hands. Her parents took her hands.

Tania swallowed and took a deep breath. "Okay," she said. "Now!"

They stepped forward together. Tania made the small side step and saw the gray stone fade away to be replaced by the familiar surroundings of her bedroom in her home in the Mortal World.

There was her bed with its yellow-and-gold-patterned duvet cover. Her cluttered desk with her new computer on it—a birthday present, hardly used. Bookshelves. A crowded chest of drawers. A bulletin board on the wall. Posters. A heap of school books on the floor. And through the window the everyday Camden skyline and a wreath of white clouds that stretched far out over London.

"Extraordinary," murmured her father.

Her mother turned and cupped Tania's face between her hands. "And now you have to go back, sweetheart," she said. "Help your sister to find a cure before anyone else gets sick."

"I will," Tania said. "But I'm still not convinced it was anything to do with Dad."

"Let's hope so," said her mother. She kissed Tania's forehead.

Her father's hand stroked her shoulder. "Best not kiss good-bye," he said.

She screwed her face up. "Stop being so sweet, the two of you!" she said. "Do you want me to dissolve into a puddle on the carpet?" She pulled away from her mother, turning and looking at them. "I'll see you soon, got me? I'll be back *soon!*"

"Be careful, sweetheart," said her father.

"And you." Gritting her teeth, Tania stepped forward and a little to one side, and her parents melted away and she was back in Faerie.

Oberon was waiting for her on the hillside, his back turned to her as she emerged from the tower, his eyes on the palace.

She stood next to him, but a little apart. "They've gone," she said.

Oberon moved closer and put his arm around her shoulders.

"It was well done, my child," he said. "I know how it grieved your heart to say farewell to them. But now we have grave work ahead of us. We must call the Conclave of Earls and await the outcome of their deliberations."

She looked up at him. "What's the Conclave of Earls?"

"A meeting of all the great lords and ladies of Faerie," Oberon told her. "When such danger as this threatens the Realm, a monarch cannot make decisions alone."

"It was *one* child," Tania said. "I know it was awful,

but it was only one child."

The King's eyes seemed to burn into her. "Heed me, Tania," he said, his voice deep and severe. "If you have not understood yet, then understand now: The child's death was not of natural cause. If your Mortal father did not cause it, then some great evil attacks this land. And for all his sorceries and subtleties, the King of Lyonesse did not have the power to extinguish without trace the life of a Faerie child."

Tania gazed up at him in growing alarm. "You mean it could be something worse than the Sorcerer King?"

The King nodded, gazing out over the palace and the deep woodland that lay beyond the curl of the river. He spread his arms as if to embrace the soft, heathered hills that rose to the northern horizon.

"I am Faerie," he intoned, his voice so deep that Tania felt it like thunder in her belly. "As thrives the land, so I thrive. I am tied to this land mind, body, and soul. Every death pierces me—and the death of Gyvan has thrust a thorn into my heart."

As she watched her Faerie father, Tania finally realized the dreadful truth. She had been hoping that her Mortal father had not caused the child's death, but for the people of Faerie, an imported Mortal disease was better by far than the alternative: that some evil power had reached into their land and squeezed cold fingers around Gyvan's small body.

The King started, as if some sudden sound had

shocked him. "There is fear and dread in Leiderdale," he said, peering into the west. "Come, we must return!"

Tania reached for his hand and was swept up in racing lightning.

Earl Valentyne lay on a low cot, his head propped on a pillow, his face gray. Eden sat at his side, holding one bony hand in hers, looking at him with anxious, frightened eyes.

Lord Brython put his hand under the earl's head, lifting him so that his lips came to the rim of a small wooden bowl held by Hopie.

"Drink, my lord," Eden urged.

The earl sipped and coughed. Eden wiped sweat from his forehead.

Tania stood at the end of the bed. Oberon was behind Eden, leaning forward, looking down at the earl with anxious eyes.

"When was Earl Valentyne taken sick?" the King asked.

"It happened only moments after the horse of air took you," Rathina said, standing at Tania's side. "He stumbled and would have fallen if Eden had not been to hand."

"He has a high fever," said Hopie. "This tincture of yarrow and elderflower will bring out the sweat, and I have added echinacea, chamomile, and goldenseal to give him strength." She glanced up at Tania. "These are physics I use to fight the fevers that come with broken limbs, but I do not know how effective they may be against . . . against this plague that you have brought on us."

Tania stared at her. Was even Hopie blaming her for this?

"Hist, now, Hopie," said Titania. "Do not strike out blindly in your grief and helplessness. This is not your sister's fault."

"No, I spoke in anger," Hopie said, looking at Tania with hooded eyes. "This thing is not of your doing— and yet as we speak three more infants sicken."

"Oh, god . . . *no* . . ." Tania groaned. "Not more."

She felt Rathina's arm around her waist. "Brave heart, my love," her sister murmured in her ear.

"Are they dying?" Tania asked.

"My potions tether them to this world for the moment," said Hopie. "But I know not how long my herbs and simples will suffice."

"We must prevent the disease from spreading further," said Titania. She turned to the King. "None must be allowed to leave here, my lord," she said. She frowned. "And yet this is no place for the sick. We came prepared for a day of festivities, not to feed and house hundreds while this fever takes its course."

"We should return to the palace," Sancha said. "In the library there are many lore books; perhaps I will find a cure in their pages."

"The cure for a Mortal disease?" Cordelia said dubiously. "I fear not."

"Nevertheless—" Sancha began, but Oberon interrupted her.

"We will not dwell here," he said. "But neither will we return to the Royal Palace. Many folk remained there who may have none of this pestilence in their veins; I would not put them in danger. Let us go to Veraglad upon the high southern cliffs. There shall we stay until this thing is defeated or until its evils are spent."

Tania knew of the Summer Palace of Veraglad, although she had no memories of the times she had spent there with her sisters in her lost Faerie childhood.

The King turned to her. "Tania, go with Rathina and Sancha. Spread the news of our departure; have all make ready to board the ships."

Tania nodded and with a final miserable glance at Earl Valentyne, she left the tent with her sisters, intending to let everyone know that they should start packing up and making their way to the harbor.

Edric was standing just outside the tent.

No, she thought. *Not now. This isn't the time.*

He stepped into her path. She lifted her hand, as though trying to ward him off.

"Will you talk to me, please?" he said.

She paused, aware that her sisters were looking at her. "You go on ahead," she said to them. "I won't be long."

She felt the quick squeeze of Rathina's fingers in

hers, and then she was alone with Edric. She looked into his face, holding her emotions in check, caught between the need to be comforted by him and the urge to launch her fist into his face.

"Well?"

"You're blaming me for what happened, and that isn't fair," he said quietly. "I didn't accuse your parents of anything. They came to me."

"But you were quick enough to agree with them, weren't you?" Tania said, glad that her voice sounded steady and level. "You were happy enough to let them be punished for it."

"No, I wasn't happy. But what else could I have done?"

"You could have stood up for them like I did!" A poisonous edge came into her voice. "Ever heard the phrase 'innocent till proven guilty'?"

A muscle twitched along his jaw. "Ever heard the word 'epidemic'?" he retorted. "Don't you care about what happens here? Because I do. This is my world, Tania, and your Mortal father has put it at risk."

"You don't *know* that!"

"Oh, wake up, Tania! What else?" His eyes burned. "Tell me!" he said. "Tell me what else could be going on here? You're so blinded by loyalty to them that you're not thinking straight."

"Loyalty? Is that all you think I feel toward my parents?"

"I presume you mean your *Mortal* parents," Edric said coldly.

Her eyes narrowed. "Oh, you're very quick to remind me of that, aren't you?" she said bitterly. "Tania the not-really-full-blood Faerie. Who is she? Who is this strange girl? She's neither one thing nor the other; she's Tania the half-breed!"

"I never said that. I never thought that for a single moment," said Edric. "Why would I have asked you to marry me if I felt like that about you?"

"Who knows?" Tania exclaimed, the anger surging unstoppably through her. "Nothing in this stupid world makes any sense. Maybe you were thinking of starting a freak show with me as the main attraction."

Edric moved toward her, his face now more concerned than angry. "Tania, calm down," he said.

"Get away from me!" she exploded. "Don't *touch* me!"

He backed off, his hands raised. "Okay, okay," he said. "I'm going. You obviously need to cool off. We'll talk again when you're being a bit more rational." He turned and walked rapidly away.

She seethed with rage, her hands knotted, her knuckles white. She wanted to run after him and throw herself at him and beat him with her fists until all the pain in her mind was gone forever.

I can't believe he's just walked away from me, she thought furiously. *He's meant to love me!*

She wished she had never met Edric. She wished she had never even *heard* of Faerie. She wished with all her heart that she could go back three months and just be a normal girl again.

She turned and followed her sisters.

She was so sick and tired of feeling this way. All she wanted was to wake up in bed back in London and find this had been a bad dream.

VI

Tania stood at the forecastle rail of the *Cloud Scudder*. She was alone at the bow, a breeze sending her hair flying around her face. The silver ship had been sailing all through the night and dawn was now close.

A white light caught her eye, sparkling and winking low on the dark horizon. At first she thought it was a star, till she heard the lookout's voice ringing out from high at the masthead.

"Rhyehaven, ho!" came the call. "Voyage's end!"

The *Cloud Scudder* sailed in under the rearing chalk cliffs of Udwold just as the sun was rising in a sky banded with clouds of pale crimson. Perched on the highest cliff, far above the topmost mast of the Royal Galleon, was the Palace of Veraglad, its elegant curved walls and slender turrets and needle-sharp steeples fashioned from a white crystal that shone so brightly Tania could hardly bear to look at it.

A voice came soft in her ear. "Do you remember?" It was Sancha, standing at her shoulder and also gazing up at the palace. "The long golden weeks of summers long past when the whole court of Faerie would sally forth to Veraglad Palace for the Solstice Revels . . ."

"No, I don't," Tania said sadly. "I wish I did."

"Perhaps memory will return when you enter your old bedchamber high in the Sunset Tower."

"Here's hoping." Tania sighed. She had spent sixteen years as a princess in Faerie, but of that life she knew nothing apart from what she had read in her Soul Book or had had explained to her by others.

The loss gaped inside her like a wound that would never heal.

She turned and looked down the bustling decks. Beyond the high stern of the *Cloud Scudder* she saw the other ships following in their creamy wake. The quarantine ship was at the rear, a dark red flag snapping at the head of its mainmast.

"I'm praying no one else has died," Tania whispered.

"Hopie has great skill," said Sancha. "I have faith that our sister will prevail."

Hopie was aboard the quarantine ship with the Queen, mixing what potions she could and giving them to the sick. Apart from a small crew, mother and daughter had insisted on being alone with the plague victims.

"Yes. Faith is good," Tania murmured. "I like faith. . . ."

But would faith be enough?

* * *

Rhyehaven nestled in a deep slot between rearing cliffs, its round harbor protected by two curved breakwaters of natural rock reaching into the sea and leaving only a narrow gap of open water between. Beacons stood at the extreme end of each, their lights still glimmering in the early light as the *Cloud Scudder* led the ships into port.

Tania looked out at the small town, its seafront a tumble of tall black wharves and slatted drying huts, its streets narrow and twisting, its houses and shops of stone or half timber. The quayside was hung with fishing nets stretching out like spiderwebs over the cobbles. A flotilla of small fishing boats was gathered to one side of the harbor, the crews busy unloading the night's catch while seagulls wheeled and screamed.

The salt air had a strong sea tang to it and the scent drove Tania tumbling back to her childhood holidays in England. A green-and-white wooden chalet behind the sand dunes. A carousel and a games arcade on a stretch of cracked concrete above the beach. Ice cream cones. Fish and chips wrapped in paper. Vast golden sands at low tide, the sea a silvery glimmer on the horizon. Building sand castles with her dad. Searching for cockles on the sand flats before the long tide came sweeping in. Running through the surf, sand clotted richly between her toes.

Such strong memories.

Is that who I am really? Not Princess Tania of Faerie

at all? Anita Palmer, only child of Clive and Mary Palmer of 19 Eddison Terrace, Camden, London. Was Dad right? Have I just been hypnotized by all this? Should I go back now and let all this fade away like a dream?

"Tania!" Sancha's voice dragged her back to reality. "Come quickly. The earl is worse. Eden is asking for you."

Earl Valentyne's bed had been brought onto the deck of the quarantine ship. The crew would come nowhere near him, but Eden was at his side as Tania boarded the ship and ran across the deck.

"What is it?" she asked. "What's happened?"

"I cannot rouse him!" cried Eden. She stared into Tania's face with haunted eyes. "You know this ailment; what does this mean?"

Tania looked down into the earl's ravaged face. His skin was gray and had a sickly sheen to it. His deep-set eyes were closed, but his face was not peaceful. There was a tension around his eyes and mouth as if he was in pain.

"I don't know," Tania said helplessly. "Where are Hopie and our mother?"

"Belowdecks, tending the children." Eden snatched at Tania's hand, her fingernails digging into her flesh. "I fear he is dying. He cannot die. You must not let him die." Her voice was almost hysterical now, her eyes pleading. Tania couldn't bear to see her sister like this; she had only ever known Eden calm and steadfast.

"I don't know what to do," Tania said, her voice shaking.

Eden turned to the earl, her hands cradling his face, leaning over him so that her face was just above his. "My lord," she cried, "do not leave me."

Close to panic, Tania ran to the hatch that led belowdecks. She shouted down, "Mother! Hopie! Come quickly!"

She had returned to Faerie to try and help, but now it came to it—what use was she? *None at all*, she thought bitterly as Titania's face appeared in the half darkness at the foot of the ladder. *I'm useless.*

"What is it, Tania?" called the Queen.

"The earl has fallen into some kind of coma," she called down. "Eden thinks he's dying."

"There's nothing we can do," called her mother. "Two of the little ones have also lapsed into unconsciousness. Hopie is doing all she can for them, but . . ." She didn't need to finish the sentence.

"It's okay," Tania called down. "I'll think of something."

She ran back across the deck and pounded down the bouncing gangplank to the quayside.

I have to find Oberon, she thought desperately. *He has so much power. Surely he'll be able to stop this.*

The King was standing on the quay with the earl marshal and Lord Brython. They were deep in discussion as Tania came running up.

"Father, you have to come—*now!*" she said gasping,

clutching at the King's arm.

He frowned at her. "Tania, be calm! What is the matter?"

"Eden's husband is dying!"

"No!" exclaimed Cornelius. "Earl Valentyne dying? It cannot be so."

Tania looked into his horrified face. "Yes," she said firmly. "It *can*."

"I shall come," said the King. "My lords, see to our people. Have the townsfolk keep to their homes as we pass through. I would not have this sickness spread to the people of Rhyehaven. Ensure all pass through the town and onto the cliffs as swiftly as may be."

"We will, sire," said the two lords.

"Please come quickly, Father," Tania urged the King. "You have to do something *now* or more people will die."

The King strode rapidly toward the quarantine ship. "I have no cure for this malady, Tania," he said. "You must reconcile yourself to that. But mayhap I can thwart death for a while. . . ."

They came up onto the ship. Eden was huddled by the bed, her head fallen forward, her hands spread on the earl's chest.

"Stand back, my child," said the King. "It is time for the Gildensleep."

Eden looked up, a new hope in her eyes. She got to her feet and stepped away from the bed.

Oberon reached out one spread-fingered hand

over the earl. A deep stillness came over Faerie. Even the seagulls were silenced, and Tania could no longer hear the creak of timbers or the slap of waves on the hull.

Oberon's hand began to glow. Drops of gold fell like honey from his fingertips. They splashed just above the earl's chest as though they were hitting an invisible glass dome. The golden drops ran down to either side in curved streams, spreading and forking into a fine filigree of shining threads. And then Tania saw the earl's thin body rise slowly from the bed. The threads of golden light spun beneath him so that he was cocooned in their radiance.

Eden let out a gasp of amazement as the shell of golden strands twined and twisted together, completely encompassing the earl, his floating body still visible through the corona of light.

Tania looked into the King's face. He was frowning and his mouth was tight, as though the enchantment was putting a strain on him. He let his hand fall. The cocoon of glowing golden threads hung still in the air.

"There, 'tis done." The King gasped. "The earl will slumber deeply now in the embrace of the Gildensleep. No evil will come nigh him. The despoliation of his body is halted." Tania saw that a serenity had come over the earl's face now—as if the pain had been drawn away from him.

Tania gazed at her father in awe. "That's totally

amazing!" she said. "You've put him in some kind of cryogenic suspension."

"I do not know the words you use, daughter."

"You've frozen him, haven't you?" said Tania. "He'll stay like that till we find a cure."

"Or until I can no longer keep the enchantment alive," said Oberon.

"Is it hard, then?" Tania asked. "It looked hard."

"Hard?" The King looked pensively at her. "Nay, the charm did not tax me overmuch, child—but it will only last so long as I remain wakeful."

"For the Gildensleep to exist, the King must not drowse," said Eden.

Tania looked up at him. "How long can you stay awake?" she asked uneasily.

Oberon didn't reply.

"My Lord Father," said Eden, taking the King's hand. "Others are on the threshold of death below-decks. Can you bring aid to them also?"

"I can." The King went to the hatch and climbed down.

Tania looked at her sister. "How long *can* he stay awake?" she asked.

"I do not know," Eden replied. "But the enchantment of the Gildensleep will quickly drain his strength." She looked at Tania. "And the more of our folk he has to protect, then the swifter will he tire."

"Then we probably have a few days at most?"

"Aye, mayhap—but with each new victim, our time

dwindles." She touched her hand against the golden cocoon and it glided silently and smoothly through the air. "Come now, sister. The sooner we are all within the walls of Veraglad, the sooner will the folk of this town be safe from danger."

The interior of Veraglad Palace was delicate and graceful beyond anything Tania could have imagined. Its rooms and hallways were full of dancing light and the subdued play of soft colors, the white surfaces sending pale shadows leaping and colliding. Gentle music played everywhere, coming from the trembling crystal droplets of chandeliers and from water that ran in fountains of colored glass.

People gathered at first in the airy atrium inside the gatehouse, putting down their burdens and waiting patiently while Lord Brython and the earl marshal spoke with the palace retainers and made preparations for this sudden influx of unexpected and uneasy guests.

Tania stood to one side, wishing she could help but knowing at the same time that she would only make the Faerie folk more fearful if she approached them. She felt useless—and worse than useless: She felt a crushing responsibility for what was happening. She could no longer pretend this was anything other than a Mortal disease brought into Faerie by her Mortal parents.

She heard a sudden murmuring and the rustle

of hasty movements behind her. She turned to see Titania and Hopie lead the floating golden cocoons of Gildensleep in through the gateway, pushed gently forward by wardens. The other folk backed away from the cocoons, their faces filled with fear as they huddled in the far corners of the wide antechamber of the palace.

"We will place the sick all together in Cerulean Hall," said Titania. "Its windows face east to the rising sun. Though they will see it not, the sun may comfort their souls."

Tania watched in sorrow and distress as the cocoons were guided through the doors of the hall and into a soft blue radiance. More folk came in through the gateway, and Tania saw that Sancha was among them.

"Well, my love, will you aid us now?" Sancha asked, looking solemnly at Tania. "Our need is great."

"I know that," said Tania. "But what can I do? Everyone is scared of me. They think I brought the plague here."

"I am not scared of you," Sancha said simply. "The library here is not so extensive as my own in the Royal Palace, but mayhap there are books that will be of use to us. Would you come with me to fetch them?"

"Of course." Tania was glad to be asked; she was desperate to help in any way that she could.

Sancha led her up a long winding staircase to the first of a series of wide galleries that overlooked the entrance hall. She pushed open a door, and Tania saw a room filled with laden bookshelves. "We will take those books I deem relevant down to Cerulean Hall. I would be with Hopie and our mother while I work. Together we may find a way to defeat this thing."

It took Sancha a while to pick the books she wanted. They smelled old and timeworn to Tania as Sancha heaped them into her arms.

At last the two of them made their way back down the stairs. The atrium was beginning to empty as people were allocated rooms. Tania noticed Edric a little way off helping a woman with three small children. It was the first time she had seen him since Leiderdale.

If he saw her, he showed no sign of it, and she made no attempt to speak to him. What could she possibly say? Even *looking* at him tied knots in her stomach.

A warden had been put on the door of Cerulean Hall, but he stepped aside to let Tania and Sancha through. A floor of pale blue marble stretched away from them between sapphire walls. The hall was long and slender and empty of furniture or decoration; it seemed to Tania to be a place where grand balls might take place. The air all around her was awash with light that shimmered as it poured in through the huge open windows.

The cocoons of Gildensleep had come to rest along one wall, hovering a little above the ground, sending out their own golden glow. Tania's heart ached to see them. The number of sick children had grown to eleven—and there were now seven sick adults as well:

four men and three women. At Eden's insistence Earl Valentyne had been taken to a separate room, where she remained at his side behind a locked door.

Tania looked through the glaze of gold at the faces of the sleeping patients. They seemed peaceful, giving the impression that Oberon's enchantment had washed them clean of the sickness that was really only being held at bay.

A table had been set up on trestles under a window. It was filled with beakers and vials and bottles and jars of liquid and dried herbs and powders. Hopie pounded a mixture with mortar and pestle.

As Titania saw them enter, she stepped forward. "Tania, you should not be here," she said. "We cannot risk you falling ill."

Hopie pushed her long hair out of her eyes with one arm, her fingers darkly stained by her work. "No, Mother, by your leave, let her stay. She may be able to assist me."

Tania looked beseechingly at her mother. "Please? I have to do something to help."

The Queen nodded. "So be it. Stay, then, for a little while."

"Put the books on the floor by the table," said Sancha. They spread the ancient leather-bound volumes on the floor. Sancha knelt, opening some of the books, leaning in close to read the fine gothic script.

Tania stood at Hopie's side. A sharp, tangy scent rose from the stone mortar.

"What can I do?" Tania asked.

"I have mixed and brewed such potions and nostrums as I know," Hopie said. "But I am working in darkness, Tania. I need you to tell me all that you know of the remedies that Mortals use for such ailments."

"I don't really know anything about medicine," Tania said. "It's all chemicals."

"Indeed," Hopie said with a hint of impatience in her voice. "But even in the Mortal World, these chemicals must surely come from natural sources? I must try to find these sources and replicate the formulas used by Mortal apothecaries. Think, now, Tania. Is there anything you can remember, any medicinal herb or plant or root of the Mortal World that grows also in Faerie? Something that I can use?"

"I'm not sure," said Tania. "I know that aspirin has something to do with tree bark, but I don't have any idea which tree. And I have no idea at all how antibiotics are made."

"A tincture of the bark of willow and myrtle relieves pain," Hopie mused. "I know this, already, Tania. I need more."

"I don't *know* any more," said Tania, becoming frustrated by her own ignorance.

"What of the petals of the nasturtium flower?" said Sancha, looking up from her books. "A healer from centuries past wrote, 'combined with honey and pure water, these petals purify the lungs and will eradicate fevers.'"

"Good. Good, Sancha. I will add a tincture of nasturtium," Hopie said. "Tania, hand me the bottle with the red liquid in it."

Tania watched as Hopie made up a new mixture, but she could not help glance every now and then at the golden cocoons, beautiful but sad in the blue light.

"How will you know when you've got the right formula?" she asked her sister. "Can you treat people while they're inside that . . . *light*." She didn't quite know what to call the glowing shells of the Gildensleep.

"I will not have to," said Hopie. "I will know when the potion is true." She looked at Tania. "Did you think that my gift resided only in my hands, sister? Nay, it runs through my whole body. I will know if I find the cure. I will feel it in my soul."

Sancha looked up again. "It is written here that the feather of an ossifrage can be of assistance in treating colic." She frowned. "I do not know what manner of bird an ossifrage is."

"I do!" exclaimed Tania. "It was in a crossword. My mum does them all the time." She looked at Titania. "My other mum, I mean. It's an old-fashioned name for a lammergeier. It's a kind of vulture."

"Such creatures dwell only in the crags of the far north." Hopie sighed. "If all fails, mayhap Eden will ride the horse of air into far-off Prydein and fetch for us this feather." Her voice became brisk. "In the meantime, Tania, you will assist me with my potions even if you cannot unlock for me the secrets of Mortal medicines." She looked sharply at Tania, and there was a glimmer of understanding in her eyes. "Fear not, sweet sister; I will work you hard. Under my tutelage you will have little time for brooding over things you cannot change. Now then, let us bind the tincture of nasturtiums with rosemary and rue, for repentance and for grace. Swiftly now, Tania. All the bottles are labeled. Be *helpful*!"

For the rest of the morning, as Sancha read the age-old texts, Tania sifted powders and poured thick liquids into spoons and cut dried herbs with a sharp double-bladed, crystal mezzaluna while Hopie brewed potions and elixirs that filled the air with a heady brew of pungent smells.

They could only hope this would help.

A sudden knock sounded on the doors of Cerulean Hall.

"Who can this be?" muttered Hopie. "Have we not work enough without interruption?"

The knocking became an urgent hammering.

"Bid them depart!" said Sancha.

Tania nodded and ran to the closed doors.

"Do not let anyone in!" called Titania.

"What do you want?" Tania called through the doors.

"Tania—quickly—open the door!"

"Edric?" She jerked the bolt free and pulled one of

the doors open a fraction.

"Edric, you can't come in here, it's not—" She stopped dead as she saw the disturbed expression on his face.

"Quickly," Edric said. "It's Cordelia. She's ill."

VII

Tania arrived at Cordelia's bedchamber to find the door locked against them and Bryn hammering on the white wooden panels.

"Let me in, Cordelia; you are not well. Hopie is here." He paused but there was no reply. He banged the flat of his hand on the door. "Cordelia? You must open the door."

Bryn looked at Tania. "She is alone in there. She will not even speak with me."

Tania pressed her ear against the door. "Cordelia?" she called. "It's me. What's wrong? Open the door, please."

There was no reply.

Hopie rapped on the door with her knuckles. "Cordelia? What nonsense is this, sister? Come now, open the door and let me in. I shall not harm you." She listened for a few moments then shook her head and turned to Bryn. "Does she have the symptoms of the plague?"

Bryn's voice shook as he replied. "All was well but then she became pale and complained of a tightness in her chest. She collapsed onto the floor, clutching at her stomach and coughing. There was blood on her lips. I tried to help her, but she screamed at me and tore at my face. I ran for help. When I returned, the door was barred against me and Cordelia would not speak." His eyes were full of dread. "I fear she is too sick to respond."

"But why bar the door?" asked Hopie. "No matter. Edric, Bryn, use what force you must."

The two young men hurled themselves at the door. Once it resisted, the second time Tania heard wood splintering, and the third time the door burst open. Hopie was the first into the room, Tania close behind her.

They came into a white chamber with open windows and silk curtains flying in the wind. But there was no sign of Cordelia.

They moved quickly into the bedchamber.

"Cordelia!" called Hopie. "You must let us help you."

Tania noticed that the bedclothes had been torn from the mattress. An odd, sick feeling grew in her stomach as she walked slowly around the bed. She swallowed hard.

"She's here," she said. Cordelia was huddled in the corner of the room wrapped in sheets and blankets so that only her face was visible, flushed and running with sweat. There were flecks of blood on her lips and chin. Her eyes were strained wide open.

Tania knelt in front of her and reached out very slowly. "Cordie? Don't be scared. It's only me."

The feral eyes focused on her, and Cordelia's mouth twisted into a bloodstained snarl. She shrank away, pulling the covers closer around herself.

"Why is she like this?" murmured Edric. "No one else is showing these symptoms."

"None other have animal spirits so deep in their souls," said Hopie. "Her gift of empathy with the beasts of Faerie runs through her like the blood in her veins, and the sickness has set her animal spirit loose. She is lost in it."

Now Tania understood. *She's acting like a sick animal would.*

"Cordelia, my love?" Bryn moved closer to her, a hand reaching tentatively out. "Have no fear—"

"Touch me not!" Cordelia's voice was guttural and savage.

"No, Cordie," Tania said. "Don't be daft. It's Bryn. He won't hurt you. He loves you, remember?"

Cordelia's face turned to her.

"Tania . . . ?" she said hoarsely, a glimmer of recognition igniting. "Leave me, dearest sister. Leave me now. I would die alone."

"Listen to me, Cordie. You're not going to die," Tania said. "Hopie will give you some medicine—and if that doesn't work quickly enough, the King will come and put you in a lovely deep sleep." Cordelia still stared at her, but her lips had relaxed and the manic snarl faded.

"You stay. . . ." Cordelia rasped. "It is acceptable. You are not of Faerie born. But the others must go—" She spread her hand over her face. "They cannot see me die."

"No!" cried Bryn. "I won't leave you."

Cordelia's mouth opened wide and she let out a shivering, wailing howl that chilled Tania to the heart. There was nothing human in that howl; it was the wretched screaming of a trapped and dying animal.

"You'd better go!" Tania cried. "All of you. I'll make sure she's okay. Get Oberon."

"Come," said Hopie. "Do as she says. Master Chanticleer, fetch the King, and quickly!"

Hopie and Edric went, but Bryn stood hesitantly in the doorway, reluctant to leave his new bride.

"I'll look after her," said Tania. "I promise."

His face misshapen by grief, Bryn turned and left. Cordelia's howling died away to a harsh, grating panting, but her eyes still brimmed with a wild light.

"They're gone now, Cordie," Tania said, her voice soft and low, using a tone she would have used on a frightened cat or dog. "Come on, there's no need to be scared. I'm here. No one's going to hurt you. It'll be fine."

Very slowly Tania drew the covers back. She saw that Cordelia was still wearing the blue-and-gold wedding dress. Fear filled Cordelia's eyes. She was taking quick shallow breaths now, her whole body trembling. Tania shifted so that she was beside her sister, holding her against herself, pressing Cordelia's head to her shoulder.

"That's it, Cordie," she crooned, wrapping her arms around her. "Nothing to be scared of. Everything's going to be all right."

But although Cordelia allowed herself to be held, her body was rigid, every muscle tense as a bowstring. And the trembling did not stop.

"How fares my daughter?"

Tania looked up at the sound of Oberon's voice. Her arms were still around Cordelia, but her sister's breathing had calmed to a low rasp. Her eyes were closed now and her head was resting on Tania's chest.

Tania looked into her father's face and saw his agony as he gazed at Cordelia from the doorway. She knew what he must be feeling. It was only a few short weeks since Zara had been killed, and now death threatened another of his children.

"Can she be lifted to the bed?" asked Oberon.

Tania nodded. She kissed the top of Cordelia's head and smoothed her hair. "Cordie?" she crooned. "I need you to get up now, just for a moment or two. Will you do that for me?"

Cordelia's head snapped up. Her eyes were insane and her body rigid. She hissed, her fingernails digging into Tania's arm. Tania winced but tried not to flinch away.

"It's all right. It's me."

"Tania?" The voice was puzzled. "Have you walked with me into death?"

"No. No one is dead. I need you to get onto the bed. You'll be more comfortable there."

Tania got slowly to her feet, drawing Cordelia up with her. Suddenly Cordelia lifted her face and sniffed the air. A confused, startled look came into her eyes, and she turned her head to the doorway where the King stood.

"Ahhh!" she breathed, her eyes widening, her body trembling from head to foot. "My lord . . . the noble beast . . . eagle of the mountain, lion of the vale, stag of the forest . . . He has come for me. . . . He will lead me safe into the Great Darkness, where my furred and feathered and scaled brethren await me." She pulled away from Tania and stumbled toward Oberon, her hands reaching out for him.

He opened his arms and gathered her to him, holding her against his broad chest, lowering his head to kiss her hair. "Daughter, mine!" he murmured. "I am not the harbinger of death. I am your father, and while I have breath in my body, I will stand forever between you and that deadly portal." His arms tightened around her for a moment. "Sleep now, Cordelia, and awake to the eternal bliss that is your birthright." His voice rumbled. "Sleep!"

Tania watched as the golden light came threading out from his fingers, writhing and braiding in the air, encompassing Cordelia's quivering body, surrounding her with its gentle glow.

Cordelia's feet lifted from the ground, and she turned slowly as the cocoon of the Gildensleep knitted around her. Tania saw the desperate animal light fade from her eyes; tranquillity suffused her face as her eyelids peacefully closed.

The golden cocoon floated to the bed. Tilting and adjusting so that Cordelia was lying now on her back, it came lightly to rest on the mattress.

Tania stared at her father. "Will she recover?" she asked. "I mean, will she get *completely* better?"

She was thinking of what Hopie had said about Cordelia's animal spirit. *The sickness has set her animal spirit loose. She is lost in it.*

"I know not," said the King, standing at the bed-side. "I have done all that I can for her."

Tania turned as she heard others coming into the room: Bryn and Hopie, with Edric close behind.

Bryn looked at Cordelia, and tears ran down his cheeks. "Be well, my darling, in good time," he murmured. "I will not leave you again."

They stood in silence around the bed. Hopie was the first to speak. "I must away," she murmured. "Farewell, Cordelia, for the moment. I go to seek a cure."

"And I must also go," said the King. "Sickness stalks the corridors of this place, and there are others who need release from the turmoil of the plague."

They departed together.

Tania was acutely aware of Edric standing at the foot of the bed with his head bowed. She glanced at him, hoping that maybe he would look at her and hold out a comforting hand, that he would offer her some small moment of love or shared grief or understanding.

But it didn't happen. He walked silently from the room.

Bryn knelt at Cordelia's head.

Tania heard him singing softly to her.

> *"And I will guide you there*
> *Beyond this shallow land*
> *What lady is more fair*
> *What lord to take your hand*
> *As ever on we dance*
> *Among high heaven's host*
> *And I see at every glance*
> *The one I love the most."*

Tania couldn't bear the sorrow that bled through the lovely melody. There was a pain in her chest like stones grinding her heart as she made her way into the corridor. She went back to her own chambers and lay on her bed, utterly exhausted. When had she last slept? Not for two nights now: one long night with Mallory, the second aboard the *Cloud Scudder*.

But how could she sleep when all around her people were succumbing to the plague that she had brought on them? How could she ever hope to sleep again?

When she awoke, the bedchamber was full of shadows and there was the steady patter of teeming rain.

She sat up. Beyond the tall open windows the sky was dark. Not the beautiful starry, velvet blue of a clear Faerie night, but the deep, brooding gray of rain clouds. She got up and walked to the window. The sill and the floor were wet from the windblown rain that pricked cold on her face.

Not for the first time she wished they had clocks in Faerie. It was disorienting never to know the exact time of day—and for all she knew she may have slept half the night away.

She lit a candle and caught her reflection in a circular mirror above the washstand. She leaned close, looking into her weary eyes. The sadness in her face startled her.

She remembered her dad's words. *What happens on the morning* after *happy ever after?*

"Well? We're there now, that's for sure," she said to herself. "So what's the answer? What happens now?"

Her reflection shook its head and said nothing. She straightened up, listening to the endless rain. She could hear no other sound.

Out of nowhere a sudden panic gripped her: the terror that she was the only person left alive in the whole of the palace—the overwhelming conviction that the plague had taken everyone else in Veraglad. That she was surrounded by corpses.

She ran for the door. The candle fluttered and went out. She paused, breathing heavily, trying to calm herself. She turned to the nightstand and relit the candle. This time she moved more slowly, cupping the flame. She opened the door to her chambers and stepped out into the corridor.

The hallway was bright with candles set in crystal sconces all along the walls. Someone must have lit the candles; someone must still be alive.

She snuffed out her own candle and walked to the curved gallery that overlooked the main entrance hall to the palace, five floors below her.

Voices drifted up. Almost breathless with relief, she leaned over the banister. The hall far below her was awash with candlelight and movement. Figures were gathered there. She saw the King and the Earl Marshal Cornelius as well as several other folk of the royal court. They were greeting a tall silver-haired man clad in a heavy, rain-soaked black cloak. His deep, powerful voice came up to Tania. It was a voice she recognized, and the sound of it made her shiver.

"Ill met on a storm-wracked night, my lord Oberon," said Lord Aldritch of Weir, father of the Great Traitor Gabriel Drake. "Are all yet gathered? The summons of the Queen was most urgent. The great lords of Faerie have stern work ahead, I deem."

"Greetings, Lord Aldritch," replied the King. "Not all the earls have yet arrived. Lady Kernow came with us from Dinsel, and Lord Tristan is with us, as is Fleance of Gaidheal. Marchioness Lucina and Lord Brython are also in attendance."

"How fares Earl Valentyne?" asked Aldritch.

"I have bound him and many another in the Gildensleep," said the King.

"Then time presses hard on us. Let us to Conclave ere all is lost."

"We await the arrival of Lord Herne and Lady Mornamere," said Cornelius. "Conclave cannot commence until all are present."

"Then let us wish them good speed in their journey," said Aldritch. "Who will deputize for Earl Valentyne?"

"Princess Eden, if she can be spared," said the King.

"That is well. But I have given thought to our plight. I have summoned one who may be the surcease of all our woes."

Tania leaned farther out, listening intently. She had begun to get used to the courtly manner in which the Faerie folk spoke to one another. "Surcease of all our woes" meant Aldritch believed he had found a possible cure for the plague.

"Of whom do you speak?" asked the earl marshal.

"His name is Hollin. He is a Healer, a wise and skillful apothecary."

"I have not heard of this man," said Cornelius. "Whence comes he?"

Aldritch's voice was sharp as he replied. "I will vouch for him, Earl Marshal," he said. "And if the lords and ladies of the House of Aurealis traveled more often in the north, then perhaps his name would not be unknown to them."

"And if Weir showed a warmer welcome to wayfarers on the northern roads, then perhaps it would not be perceived by so many as a nest of darksome secrets," said another lord.

"Hush, Fillian," said the King. "Weir is our ally." He turned to Aldritch. "Speak on, my lord. What of this man?"

"I have bidden him and those acolytes that follow him to come here with all dispatch," Aldritch replied. "They left Weir upon a swift ship and if the wind is fair, they should be with us by dawn of tomorrow's tomorrow." He gave a formal bow. "It is for you, Lord Oberon, to judge his merits. If you find him wanting, then dispatch him whence he came." He put a hand to his chest. "But upon mine honor I do believe he may find a firm footing in the mire upon which we stand."

"So be it," said the King.

"You are sure that this man has the craft to battle the plague?" asked the earl marshal.

"Nothing is certain till it be tested," said Aldritch. "But it may prove so, my lord earl. The knowledge of Hollin is deep and subtle."

"Then may the spirits of the wind and of the sea speed his arrival, my lord," said Oberon. "But come; you must be weary after your long journey. There is food and drink in the Star Chamber."

The King led Lord Aldritch away out of Tania's sight. She stood, still leaning over the banister, the rail digging into her stomach.

The last time she had heard that sepulchral voice had been in Caer Liel in Weir. Lord Aldritch had been speaking to his son and agreeing not to come to the King's aid in his fight against the Sorcerer King of Lyonesse. Queen Titania had insisted that Aldritch was not a traitor—but all the same Tania still feared and distrusted him.

But he had spoken of a Healer. Could there really be someone in Faerie who would be able to prevail against the illness?

She heard footsteps along the corridor.

It was Rathina. "You look as pale as aspen leaves, Tania," Rathina said, scrutinizing her face. "What's the matter? Why are you not abed? Has sleep deserted you as it has me?" A flicker of fear crossed her face. "Or are you unwell?"

Tania shook her head. "I'm not ill," she said. "Lord Aldritch has just arrived." She shuddered. "I'm sorry, but he gives me the creeps."

A bleak smile curled Rathina's lips. "'Tis a good phrase," she said softly. "Aye, there is something about the lord of Weir that makes the skin crawl, I cannot deny. But you should not fear him. Were our father in any doubt, Weir would have been excluded from the Conclave."

"I heard him say something about a Healer—a man who might be able to deal with the illness. He's already on his way."

"Glad tidings, indeed, if it proves so," said Rathina. "But I shall not dance on a needle's point till the deed is done."

Tania looked into her sister's face. "Rathina . . . I

know this sounds weak," she murmured. "But I need a hug. . . . I need it really badly right now."

Wordlessly Rathina moved close to Tania and folded her in her arms. It was a comfort for Tania to close her eyes and rest her head on Rathina's shoulder, to feel her sister's long, thick dark hair against her face, to smell her, and to relax into her embrace.

"These are hard times for all," Rathina murmured. "The disease strikes us down like a quarter-ball at pitch-pin, and none may feel safe."

Tania lifted her head. "Like a what at *what*?"

"A quarter-ball at pitch-pin. 'Tis a game, Tania. The purpose is to roll a wooden ball and strike down the pins. We played it often as children."

Tania nodded. "Bowling. I get it." She moved out of Rathina's arms. "It does feel a bit like that—except that I'm the one who rolled the ball. I set all this in motion and now I can't stop it."

Rathina raised an eyebrow. "You would speak to me of guilt?" she said. "Sister, I could trade you guilt for guilt ten times over and leave you groaning under the burden of my misdeeds."

Tania didn't have an answer to that. She pulled back the sleeve of her gown. There were four small crescent-moon marks on her forearm, dark red with dried blood. The wounds of fingernails. "Cordelia did that," she said. "She was so frightened, Rathina."

"As are we all, sweet sister, as are we all." Rathina linked her arm with Tania's and drew her along the high gallery. "But we shall banish melancholy with naughty deeds." She gave a sly grin. "Would you visit in secret the Chamber of the Conclave of Earls?"

"Are we allowed?"

"Nay—that is the whole point. 'Tis a place most solemn and private, and none but the earls may enter. Come." Rathina began to run, towing Tania along with her.

They passed many closed doors. Tania wondered about the folk who filled those silent rooms. The palace was full of people, but were any of them able to sleep, or were they all lying wide-eyed in the rain-filled night, dreading the coming of the plague?

She was sure at least that Hopie and Sancha and the Queen would not have taken to their beds. The most they would have allowed themselves was a brief nap to sharpen their wits. Tania wished she could be with them—wished she had some knowledge that would make a difference.

But she didn't. Oberon had hoped she would be able to help, but so far that hope had proved in vain. For all the use she was being she may as well have remained in London with her mum and dad.

Tania soon lost track of where she was as her sister pulled her along the maze of corridors, but at last they came to a pair of tall white doors of carved crystal.

Rathina lifted a candelabrum from its wall sconce and pushed at the doors. They glided open into a large dark space. Tania followed her sister through, sensing immediately that this was a place where she should tread lightly and speak in whispers. The sound of pattering rain echoed off the walls.

Rathina closed the doors behind them and held up the candelabrum.

The Chamber of the Earls Conclave was a lofty, circular room made entirely of glass. Tall pointed windows swept to a high vaulted ceiling, their dark faces stippled and streaming with the rain. The thin spires that framed the windows were a milky color, hardly seeming substantial enough to hold off the pelting rain.

But most extraordinary and unnerving of all was the floor beneath Tania's feet. It was of a glass so clear that Tania felt as if she was standing on nothing.

"Oh!" she gasped, and clutched at Rathina, suddenly realizing that she was looking through fathoms of rain-lashed air to the dimly visible sea far below. The chamber overhung the cliff, and there was nothing but the thin veil of glass under her feet to prevent Tania from plunging to her death.

Smiling at her unease, Rathina took Tania's arm and walked her in a slow circle around the chamber. Set in crystal niches around the walls were simple, high-backed chairs made of smooth white stone.

"These are the Thirteen Sieges of Faerie," Rathina explained. "Ten are reserved for the lords and ladies of the ten caers, and two for our father and mother."

"You said thirteen," Tania said. "Who sits on the last one?"

"No one," Rathina replied. "It is always empty: It is

called the Siege of the Lost Caer, but I have no notion why it is so named, for there is no such castle in all of Faerie."

Tania noticed that there was a symbol carved in the crystal above each seat. She recognized the radiating sun of the King and the full moon of the Queen, but there were many others: a bird, a coiling dragon, a tree, a unicorn—a different symbol for every chair save one. The Siege of the Lost Caer.

For some reason Tania felt a shiver run down her spine as she stood in front of the thirteenth chair.

"As soon as Lord Herne of Minnith Bannwg and Lady Mornamere of Llyr arrive, the Conclave will commence," Rathina said. "Earl Valentyne will not be able to attend; Eden will take his place and represent Mynwy Clun, if she can be persuaded to leave his side. Lord and Lady Gaidheal were killed by the Sorcerer King, so their son Fleance, a lad of but ten summers, will represent their Earldom. And of course there is no lord nor lady of Caer Regnar Naal, nor has there been from time immemorial, so our uncle the earl marshal shall sit in the Siege of Sinadon."

"And where will Lord Aldritch sit?" Tania asked.

"Under the charge of the wild unicorn of Caer Liel," said Rathina. "Dinsel is represented by the leaping salmon, Minnith Bannwg by the stag—each of the Earldoms of Faerie has its own charge. For Gaidheal the oak tree, for Talebolion the sea horse, and for Sinadon the two crossed keys." Rathina looked at Tania. "'Tis shame indeed that we come here on a stormy night. When the sky is clear, the stars do shine so very bright!"

"Sorry? What were you saying?" Tania had been staring at the Siege of Weir, seeing in her mind the thin, dour face of the sinister old lord.

"It matters not," said Rathina. "Come, let us to bed now, sweet sister. Sleep offers peace and ease, and mayhap the new morn will bring clearer skies to our wounded Realm."

Tania linked arms with her and walked out into the corridor. She was glad to leave the Chamber of the Conclave of Earls. It was beautiful with its soaring walls of glass and crystal, but it was also a strange and uncanny place to be on a rain-swept night.

VIII

"Tania. Wake up now."

Tania opened her eyes to darkness. A heavy, blue-gray darkness, as if the world had turned overnight into burnished lead.

"Cordelia?"

"Yes, sweetheart. You must get up now. I have something to show you."

Tania climbed out of bed and followed her sister along a curved corridor.

"Where are we going?"

"You will see."

Cordelia led her to a pair of tall crystal doors. The doors opened without being touched, and Cordelia and Tania stepped into the Chamber of the Conclave of Earls. Beyond the slender windows the sky was full of towering mountains of cloud black as sloes, shining dully. Under their feet the sea moved like molten rock.

"I'm not too keen on this place," Tania said. "Do we have to be in here?"

"Yes. You must see!"

"Okay. But quickly, though."

Cordelia ran across the glass floor to the Siege of the Lost Caer. She turned and sat, smiling darkly.

Suddenly Tania was aware of the rippling sound of a harp and of a deep, rich woman's voice singing a sad, beautiful lament.

> *Years do pass, and in passing, spin out threads*
> *   of the future*
> *Alive upon the weaver's loom as she weaves her*
> *   net of doom*
> *Silence drowns this wound of passion*
> *Is this our song we hear come a-singing?*
> *So fierce and bright was the sun, so huge and full*
> *   was the moon*
> *The night once filled with lambent and fragrant*
> *   stars*
> *Lovers' jewels, in timeless reverie they twined*
> *They are lost now and we drowned deep*
> *Our song is stilled now, never to give voice*
> *   again*
> *Yet ever the echoes ripple to the shore*
> *Along the road of faith we will walk nevermore*
> *Lost in the deep Ocean is our harbor*
> *Lost in the deep Ocean is our home*

"What is that song?" Tania asked.

"It is the Song of the Lost Caer," said Cordelia. "It is the Song of Our Redemption. If you would cure me—if you would cure us all—seek the Lost Caer, sweet sister. Seek the Lost Caer. . . ."

The floor gave way under Tania's feet and with a shriek she fell, to be swallowed by the ocean.

Except that she didn't land in the sea at all. She was enveloped by night air thick as wine, dark as caverns under countless fathoms of seawater. And she was not swimming; she was flying on gossamer wings, and below her she could faintly make out the shapes of dark and sinister buildings that thrust towers and spires into the gloomy air.

If you would cure us all—seek the Lost Caer, sweet sister. Seek the Lost Caer. . . .

Tania awoke with Rathina's voice ringing in her ears. "Breakfast, Tania! Although if it can be called so when the sun is at the zenith, I do not know."

Tania sat up as Rathina lowered herself onto the bed, carrying a tray laden with bread and butter, cheese and fruit, and cups of yellow Faerie cordial.

Tania knuckled her eyes. "I must have slept like a log." She yawned.

"Indeed," said Rathina. "Like a log being sawn into firewood. You snored like a sow!"

"I do not snore!" Tania protested.

They had come back late in the night, tumbling together into Tania's bed and falling quickly asleep.

Tania looked sharply at her sister. "Has the meeting of the earls begun?"

Rathina nodded. "A while ago," she said. "Lord

Herne arrived before dawn, and Lady Mornamere rode in as the sun was rising."

Tania frowned. "You shouldn't have let me sleep in," she said. "I wanted to be there."

"They would not have allowed you into the chamber," Rathina said, buttering a slice of bread and handing it to Tania. "None but the earls or their representatives may enter—most especially not when a Conclave is in session."

"They've been at it all morning, then?" Tania asked. "The Healer Aldritch mentioned isn't supposed to arrive till tomorrow. What can they be talking about that takes so long?"

"There is much to debate over how the plague came to Faerie," Rathina said, curling her legs up under her and taking a sip of cordial. "And how to prevent such a thing from ever happening again."

"Oh, for heaven's sake, we know what happened; my parents brought it here. But they've been punished already. What else is there to do about that? It's done; they've gone. End of story."

Rathina looked carefully at her. "Tania, can it be that you do not realize the true purpose of this Conclave?"

Tania gave her a puzzled look. "The *true* purpose? What are you talking about?"

"The earls do not debate over the fate of Master Clive and Mistress Mary," Rathina said gravely. "The focus of their deliberations is *you*, Tania. Everyone knows this; how is it that you do not?"

Tania stared at her. "Me?" she said. "What about me?"

Rathina reached out and cupped Tania's cheek in her hand. "They are gathered in Conclave to decide your fate, Tania: to deem whether you may remain in Faerie, or whether you should be sent back forever to the Mortal World."

"*What?* Why would they do that?"

"You are half Mortal, Tania. They fear you may also be the harbinger of Mortal disease. I thought you would have understood that." Rathina's expression became urgent. "I have a boon to ask, sister," she said. "If it must be that you are doomed to exile in the Mortal World, will you take me with you?" She gripped Tania's wrist with fierce fingers. "You are my dearest friend," she continued. "I could not bear to be here without you."

But Tania hardly heard what she was saying. How dare the earls decide her fate without hearing her side of things, without even allowing her to be present while they talked about her?

No! No way!

Tania jumped out of bed, spilling the tray. Ignoring Rathina's protests, she ran to the closet and quickly chose a gown: gray satin, simple and unadorned.

"Tania? What is the matter?" Rathina asked.

"There is no way they're going to make any decisions about my life till they've heard what I've got to say on the subject!" Tania replied. She smoothed out the long skirts of the gown. "I can't remember how to get to the glass room; take me there, please."

"It is pointless," Rathina said. "They will not allow you in."

Tania's eyes narrowed. "Want to bet?" she said.

Two wardens stood at the white doors of the Chamber of the Conclave of Earls. Each held a tall crystal halberd, the axe-heads glinting in the light.

Rathina hung back as Tania approached the men in their dark red livery. As she tried to move between them, the halberds snapped diagonally across her path, bringing her to a halt.

"None may pass, my lady," said one of the men.

"Get out of my way," Tania said, pushing one of the halberds aside and reaching for the door handle. "I'm not in the mood!"

"My lady!" One of the guards put a restraining hand on her shoulder, but she shrugged it off and pushed the door open, stepping into the chamber before either of the wardens could stop her.

She paused just inside the sunlit chamber, quickly taking in the scene. The tall windows were full of blue sky. Of the thirteen crystal sieges, all were occupied save one. Eden was among those gathered, seated under the heraldic charge of the dragon of Mynwy Clun. Tania also noticed that a fresh-faced lad with close-cropped blond hair sat on the Siege of Gaidheal: the son of the lord and lady who had died at the hands of the Sorcerer King of Lyonesse, his hidden wings the merest bulge under his clothes.

As she entered, the boy, Fleance, was speaking. ". . . cast as I was too soon into the high politics of Faerie by the deaths of my mother and father—" He stopped dead, staring at Tania.

The other faces that turned to her were grave and solemn, and in Eden's and Titania's expressions Tania saw deep anguish. It must have taken a lot to persuade Eden to leave her husband's side.

As Tania stared around the gathering, she was aware of the clear floor under her and the sunlit drop to the wrinkled face of the ocean far below.

"Tania?" growled Oberon, a frown gathering on his brow. "You cannot enter here."

"You're talking about me," Tania replied, aware that the wardens were at her back now, ready to take hold of her. "I want to know exactly what you're saying."

Lord Aldritch glared at her. "None but the earls of Faerie or their representatives may enter this chamber when the Conclave is in session," he said. "Be gone, Princess Tania; you cannot defy the will of the nobility of Faerie."

Tania stepped forward, moving out of reach of the wardens. "If this gabfest concerns me, then I have a right to be here," she said. "Do you think I'm going to sit around doing nothing while you decide what's going to happen to me?"

Lord Aldritch reached out his hand toward her. "The princess's actions serve only to prove the point I made earlier, my lords and ladies: She is not a native of Faerie; she is more than half Mortal. Her sojourn in the Mortal World has changed her utterly from the child we knew before the coming of the Great Twilight." His eyes glinted. "We should not risk our lives for this half-thing!"

"Peace, my lord!" snapped Titania, her eyes flashing dangerously as she looked at Aldritch. "Watch your tongue; you speak of my child."

Lord Aldritch bowed his head, but did not apologize.

A light, thoughtful voice sounded. "I have listened to much talk of the strange history of the Princess Tania," said Fleance, "but it is hard to understand *what* she is." He looked at Tania. "I have been told that you were Mortal-born, but that your spirit is Faerie—is that true?"

Tania was silent for a moment, acutely aware of the piercing looks of the people who surrounded her. "I don't know," she admitted at last. "I don't know what I am."

"A troubling admission," commented Lord Herne, a broad-set man with a great russet beard and eyes like blue ice. He looked keenly at her. "For in your soul surely lies hidden the answer to the conundrum we debate today. Are you Faerie or are you Mortal?"

"She is both," said Titania. "And before you condemn her for it, bear in mind, my lords and ladies, that were it not so, she could never have defeated Lyonesse."

"'Tis true," added Eden. "My husband knew the legend—that neither true-born Faerie nor one of Mortal kind could slay that evil thing. Had my sister not been the person she is, we would not be seated here today, but would rather be under the yoke of Lyonesse."

"And for her help we are all most grateful," said Lady Kernow of Dinsel, a woman with flowing gray hair and a face like carved marble. "But we face now a new peril: a disease brought into our land by Mortals." She frowned at Tania. "Do all Mortals carry disease with them, Princess?"

"I . . . I don't know what you mean—"

Titania broke in. "All Mortals can fall prey to disease," she said. "Just as any man or woman in Faerie may succumb to the evils of the Dark Arts. But they do not carry the seeds of disease within them. It invades their bodies from outside." She turned, holding each of them for a moment in her fierce glance. "And I tell you true, my lords and ladies, if Tania had the sickness, it would have shown in her by now. We have nothing to fear from her."

"You speak as would any mother," said Lord Brython. "And I do not doubt your words are true, but is it not also true that Princess Tania's gift—her ability to step between the worlds—is a constant threat to us? Were she allowed to pass at will between Faerie and the Mortal World, do we not risk her bringing some further disease into our Realm?"

Tania looked at the tall bearded lord, alarmed that a man with whom she had fought side-by-side should turn on her.

"Lord Brython touches the very heart of the matter," said Aldritch. "If we are to live without fear of Mortal disease, then we have but two choices before us: either Princess Tania must be sent forever from this Realm and locked in the Mortal World behind unbreakable enchantments, or if she is to remain here, her gift must be taken from her for all time."

Tania stared at her father. "No!" she cried. "You can't make that kind of decision about me like . . . like it's *nothing*!"

"Heed me, daughter," said Oberon. "A choice must be made. But you speak true: This is too weighty a matter for us to make the choice on your behalf." He rose from his chair, moving slowly, as though his body ached. Moment by moment the Gildensleep was draining all the energy out of him. But there was still great majesty in him, and all eyes turned to him. Tania felt a warm hand slip into hers. It was Rathina, silent at her side.

"We have debated long, my lords and ladies," Oberon said. "We have spoken of Tania's gift and of its mystic origin. We have spoken of our hopes and our fears. We have spoken of what enchantments or remedies may lie in Faerie to halt this Mortal plague. We have spoken of the Mystic Arts and of the spirits that live in all things. We have spoken of how our people may be saved and of how the Immortal Realm may survive. I have weighed all your words in the balance, and here then is the doom I decree.

"For the safety of the Realm of Faerie Princess Tania can no longer be allowed to use her gift—save once more if she so chooses. She stands at a fork in the road of her life. She alone can decide which path to take: either to remain with her loving family in Faerie or to depart forever and live out her life in the world of her Mortal parents. I give her until tomorrow eve to ponder the question of her life. But in that time she must give her most solemn oath that she will not use her gift, that she will remain in Faerie. And whatsoever her choice be, I decree that all the portals between Faerie and the Mortal World will be closed forever at dawn on the following day. By that time Tania must either have departed this Realm or she must embrace Faerie for all eternity."

Tania could hardly take this in. The King was only allowing her a day and a half to make a decision that would change the rest of her life.

For a moment she thought she was going to faint. If she had not felt Rathina's hand tight in hers, she could easily have collapsed onto the glass floor.

"Do you accept my doom?" she heard Oberon asking.

She gazed at him, her brain refusing to work.

"I will vouch for her," said Eden, looking at Tania with pity and understanding. "She will not disobey."

"Then are all in agreement?" Oberon asked.

Tania was vaguely aware of voices saying aye.

"The closing of the ways between the worlds will save this Realm from further harm," she heard Aldritch say. "So let us turn now our thoughts to the coming of the Healer, for I deem that none other can hope to find a cure for the plague."

"Who is this man?" asked Titania. "You say his name is Hollin and that he has followers—but whence comes he, and what is the wellspring of his skills?"

"Aye," added Eden, frowning at Lord Aldritch. "I would know that, too. My sister the Princess Hopie is the greatest Healer in all of Faerie—and yet, my lord, you tell us that this Hollin can outdo her in her own craft? How is that so?"

"He is not a native of this land," said Aldritch. "He came to Weir from Alba—from across the Western Ocean." He looked at Titania. "As you did yourself, in glad times long past, your grace."

Tania stared at her mother. She gasped. "You're not from Faerie? You never *said*—"

"It was not kept from you as a secret, Tania," said the Queen. "I was born in Alba, and I came to Faerie as a young woman, following a prophecy that was made at my cradle." She turned to Aldritch. "But I do not recall that there were any Healers in the land of my birth to outrival Princess Hopie, my lord."

Aldritch straightened his back, his eyes proud as he looked at the Queen. "If Hollin proves inadequate to the task, then may the curse of the plague fall upon me and all my House, your grace," he declared. "I know of

Master Hollin only that he has great healing powers—powers that I have witnessed with my own eyes." He glanced around the chamber, his voice cold and angry. "But if any doubt me, then shall I gladly quit this palace and return to my own Earldom with Master Hollin in my train."

"Peace, Lord Aldritch. We do not doubt you," said Oberon. "But let us hope that this man is all that you say he is. When is he expected?"

"He comes by sea and will make landfall here at first light tomorrow."

"Then all is decided," said Oberon. "We shall arrange that the Healer from Weir receives a goodly welcome on tomorrow's early morn." He turned his gaze on Tania. "In the meantime you must go, daughter, and give thought to your future. We shall meet here tomorrow eve to hear your words and thus to welcome you forever to this Realm, or if you so choose, to bid you a final, sad farewell."

"Who am I, Rathina? I mean, really—tell me: Who am I?"

Tania was sitting at the top of a broad set of marble steps, her chin propped on her arms and her elbows resting on her up-drawn knees.

She and Rathina were alone in a wide, terraced garden that lay within the walls of the palace. It backed onto tall crystal towers and stepped down in gentle grassy gradients to a low balustrade that stretched in a curve along the cliff edge. Gravel paths wound between the clipped lawns, and in pots and stone troughs grew yellow and blue flowers and tall fountains of red and golden grasses. Every stone surface in the garden was encrusted with elegant designs fashioned from seashells—from scallop shells as large as Tania's open hand to cockleshells and mussels, and green limpets and yellow nerites, and tiny blue periwinkles no bigger than a child's fingernail.

Rathina was sitting on the polished top of the balustrade, picking pieces of dove gray gravel from her hand and idly tossing them down the cliff face into the sea. She looked at Tania through a veil of windblown hair. "You are my sister," she said with a slight shrug. "What else would you have me say?"

Clusters of hanging crystal tubes chimed together in the breeze, filling the air with a gentle bell-like music.

"I am so sick of feeling torn apart," Tania said heavily. And that was not the worst of it; she ached for Edric. It was so hard to make this impossible choice without him, and yet she had seen nothing of him since he had left Cordelia's chamber yesterday. She had no idea where he was or what he might be doing.

The love of her Faerie parents and of her sisters meant an enormous amount to her—but their love was a comfort that came from outside. It had always felt as though somehow Edric's love warmed her from deep within.

She remembered something he had said to her once: that home for him was wherever *she* chose to be. She lifted her fingers to the black onyx pendant that he had given her. It hung from a necklace woven from the hairs of a unicorn's mane, slender as light, finer than silk. A token of his love—of his undying love, he had said.

So where's that love now, Edric?

If she chose to live in the Mortal World, would he still want to be with her? Would he take her hand and be led into permanent exile? Did she even want him to make such a sacrifice?

Tania had tried to explain details of her old life in the Mortal World to her sisters. She had hosted show-and-tell sessions with them—bringing things through from the Mortal World to intrigue and amaze them. And she had tried to explain other stuff like movies and recorded music and iPods and the Internet. Airplanes, cars, trains, skyscrapers.

Sancha and Cordelia and Zara had been to London, so they understood some of these things, but Rathina found everything about the Mortal World strange and compelling. Tania could still remember Rathina sitting on her bed in the Royal Palace, turning Tania's debit card over and over, trying to grasp its purpose.

Tania walked to the balustrade and leaned against it, turning to gaze up over the garden. She spotted a shell picture that she had not noticed before. It was of a small unicorn trotting along with periwinkle shells hanging from its silvery horn.

"Percival . . ." she murmured. "My pet unicorn, Percival, is buried there."

Rathina stiffened at her side. "You remember him?"

Tania nodded. "I read about him in my Soul Book."

"Ahh." Rathina sounded disappointed.

"No, you don't understand," said Tania, excitement growing in her. "I read some stuff about walking along the beach with him when I was young—but I never read anything about what happened to him." She looked at Rathina. "I never read that he died and was buried here."

"What did he die of, Tania?" Rathina's voice was urgent. "Think now."

Tania struggled to beat down the locked doors in her mind. "No," she gasped. "I don't remember."

"Southern unicorns only live for three years," Rathina said.

"He died of old age—of natural causes," Tania blurted. "I cried for days and days." She began to speak ever more rapidly. "And . . . and Hopie said I should be given another unicorn to take his place, but Mother said no—because they live such a short time and she couldn't bear to see me so unhappy again." She turned to her sister, her eyes wide. "Rathina—I remember all that. It came to me out of nowhere. I *remember*!"

"What else?" urged Rathina. "Do you remember that song we used to sing, 'The Ballad of Perfect Love'? You would play the lute and Zara would play the spinetta and we all would sing."

She began to sing a simple melody.

> *"And he shall wear a crimson cloak*
> *His hair shall be black as the raven's wing*
> *And he shall ride a tall white charger*
> *And he shall have hawthorn spurs upon his*
> *heels."*

The words of the next verse flooded Tania's mind and she joined in.

> *"And he shall laugh and take me in his arms*
> *And my head shall lie upon his shoulder*
> *And he shall smell of woods and wild things*
> *And he shall kiss my forehead and smile*
>
> *"And we shall live in a tower of gray stone*
> *And he shall never, ever leave me*
> *And he shall call me his beloved and bow*
> *And he shall fight dragons for me."*

Rathina jumped from the balustrade. "Your memories are returning at last, praise the good spirits!" she cried.

But Tania shook her head. "They're still only bits and pieces," she said. "Just . . . *scraps*. It's no different than before. I remembered a song the very first time I was here—I sang it with Zara—but there was nothing else."

"Yet every new memory adds a thread to the tapestry of your past," Rathina said. "Have patience, Tania; you shall come back to us."

Tania looked at her. "But that just makes it harder," she said. "The more I remember of my life here, the harder it is to decide what to do."

"Do not attempt to decide alone, Tania. There are many here who love you, who would help you with the burden you must bear."

Tania gave a bleak smile. "Yes, I know—and I know what most of them would say: They'd tell me to stay here in Faerie."

"Is that such bad counsel?" Rathina asked softly.

"Ask my mum and dad back in London that question," Tania said.

Rathina frowned deeply but said no more.

Tania gripped her hand. "I need to be on my own for a bit," she said. "Is that okay?"

Rathina nodded. "It is. Go. Think. Decide." Rathina's fingers wrapped firmly around Tania's. "But remember what I asked of you, sweet sister: If you choose to go to the Mortal World, take me with you."

"Yes," Tania said quickly. "Yes—if that's what you really want, of course I will." She didn't share her other thought. *But if you think that going to the Mortal World will help you to outrun your bad memories, then you're going to be disappointed.* Tania ran up the broad steps and pushed through the door that led back into the palace. Crystal chandeliers chimed in the breeze as she closed the door behind herself.

"Tania."

She spun around. Edric was standing against the wall behind her.

"Oh! You startled me!"

He didn't smile. "I'm sorry. I didn't mean to."

"What are you doing here?"

"Waiting to catch you on your own. You didn't see me, but I was in an anteroom close to the earls' chamber when you"—now he almost smiled—"when you made your grand entrance. You made quite an impression. I heard it all."

"So you know what's going on."

"Yes. I know what's going on."

Her mouth twisted. "Any helpful suggestions?"

"Remember that Sunday afternoon when we watched *The Wizard of Oz*? What was it Dorothy said? 'There's no place like home.'" His eyes widened. "Close your eyes and click your heels three times. What do you long for? Faerie or London?"

There was a pause, and Tania suddenly had the horrible sensation that Edric was moving away from her, that a gulf was opening between them—that if she didn't do something immediately, he would be forever out of her reach.

"You," she whispered. "I long for *you*."

A look came over his face: a fusing, she thought, of love and desire and sadness and loss.

She ran into his arms and buried her face in his shoulder, her arms tight around him. "I'm sorry," she gasped. "I'm so sorry. Please—Edric—help me, please.

Tell me what to do. I can't stand it anymore." The words came pouring out of her, and it was almost as if she was listening to someone else speaking. "I'll do anything you want. I don't care anymore. I'll marry you if you still want me to. Let's do that right now. Let's get married and go right away from here—somewhere all on our own. Let's forget *everyone*." She lifted her head and looked into his face, so close that she could feel his breath on her skin, see her smoky reflection in his chestnut brown eyes.

"You don't mean that," he said gently. "The thing about getting married and running away. You don't really mean that."

"Don't I?" She blinked tears away, squeezing him fiercely in her arms till she heard him gasp for breath. "I'm sorry I hurt you. I love you *so* much." She looked deep into his eyes.

He didn't reply. She pulled away from him, looking searchingly into his face.

"Edric? Are we okay?" she asked.

He swallowed. "There's something I have to tell you," he said.

"That sounds ominous," she said uneasily. "It can't be that you don't love me anymore. Rathina told me all about falling in love here. Once you're in love, you're stuck with it. So you're pretty much stuck loving me, Edric—no way out of that one!"

"Tania—stop!" he said.

"No, no, you're going to tell me something unbearable. I know you are."

The Queen and Hopie and Sancha all have the plague.

Oberon is too exhausted to keep the Gildensleep working; everyone is going to die.

"I have to leave here," Edric said.

This was so unexpected that for a few moments Tania just stared at him. "What do you mean? *Leave* here? Leave for where?"

"For Weir, for Caer Liel."

"What do you want to go there for?"

"Lord Aldritch has called me into his service," Edric said. "I am to return to Caer Liel with him when the business of Conclave is finished."

Tania stared at him in disbelief. "And you decided this *when*?"

"I didn't *decide* at all," said Edric. "My family have always been bondsmen to the lords of Weir. I hoped that Lord Aldritch would release me from my duty to his House—but he's ordered me to return to Weir with him."

"I'm sorry—*ordered* you? What gives him the right to order you to do anything? And even if he does think he can give you orders, you don't have to go along with them. Tell him to get lost. You don't owe him anything."

"I owe him my allegiance, Tania," Edric said. "I have to do as he commands." A kind of forlorn hope came into his voice. "But I may be gone only a short while, possibly only a few months. I'll do everything I can to get him to release me—and then I'll come back to you."

"And what if I'm not here? What if I decide I want to spend my life in the Mortal World?"

Edric didn't reply.

"Don't do this, Edric."

"I must."

"Even if it means us never seeing each other again?"

His voice was barely above a whisper. "I'm sorry. It's my duty. I have no choice."

IX

The streets of Rhyehaven were deserted. A few fearful faces watched from shuttered windows or peered out from between the slats of bolted doors, but most of the inhabitants had heeded the warnings of the King's wardens and had shut themselves away when the delegation from the palace had walked through the town to the harbor.

They stood now on the quayside. Silent. Waiting.

Tania and Rathina were standing side-by-side at the water's edge, slightly apart from the other lords and ladies of Faerie.

Lord Aldritch was at the head of the gathering, clad in a black cloak lined with sable fur. Edric stood attentively just behind him, also now dressed in black. He glanced toward Tania for a split second, then looked away again, his face emotionless—unreadable.

I've lost him, Tania thought. *Lost him forever.*

As though sensing her pain, Rathina slipped her arm into Tania's. Tania gave her a bleak smile, glad to have her sister close.

All the Earldoms were represented in the welcoming party, all save Mynwy Clun: Valentyne could not come to greet the Healer and Eden would not leave his side a second time. Earl Marshal Cornelius represented Oberon. The King had also remained at the palace; the need to maintain the power of the Gildensleep consumed all his energy. Titania and Hopie and Sancha had stayed there as well, watching over the sick and the healthy, still searching for a remedy to the plague, unwilling to cease their labors until the Healer made landfall.

Tania gazed out over the sea, trying not to think of a future without Edric.

"He comes!" Aldritch's voice cracked the pensive silence.

Tania saw a masthead beyond the breakwaters coming in from the west. A bright yellow pennant snapped in the wind. Yellow sails glided into view. A subdued murmur ran through the crowd as the Healer's ship rounded the stone breakwater and sailed into the harbor.

It was a schooner, skimming the sea under full sail, its wind-stretched canvas as yellow as the sun, its hull slender and graceful as it clove the foaming water.

A strange joy came into Tania's heart as she watched the bright sails being reefed. She hadn't known what to expect of the Healer from Weir—something dark and maybe a little sinister, perhaps? Black robes and stern faces hidden under deep cowls.

Ropes spun out from the ship and wardens ran to

catch them and secure them to stone bollards. A gang-plank was run out onto the quayside.

Lord Aldritch stepped forward as a man appeared.

Tania almost smiled as she looked at him: He was tall and wide-shouldered, dressed in a simple yellow robe tied at the waist. He had an ageless face with a high forehead and deep-set emerald eyes. His hair was tawny and hung about his shoulders. A thin white band circled his forehead and in its center was a bright blue stone that flickered like sapphire flame in the sunlight.

"Well met, Master Hollin," called Aldritch. "You come in good time to our aid."

"'Tis hoped so, my lord," replied the Healer. He paused at the head of the gangplank, his head turning slowly as he looked from face to face. Tania thought she saw a slight frown pucker between his eyes when his gaze fell on her, but it happened so quickly that she may have imagined it.

Rathina's voice whispered to Tania. "I had expected someone . . . I cannot say . . . darker, mayhap, coming from Weir. This man seems filled with sunlight. 'Tis a good omen, I am sure."

"Let's hope so," said Tania.

Hollin walked down the gangplank to the quay. He came briefly to one knee before Lord Aldritch. "My lord."

"Rise, friend," said Aldritch. "There is much to be done."

More men now appeared on the ship, the Healer's acolytes, their tunics and leggings a fresh leaf green. They began to walk down the gangplank. Tania noticed that they carried staves of white wood and that one had a fur bundle in his arms.

"You are thrice welcome, Master Healer," said Cornelius, coming forward as Hollin got to his feet. "Our need is very great. Will you come with us to the palace?"

"In a moment, with your leave, my lord," said Hollin. He turned and gestured to the man carrying the fur bundle. "First I would lay a blessing on the voyage."

The man crouched and carefully spread the bundle. Tania moved in closer. The bundle was an animal skin and gathered in the center was a collection of colored gemstones.

Hollin knelt and picked a browny green stone, touching it to his forehead then placing it on the ground. "Agate for the earth," he said. He picked another stone: creamy white this time. "Quartz for the air." He laid it next to the first. Two more stones joined them, one red and one blue. "For fire and water," Hollin intoned. He passed his hands over the four stones. "Earth, water, fire, and air. I place the four paradigms of the unanswerable riddle upon the white bull's spotted hide. Bless this time and bless this place and bless all my actions."

Tania held her breath, half expecting something magical to happen, but Hollin simply got to his feet and gestured to the man to put the stones back into the skin.

"Have you seen anything like this before?" Tania whispered to Rathina.

"Nay, never," her sister said. "'Tis most curious. What can it portend?"

"I have absolutely no idea."

"Take me to the sick," said Hollin. "I would begin my work."

Cornelius and Lord Aldritch led the delegation as it made its way solemnly through the rising streets of Rhyehaven. Hollin walked between them, his head bowed as they explained to him their troubles. His acolytes trooped along behind, their staves clicking on the cobbles as they went.

Tania walked alongside one of the men. "Did you have an easy journey?" she asked.

He smiled and inclined his head politely.

"We're all hoping you can work miracles," Tania added. "Is . . . um . . . Hollin good with miracles at all?"

The smile widened for a moment then the man looked away without replying.

Not too chatty, then. But so long as the Healer could cure the plague, she didn't mind if none of them ever said a word.

The Healer stood at the entrance of Cerulean Hall. The doors had been thrown open and the blue chamber glowed with the golden light of many floating cocoons. There were fifty or more patients now, all of them cradled in Oberon's Gildensleep, their symptoms suspended just so long as the King's mind held fast to the reins of his Mystic Arts.

Titania pushed a stray lock of hair from her face as she approached, her expression resolute but weary as she greeted the Healer. "I am told you come from the land of Alba," she said. "I would learn more of your life and of your travels when time permits."

"I will welcome such discourse, your grace," Hollin replied.

"My daughters have sought long for a cure without success," Titania continued. "Neither book nor herb can offer us salvation. I fear the answer lies beyond our ken."

"Be at peace, your grace," said Hollin. "I will do what I can." He frowned. "There is much suffering here. The auras of these folk are cracked and bleeding." A spasm of disgust twisted his face, and he backed out of the doorway.

Almost immediately his acolytes surrounded him, facing outward, their staves held up, their faces oddly blank.

"What is the matter, Master Hollin?" asked Aldritch.

But by now the Healer's face had cleared. "The sickness is too furious when many are brought together," he said. "I would meet with but a single victim if I am to know this disease."

"Cordelia is alone," said Rathina. "She is close by;

we can take you there."

"So be it," said Hollin. The protective ring of his followers opened and Rathina led them across the hallway and toward Cordelia's chambers.

He used the word "disease," Tania thought. He seemed quite familiar with it, even though few here had known the word before the illness had appeared. But then, he wasn't a native of Faerie. And if the people of Alba understood disease and sickness, then there was a good chance he would be able to do something to cure them.

They came into Cordelia's chambers. Bryn was sitting on the floor with his back to the door. He looked exhausted.

He got to his feet as Hollin approached. "You are the Healer?" he asked, his eyes narrowing. "You come from Alba, so they say. But save for our Queen, none have sailed to the shores of Faerie from that distant place for many thousands of years. Why came you to Weir?"

"Stand back, Master Bryn," said Aldritch. "It is not for you to question this man."

Bryn looked guardedly at the lord, as if debating whether to get into a dispute with him.

Edric stepped forward, placing a hand on Bryn's arm. "Trust that Master Hollin means no harm, Bryn," he said gently. "He may have a cure—for Princess Cordelia, for everyone."

Bryn nodded briefly and stepped aside. "Beware," he said. "Cordelia is not alone."

Tania was puzzled by this remark—until Edric opened the door and she was able to see into the room beyond.

Cordelia's bedchamber was full of birds.

They covered every surface, the sill of the open window, the furniture, the floor; they perched in rows on the high rails of the four-poster bed and on the headboard, and gathered darkly on the counterpane and even upon the pillows either side of Cordelia's head.

A multitude of different species was there: from sparrows and wrens and finches to gulls and crows and ravens and jays and jackdaws and magpies to falcons and eagles and round-eyed owls. A hundred watchful, beady eyes peered down from the picture rails and from the lintel of the door and window, and all their uncanny, inhuman attention was focused on the golden lozenge that contained the sleeping princess.

"What sorcery is this?" asked Hollin.

"It isn't sorcery," Tania said. "It's my sister's gift; she has a strong bond with animals. She loves them and they love her. But it's nothing to be afraid of; they won't hurt you."

Hollin turned to her. "Even so, I can do nothing while she is bound within yon crucible of golden light. I cannot perceive her aura. I cannot lay the divine stones upon her."

"Oberon must release her," said Lady Kernow. "Send to the King."

"Is that safe?" asked Tania. "The Gildensleep is the

only thing stopping her from getting worse."

The Healer's eyes flashed. "Would you prevent me from healing this woman?" he asked.

"No, of course not," Tania said, disturbed by the furious look that had passed across his face. "I'll go and speak to the King. I won't be long."

She ran from the chamber. She knew where Oberon would be—in the peace and seclusion of the Throne Room. So far as Tania knew, he had been alone there ever since the Conclave had ended.

A warden stood at the high door to the Throne Room.

"I have to see the King," Tania said.

The warden thrust the doors open and Tania entered. She walked the long white carpet to the simple, white stone chair.

Oberon sat perfectly still, his hands gripping the arms of the throne, his back straight, his eyes open but unfocused. He seemed unaware as she approached him.

"Father?" she asked, reaching out a tentative hand to touch his knee.

His steady gaze did not stir. Even when she moved so that she was immediately in front of his face, his piercing blue eyes seemed to look through her.

"Yes, my daughter," came the low voice, lips hardly moving.

"The Healer has arrived, Father," Tania told him. "He wants you to take Cordelia out of the Gildensleep. Can you do that?"

"I can." The eyelids flickered for a moment. "It is done. Daughter?"

"Yes, Father?"

"What make you of Lord Aldritch's Healer?"

"I'm not sure."

"He is not of Faerie, Tania. Let no harm come to our people."

"No. Of course not." She stepped back.

"Would you leave me, Tania?"

"I want to see what happens with Cordelia."

"Nay, daughter. That was not my meaning." A strange intensity came into the soft voice. "Would you leave me, Tania? *Would* you?"

A shiver ran down Tania's spine. He was asking her whether she had decided to abandon Faerie and return to her home in the Mortal World. But he sounded so *wounded*—as if the very thought of it was more than he could bear.

"Father . . ." Her voice faded. She didn't know what to say. She looked into the noble, weary face. "Can you do this for much longer, Father?" she asked.

"For a while . . ." came the whispered reply. "For my people . . . for a while . . ."

"I'd like to go back. Is there anything you need?"

"No. See how your sister fares."

Her heart aching, Tania turned and ran from the Throne Room.

When Tania came back into Cordelia and Bryn's chambers, she found most of the people gathered in the outer room, either sitting or standing in murmuring groups. The door to the bedchamber was open.

Cordelia was no longer in the protective shell of the Gildensleep. She lay on the bed, small and helpless in the rumpled wedding gown. Most of the birds had gone, but a few still remained, determined to keep watch over their beloved friend.

Rathina and Bryn stood just inside the doorway. Sancha was also close by. She looked drained and defeated, as if she was on the verge of collapse. Tania moved to her side.

Sancha looked at her with weary, red-rimmed eyes. "All my learning, all my lore, all my books," she murmured. "So far they have availed me nothing. I come to see if this man from across the seas can do for us what we cannot do for ourselves."

"I hope he can," Tania whispered.

"Indeed," said Sancha. "For if not, what then of Faerie?"

Hollin's followers were gathered around the bed, holding their wood staves high in both hands, bringing the ends together so that they formed a kind of canopy over Cordelia's prone form.

The Healer stood at her head, leaning over her, his hand spread out above her, his eyes closed as though in deep concentration.

"Her aura is in confusion," Hollin said at last, opening his arms and gesturing to the man who still held the fur bundle. "Prepare the stones, Brother Aum."

The man opened the bundle on the bedspread and once again Tania saw the collection of glittering and shining gemstones.

"Do you know what those stones do?" Tania whispered to Sancha.

"I have read ancient texts that speak of people who use crystals and gems as divining tools," Sancha whispered back. "But it was a practice I thought long abandoned. It is most remarkable to witness a Lithomancer at work." Her voice lowered so that Tania could only just hear it. "But I cannot truly believe this will aid Cordelia."

Tania looked sharply at her. "Why do you say that?"

"Hush!" murmured Sancha. "Watch!"

The Healer had picked a handful of stones from the hide and began to take them one by one from his palm and place them on Cordelia's body.

"Quartz crystal for the head, aventurine because she is a princess," he intoned in a light, lilting voice, laying the first stone on her forehead and the second against her lips. "Garnet for strength and rose quartz for love." A stone on her throat and above her heart. "Moonstone and tiger's-eye for her mother and father; mobled marble for death and black onyx for the Dark One." Four more stones were placed on her stomach. "Amethyst for temperance and carnelian for mercy. And thus are the metaphysical properties and attributes laid out that the healing may commence."

A low humming arose from the Healer's acolytes, and he stepped back, touching the fingers of his right hand against the blue jewel on his forehead.

The Healer's voice rose in pitch and volume. "Show yourselves, spirits of malevolence and mischief, the symphonious stones compel your discord to depart!" he shouted. "Leave this woman. Get you gone. Trouble her no more."

Tania felt a tugging at her sleeve. It was Sancha, her face disturbed, as she pulled Tania from the room. She brought her mouth close to Tania's ear.

"I do not think these spells and incantations will speak to the spirits," she whispered. "Mayhap I am wrong, but to my mind this is no way to compel the spirits' friendship."

"Are you sure?" asked Tania.

"Nay, sister, I am not—or I would denounce him," replied Sancha. "But I will not remain here and wait for the outcome. I will return to my books and continue to search their pages. I have more faith in the old texts than in this man's pretty stones."

Sancha swept from the room. Tania looked guardedly at the faces inside—all of them anxious, all of them tinged with hope and expectation.

What if Sancha is right? What if this so-called Healer is just a fake?

Tania went back into the bedchamber. The low, melodious humming of the Healer's followers had not changed. But neither had anything else.

Tania stepped forward, quietly circling the bed and coming up close to Hollin.

"Can you tell me what's going to happen now?" she asked softly.

"The power of the stones will call on the spirits to draw the malady out of this woman's body," murmured the Healer. "She will be cured."

Tania looked uneasily at Cordelia. She had no control over the Mystic Arts, but she had been close by on many occasions when Oberon or Eden had wielded them. There was always a frisson in the air when the spirits were called on—a tingling that felt like nothing else.

Tania did not feel it now. "How quickly will it work?" she asked.

"The spirits gather apace."

Tania looked into the Healer's face. "Actually, I don't think they do," she said. "I don't think anything's happening at all."

Hollin turned toward her like a wild thing, his eyes blazing with anger, his face twisting into a grimace. He drew back, spreading his hands out toward her. "Think you that I know you not?" he shouted. "Your aura is cracked; you are riven from the crown of your head to the soles of your feet. You hang upon a wheel of fire, and your soul is burned through to the quick!"

As he shouted this at her, the humming of his followers changed to a terrible wailing, and they pulled away from her, wielding their staves as if defending themselves from her.

"What is this coil?" roared Lord Aldritch's voice. "What chaos reigns here?" He was standing in the doorway, his eyes blazing.

Hollin pointed at Tania. "She will ruin all!" he howled. There was terror now in his face, or something that looked very like terror. "Take her from this place. Take her to a high point and throw her into the sea. Cleanse us of her decay. The evil comes from her—I see it coiling through her veins; I see it staring at me through her eyes!" He cowered away from her, his hands up to cover his face. "See—it stares at me and I am undone! She is a cockatrice. Strike her down. Destroy the thing that feeds upon her sundered soul."

"This is crazy!" shouted Tania. She glared at the Healer. "Stop it. Stop doing this. You know it's not true!"

But the Healer stumbled backward, his voice rising to an uncontrolled shriek. "Take her from me; her words burn me. Her eyes! Her terrible eyes would eat my soul!"

"Wardens, ho," shouted Aldritch above the wailing of the Healer's followers. "Come to me. Make haste."

Tania saw more faces at the door: the other lords and ladies come to discover what had happened.

The acolytes were all around Tania now, their staves pointing at her, their mouths gaping as they screamed.

"No!" shouted Rathina. "You shall not harm her!" She ran toward Tania, but three of the Acolytes turned and held her off with their staves.

Two wardens came into the room. Lord Aldritch pointed at Tania. "Escort the Princess Tania to her chambers. Keep close watch over her. She is not to leave her rooms."

"What has she done wrong?" asked Lord Brython. "By the deep spirits of love, what has happened here?"

Aldritch gestured to where the Healer sat huddled in a corner, his arms covering his head. "See what she has done!" He turned to Tania. "I counseled your father to send you from this world, but he did not heed me!" His voice rose so that everyone could hear him. "See now what this half-thing has done! She seeks to destroy our one hope of salvation!"

"This is insane!" Tania shouted. "I haven't done anything."

"Take your poisoned fangs from out my throat!" moaned Hollin. He pointed a shaking finger at Tania. "She is the source of evil in this land; it is she who has brought this sickness down upon you."

"What madness is this, my lord?" Cornelius demanded, shouldering his way into the bedchamber. "How does this man dare to speak so of the King's daughter?"

Lord Aldritch turned to him. "Think you he speaks falsehoods, my lord earl?" He gestured to Hollin. "Look you upon him: The man is in the very throes of terror."

Cornelius looked searchingly at Tania. "Are you the cause of this man's distress, my lady?" he asked.

"No, of course not!" Tania said.

"And yet behold—he is prostrate," said Marchioness

Lucina, standing alongside her husband, the earl marshal. "Why should he behave so if nothing assails him?"

"Could it be she puts her evil upon him without intent?" asked Fleance. "I have heard of such things! They say there are monsters in the far north: basilisks that can turn a man's wits with the power of their eyes alone!"

"I'm not standing here listening to this!" Tania shouted. "Can't you see what's happening? I told him I didn't think his mumbo jumbo was working, and he freaked out. He's faking it!"

Lord Aldritch looked at the earl marshal. "Will you have her taken from here, or will you risk the death of this man who has come to help us?" He pointed toward Cordelia, still lying unmoving on the bed. "And would you have this half-thing cause the death of our fair princess?"

Tania could see the uncertainty in the earl marshal's eyes. She turned from face to face: The same uneasy look was reflected over and over.

"You can't be serious!" she cried.

Rathina stepped close to her. "Sister dearest," she said, "I think you should go with the wardens. No good can be done by your staying here."

Tania glared at Rathina.

"Can you put your hand on your heart and give your oath that you did not bring the plague into Faerie?" Rathina asked, looking deep into Tania's eyes, sending her a message.

The angry retort faded on Tania's lips as she

realized that her sister was only trying to calm the dangerous situation. "No," she said, "I can't." She looked at Aldritch. "Okay, I'll go—but you're wrong. You're all wrong. That man and his troop of performing monkeys aren't going to help us at all!"

As Tania allowed the wardens to lead her from the bedchamber, she cast a final look back at Cordelia. Her pale sister was slumbering still, the Healer's stones lying uselessly on her face and body. Doing nothing. *Nothing!*

Anxious, fearful faces watched her as she left.

But could they be right to fear her?

Aldritch's words rang in her head. *See now what this half-thing has done! She seeks to destroy our one hope of salvation!*

X

"Step aside. I would speak with my sister."

It was Eden, outside the closed doors of Tania's apartments.

"The Lord Aldritch instructed that none may pass," came the muffled voice of one of the wardens. Tania got to her feet and walked to the doors.

"Since when is the Lord of Weir master in this place?" demanded Eden. "When last I heard, Oberon Aurealis ruled in this Realm. Get out of my way, or it will be the worst for you."

The voice now was deferential. "Aye, my lady."

The doors opened and Eden stepped inside. Tania opened her mouth to speak, but Eden hushed her with a gesture and turned to firmly close the doors at her back. Her face was anxious and disturbed.

"How is the earl?" Tania asked quietly. "Why aren't you with him?"

"He is neither worse nor better," Eden replied. "I have now had the time to bind about him such glamours as I am able. Wherever I go, my soul will remain to watch over him and protect him from further harm." She frowned. "And so he rests in Gildensleep until a cure may be found. Or until our Father's power fails. But I have come here to speak of other things, Tania."

Eden strode to where Tania was standing and drew her out through the open doors onto the balcony. "Things do not go well," she said in an urgent under-tone. "Aldritch called the Conclave of Earls to debate your immediate banishment."

"What? Because of what happened in Cordelia's room?" Tania shook her head in disbelief. "I didn't do anything, Eden."

"I do not doubt that," Eden replied. "But not all are convinced of your innocence. Aldritch is spinning a cunning web. He says that he does not believe you harm us with a purpose of malice. He says the very fabric of your being exudes the poison of plague as a toad produces venom."

"Oh, *charming*! So I'm a toad now, am I? What *is* it with him? Why does he hate me so much?"

"Perhaps his fear of you is genuine," said Eden. "Or it may be he has some darker motive. I know not. But do you not see the craft of it, Tania? He attacks your very nature: the fact that you are half Faerie and half Mortal. He has swayed several members of the Conclave of Earls. Lord Brython and Lady Kernow and the earl marshal and the marchioness are staunch in your defense, but Aldritch has won over Lady

Mornamere and Lord Herne and also Lord Tristan of Udwold. Fleance is young, and Aldritch works hard on his fears; I believe he will turn against you. We have adjourned to consider our positions, but Aldritch will call a vote when we reconvene. The King and Queen have no vote in the Conclave—and if Fleance sides with Aldritch, the earls will be equally divided."

"Which means what?"

"Which means that the Protocol of Prydein will be enforced."

"Eden! I have no idea what that means!"

"It means a ruby and a sapphire will be placed into a goblet and covered with a cloth," Eden told her. "Then our mother will put her hand blindly into the goblet and pick one of the gemstones. The ruby will condemn you; the sapphire will save you."

"And if I'm condemned?"

"Banishment—for all time."

A cold anger ran through Tania. "Fine," she said. "Perhaps that's exactly what should happen. If everyone here is so scared of me, maybe I should just go home!"

Eden studied her face. "You would abandon us?"

"That's not it at all. But Eden . . . what if Aldritch is right? What if I am . . . *dangerous*—without meaning to be? My dad brought this illness into Faerie, but I brought *him*, didn't I? Which means this is all down to me."

Eden nodded. "Indeed," she said. "That is true."

Tania looked at her in surprise. She'd been

expecting her sister to say the opposite—that it wasn't her fault, that she shouldn't blame herself.

"Then you agree that I should go away," Tania said quietly.

"Yes, I do, and that right quickly, before this day is over and the earls of Faerie close the portals between the worlds. But I do not suggest you should go into *banishment*. Choose what Lord Aldritch may say, I do not believe that the Healer Hollin has any powers to cure the spread of the disease. Lithomancy is a poor way of attracting the attention of the spirits; he will not succeed."

"Sancha said the same thing. So what do you think I should do?"

"Seek a cure," Eden said simply.

"How? Where? I don't know anything about medicine. If Hopie can't come up with anything, how do you expect me to find a cure?"

Eden looked steadily at her. "It is a Mortal disease," she said. "Find a Mortal remedy. Do Mortals not use medicines? Are there no Healers in the Mortal World?"

Tania stared at her. "Yes, of course there are, but even if . . ." Something suddenly hit her, something so obvious that she couldn't believe it had never occurred to her before. She had been floundering around for days now, wanting to help but not knowing how—and all the time the answer had been right in front of her!

"Connor!" she gasped. "Connor could help."

"Who is Connor?"

"He's the son of friends of my mum and dad: Connor Estabrook. He's a first-year medical student. He could tell me what antibiotics I should use; he might even be able to get them for me." She was thinking hard now. "I'd have to come up with a plausible explanation, of course. But it is possible." She got up, throwing her arms around her sister. "Eden! I'm so stupid. I could have done this ages ago. Why didn't you suggest it before now?"

"I had hopes that a cure might be found in Faerie," said Eden. "In truth, Tania, who can say what the effects of Mortal medicines might be on Faerie folk? They may have no effect—or they may do greater harm."

"Don't say that!"

"Keep in mind, too, that medicine alone may not be enough," said Eden. "Despite the dangers that Mortals pose to our world, you may need to bring a Mortal Healer to Faerie to administer the medicine."

"I can't do that," said Tania. "You know how my gift works: I can only take people from world to world if I love them. It works fine with Edric and with my mum and dad and with you and Hopie and the others, but I can't bring Connor Estabrook through. I don't love him. I had a kind of silly crush on him when I was ten and he was thirteen, but these days I see him only about twice a year."

"I have something that may aid you," Eden said. She felt inside her gown and drew out a slender white crystal bracelet. "This bracelet is made of yearnstone," she said. "It has a property that guides it always to the place where it was formed."

Tania took the delicate bracelet. It felt warm, almost alive against her skin.

"If a Mortal were to wear this bracelet and if you were to take their hand and step through into Faerie, then because of the powers of yearnstone, that Mortal would be drawn through with you. And while the bracelet is tight about the Mortal's wrist, you will be able to lead him back and forth between the Realms many times—so long as he holds fast to you. But beware: If your hand should lose its grip during the passage, the Mortal will be trapped between the worlds."

"Thank you," Tania said. "I understand." She gazed at the bracelet. "I should go *now*," she said. "Our father said he would close off Faerie from the Mortal World at dawn tomorrow. That gives me only a few hours."

"It is so," said Eden. "But you must depart in secrecy—and I would not have you travel alone into the Mortal World. As the Faerie part of your spirit has grown, so you have become vulnerable to the curse of Isenmort, and I have no black amber to protect you from its poison."

Tania remembered the time when she had first noticed her sensitivity to metal—the way it had made her fingers tingle when she touched it. The odd allergy had grown gradually more fierce until she had become as allergic to metal as any other man, woman, or child in Faerie. The bite of Isenmort was poison to her—and Eden was right: The Mortal World teemed with metal objects.

"Rathina is immune to metal," said Tania. "She would go with me. She's fascinated by the idea of the Mortal World. But I can't get to her. There are guards on the door. They'd never let me pass."

Eden smiled gently. "Not all the ways of the palace are visible to the wardens of Faerie," she said. "Come. I shall show you one of the delights of your childhood."

Puzzled, Tania followed her into the bedchamber. Eden stood by the nightstand, facing the wall with one hand raised. She spoke softly.

The nightstand began to shudder and to move jerkily forward, pivoting on one back corner.

"What's happening?" Tania asked.

Moments later she saw a low section of the wall open inward, pushing the nightstand forward. Tania found herself gazing into a small dark entranceway festooned with cobwebs.

"What is that?" Tania asked, crouching to look into the narrow passageway revealed through the hole.

"Do you not remember?" Eden asked. "I created these passageways for you and your sisters when you were little so that you could move from room to room in secret. You, Rathina, Zara, and Cordelia thought it a great game—and all the passages led to—"

"The Well Room!" said Tania. "We used to meet there. I remember! Oh, Eden! I remember!"

Eden picked up a candle from the nightstand. She passed her hand over it and a small leaf of flame sprang up. "Go to Rathina," she said. "Follow the passage to the left. You will soon see the entrance to her rooms. Go with her to the Well Room and enter the Mortal World together."

"I will," said Tania. "But I need a few things first." If she sidestepped into the Mortal World from Veraglad Palace, she would be miles from home. She'd need some money—or a means of easily getting her hands on money.

Her old canvas shoulder bag was lying by the side of the bed. She had used it to transport things back and forth between the worlds when she had been revealing a few of the lesser secrets of London life to her sisters. She rummaged quickly in the bag. Yes! The plastic wallet that had her ID pass and her bank debit card in it, along with a donor card and a few other bits and pieces. She'd been squirreling part of her allowance away into her bank account for months. A handy ATM and she'd have money on demand.

Tania hooked the bag over her shoulder. "There's one other thing before I go," she said. "I had a strange dream last night—I think it might mean something. Something important."

"Tell me."

Tania explained her dream to Eden, trying her best to get the details right. She could remember only a few broken fragments of the song, but she was able to describe the sadness and melancholy of it. And she remembered vividly Cordelia's last words. *If you would cure us all, seek the Lost Caer . . .*

"The Song of the Lost Caer," mused Eden. "I have never heard of such a lyric. And yet it is clear that the dream had weight and purpose; it did not come idly to you in this place and at this time." Her brows knitted. "The Faerie Almanac may hold the answer."

"What's that?"

"A book. It recounts the history of this Realm," said Eden. "It lies in Sancha's library in the Royal Palace. Its narrative reaches back to the Great Awakening. Perhaps it will contain some overlooked or unregarded text that will lead me to knowledge of this Lost Caer—and thus to a cure for the plague."

"Will you be allowed to go?" Tania asked dubiously.

"None shall know of my departure," said Eden. "I shall use an Altier Glamour: I shall take on the form of a swallow and skim unseen the warm airs northward." She looked keenly at Tania. "And let us pray I find what I seek. But now, get you gone, Tania, and my blessings upon you. Go!"

Tania took the candle from Eden, giving her white-haired sister a final look before she ducked and pushed into the narrow passageway.

Holding the candle out ahead of her, Tania followed the cramped passageway until she came to a wooden panel set deep in the stonework. The panel sprang open at a touch into a sunlit bedchamber.

Rathina was sitting bolt upright on her bed, her hands folded on her knees, staring straight at Tania with a wry smile on her face.

"I am ready!" Rathina said, jumping up. "The

Mortal Realm, ho!"

"You knew I was coming?"

"Indeed," Rathina said with a smile. "Eden sent her voice to whisper your plan in my mind but a few moments ago. Come, make way. We must go, you and I. Into the Mortal World to seek a cure for the plague before all the pathways between the worlds are closed."

"Are you sure you want to do this?" asked Tania.

"Who better?" said Rathina, her eyes shining. "I have no fear of the touch of Isenmort. And if it comes to it, I can fight as well as any man. Who else would you have with you?" A fierce light burned in her eyes. "And I would see the Mortal World, Tania; I would learn its secrets. Come! We must go somewhere where it is safe for you to step between the worlds."

Rathina took the candle and led the way through the passages until they came to a flight of steep rough-hewn stone steps that led down in a tight spiral. Tania's shoulders brushed the walls as she descended in Rathina's wake.

"These ways were intended for small children," Rathina said. "Are you able to pass through?"

"Just about."

Down and down plunged the winding stairway. Tania traced her hands along the cold stones of the wall as she went—the rough, uneven surfaces bringing back memories of nocturnal adventures with her sisters.

They came at last into a small circular room, into

which led more stairways and corridors.

Rathina turned, lifting the candle and looking to Tania's face. "Alas, we are without weapons," she said. "I had no opportunity to secure swords or knives."

"We won't need them where we're going," said Tania. "In any case, if we were caught with swords on us, we'd be marched straight to the nearest police station."

"Police station?"

"I'll explain later." She looked into Rathina's face. "Are you sure about this?"

Rathina smiled and nodded.

Tania held out her hand. "Stand beside me, then," she said.

Rathina took her hand. "How does it feel to travel between the worlds?" she asked. There was a hint of anxiety in the excitement that filled her voice.

"Wait a couple of seconds, and you'll know." Tania squeezed her sister's hand. "Ready?"

"Yes."

"Go."

She concentrated her mind as she stepped forward with Rathina. Then she made the side step.

They emerged into brilliant sunshine. Tania threw her hand over her eyes, dazzled by the sudden light.

She heard Rathina give a yelp and felt her hand slip away.

"Rathina?"

She squinted against the brightness—and realized that they had emerged in the Mortal World on the brink of a cliff. A moment later and she felt the ground giving way beneath her. Her feet slipped on long grass and she fell hard onto her stomach.

Then there was nothing beneath her. She was clinging to the cliff edge, and her fingers were losing their grip.

Part Two

Mortal

Children Have

No Wings

XI

"Quick! Grab them!"

"Have you got her?"

"Yes. You get the other one!"

Tania felt strong hands grip her wrists, and the next second she was being pulled away from the cliff edge. Her arms felt as if they were being wrenched out of their sockets as she was dragged through the long grass.

"Rathina?" she gasped. *"Rathina?"*

"Your pal's fine," said a voice. "Are you two out of your minds? If we hadn't looked around at the last second, you could both have gone over the edge!"

"Hey! Calm down, girl! I'm trying to help you." This came from a second voice, a little way off. Tania squirmed onto her back and finally managed to wrest her arms loose from the hands that held her.

She scrambled to her feet. A few yards away, a young man was grappling with Rathina—and not getting the best of it. He was on his back and she was sitting astride his chest, her hands going for his throat while he fought to fend her off.

"Rathina!" Tania called. "It's all right. They aren't attacking us! They're only trying to help."

Rathina lifted her head, tossing her dark hair out of her eyes.

"None may lay hands on a princess!" she shouted. "I'll beat the silly knave to a paste!"

"Rathina! *No!*" Tania ran to her sister and pulled her off the young man.

He staggered up, staring at the two of them in disbelief. "What the hell was *that* for?" he yelled. "I just saved you from falling off the cliff, you head case!"

Tania looked at the two young men: They were teenagers, maybe two or three years older than she was, dressed in jeans and T-shirts, one with long, curly blond hair and the other with dark hair that hung in his eyes.

They were just a couple of ordinary, everyday lads that you might meet in the street or in a café or at a party anywhere in London . . . or anywhere in the *world*, for that matter. A pair of quite nice-looking, totally normal *mortal* boys.

"Sorry about that," Tania said. "She's a bit sensitive about people grabbing hold of her."

"Oh, right!" said the dark-haired boy. "No problem, then. I'll let her kill herself next time!"

"Sorry," Tania said. "Really. Sorry. We didn't realize how close to the edge we were."

"How could you *not* see?" asked the dark-haired

boy. "Are you totally blind or what? And what's with the fancy-dress costumes?"

Tania had known that their clothes would stand out in the Mortal World. She was still wearing the simple gray Faerie dress, and Rathina had on a scarlet gown embroidered with heavy gold thread at the bodice and on the sleeves and around the hem.

Rathina glared at the boy. "Do not speak to the Princess Tania in such a way, knave, or I'll box your ears till your head rings like the Bells of Tamarine!"

"Rathina, remember where you are!" said Tania.

Rathina stared at her for a moment, then her face brightened. "The Mortal Realm!" she exclaimed. "Of course. My apologies, Tania. I will seek to behave more appropriately from this time forth."

The blond boy laughed. "From this time *forth*? Oh, I get it. You're part of the medieval pageant, down in Eastbourne, yeah?" His eyes were on Tania as he gestured toward Rathina. "Your friend's got the language down pat, but you need to work on ye old-ie fashioned-ie speech-ie a bit, my lady."

"And you should lose the shoulder bag, too," said the dark-haired boy, nodding toward the canvas bag that was slung over Tania's shoulder. "Not exactly a Middle Age accessory, is it?"

A pageant in Eastbourne? Excellent! And there's a train station in Eastbourne that will take us right into London.

"Good tip," said Tania. "Look, thanks for saving us. We were stupid to get so near the edge. And yes, we are part of the pageant. We just came up here to have a look around. Pretty dangerous, huh?"

"It can be if you don't watch where you're going," said the blond boy. "My name's Oliver; this is Luke."

"I'm Tania; this is my sister Rathina."

"Sisters, eh?" said Oliver. "You don't look much alike."

"We are sisters, indeed," said Rathina. She looked the two boys up and down. "Your clothes are very strange," she said. "But doubtless there is much I will find curious in your world."

Oliver gave her a puzzled look.

"She takes her part very seriously," Tania said quickly.

"Whatever," Luke murmured under his breath.

Rathina gave him a hard look but said nothing more.

"If you girls don't have anything planned, how about we all go for a cup of coffee or something back in Eastbourne? My car is just over the rise back there."

"A car?" said Tania. "That's great!"

Tania and Rathina stood on the pavement, waving as Oliver drove off.

"So, sister?" said Rathina. "Where are we going to meet the youths?"

Tania raised her eyebrows. "We're not meeting them," she said. She rummaged in her bag and pulled out her debit card. "We're going to get ourselves some money, then we're catching a train to London."

Rathina frowned. "Did you not give your word to

the boy Oliver that we would 'catch up later'?"

"I lied," said Tania.

"You *lied*?" exclaimed Rathina. "Tania, what of honor?"

"There's no such thing when you're dealing with boys," Tania explained. "Survival of the fittest is what counts here. They'll be fine; they'll just have to find a couple of other girls to practice their chat-up lines on." She pointed across the busy street. "Look, there's a charity shop. With any luck we'll be able to swap these clothes for things that'll blend in a bit better."

They waited until the traffic light turned to red again and they were able to weave their way between the standing traffic. Tania was careful not to brush against the cars. It had been tricky avoiding all the metal in Oliver's car, and sitting inside a vehicle that was effectively a metal box had given her a bad headache.

"Remember, Tania," Rathina said as they came to the far pavement. "Beware of all things made of Isenmort!"

Tania nodded. She hardly needed reminding.

But how strange. Last time she had been in this world, it had been her Faerie sisters who needed to be wary of metal—and now she was traveling with the one person in the whole of Faerie who was immune to the perils of Isenmort.

Tania stood with her sister on the platform at Eastbourne station. The amount of metal everywhere was ridiculous! Just getting to this place had been a challenge. She had not even been able to open the door to the charity shop. It had a metal handle! The clothes racks were also metal, and the jeans she had originally chosen had metal studs and a metal zipper, so they were out of the question. In the end she had gone for a plain black T-shirt and loose black trousers with an elastic waist.

Rathina had chosen a red blouse over a pair of white combat trousers. The choice had surprised Tania—not the blouse but the trousers. Women in Faerie never wore such things, and of the three sisters who had previously been in the Mortal World, only tomboy Cordelia had been prepared to wear trousers. Sancha had dismissed them immediately, and Zara had been quite appalled by the idea.

Once they had negotiated away their Faerie dresses for more modern clothes, Tania had asked the way to the nearest ATM. The buttons were again made of metal. Rathina had pressed out her PIN for her and had collected the money from the perilous steel lips of the cash dispenser.

A passerby had explained to them how to get to the train station, and with Rathina's help Tania had managed to buy two tickets to London Victoria.

Now they stood on the busy platform and waited for their train to pull in.

Once in London Tania's plan was to call Connor Estabrook's parents and track him down. She knew he wasn't living at home now. The latest she'd heard was that he was sharing an apartment with some other premed students, but she wasn't sure where.

"So who is this Mortal doctor whom we are to meet?" asked Rathina.

"Connor? Oh, I've known him most of my life, I guess," explained Tania. "He's three years older than me, which was fine when we were little—he was okay playing with me then. But when he hit thirteen he started ignoring me. I was really crazy about him at the time so I was pretty hurt. But over the past couple of years we've got more friendly again. We chat on the phone occasionally and text each other now and then. The last time I met up with him and his folks was at Christmas time to swap presents, like we always do."

"Christmastime?"

"Uh, Yuletide," Tania said. "Once we've tracked him down, it'll just be a case of convincing him to help us in time to get back to Faerie." She shrugged. "But don't bother asking how I'm going to make that work, because I don't know yet."

"But you will seek to take him back to Faerie with us?" asked Rathina.

"I think I might have to," said Tania. "Though I really wish there was some other way."

"You fear he will be in danger from Hollin and Lord Aldritch?" asked Rathina.

"I *know* he will be," said Tania. "We're going to have to be really careful, Rathina. I don't know what I'd do if anything happened to him." She shook her head. "And that's assuming he agrees to come with us." She stared down the railway track. "And that our train ever turns up!"

Time was getting on and she was impatient with the delay. She glanced at the clock display on the arrivals screen. *Come on! Look at the time! It's ten to three already. If we don't get this all sorted by dawn tomorrow, Oberon is going to shut down all the ways in and out of Faerie—and we'll be stuck here forever.*

Rathina stared about her with a frown on her brow.

Tania guessed what she was going through. Massive culture shock! "All this takes a bit of getting used to," she said sympathetically.

"'Tis like the Feast of the White Hart and the Traveler's Moon Festival and the Midsummer Revels all combined," said Rathina. "'Tis pure madness to live thus. How do these Mortals suffer it? And the smell, Tania! Spirits of air, does this whole world stink thus?"

"The towns do, pretty much," Tania admitted. "You probably won't notice it after a while." She hoped she was right. After three weeks of breathing the pure, sweet Faerie air, she was having trouble herself coping with the unpleasant odors that wafted all around them: the smell of sun-baked iron and gravel from the railway, hot diesel, hot engines, motor oil, exhaust fumes drifting in from the street, fried onions and stale coffee from the nearby café, overpowering perfume and deodorant—and worse, the smell of far too many hot humans in need of showers.

Rathina's expression changed suddenly, her lips tightening and her eyes becoming watchful. "Did you feel that, Tania?" she said.

"It's probably just the train coming—"

"Nay. I felt a shadow on my heart." She stared at Tania. "Did you feel *nothing*?"

Tania looked anxiously at her. "No. Nothing. What kind of thing?"

Rathina stared up and down the length of the platform.

"What is it?" asked Tania. "What's wrong?"

"I can see nothing from here," Rathina said. "These people mill around me like rats in a barrel!" She moved to the edge of the platform and made as if to jump onto the rails. Tania grabbed her just in time.

"No!" She dragged Rathina back through the staring people. "You can't do that," she said in a hard whisper. "You'll get killed! Now tell me what's the matter."

Rathina's eyes were dark with unease. "We are pursued," she said. "Something has followed us through between the worlds. I feel a malign presence. It is close at hand."

Before Tania could react to this, an electronic voice crackled over their heads. "The train now arriving at platform one is the fifteen fifty-eight service to London Victoria. Calling at Polegate, Lewes, Haywards Heath, Gatwick Airport, East Croydon, Clapham Junction, and London Victoria."

A few moments later the rattle and growl of the coming train filled the air.

"Sweet blessed mercy!" said Rathina, shrinking away and throwing her hands over her ears as the green-and-white train came gliding in.

"I warned you it would be loud!" Tania shouted above the screaming brakes and clanking cars and hissing doors. "This is what we've been waiting for. It'll take us to London."

But as the passengers disembarked, Tania wondered uneasily about the shadowy pursuit that Rathina had sensed. She gazed at the milling crowds.

Had something really followed them through from Faerie? Something bad? If so, why was it here—and who or *what* was it?

XII

"Does nothing in this benighted world function without hideous din?" complained Rathina.

"Not if you want to get somewhere fast," said Tania. "And we do. We're on a really tight deadline, Rathina."

"Aye, indeed, but it will take much effort to accustom myself to the noise, sister."

They had found themselves a double seat in a crowded car near the front of the train. Opposite them sat a young man plugged into an iPod and a woman talking on a cell phone.

The train was speeding through an open countryside of fields and woodlands under a blue sky bubbling with clouds.

"This train will get us to London in an hour and a half," said Tania. "How long would it take you to travel from Veraglad to the Royal Palace?"

"On a mettlesome charger such as Maddalena and

at the gallop, mayhap I could make the journey in half a day."

"There you go, then," said Tania. "Trains are good. How's your sandwich?"

She had bought them some sandwiches and snacks from the cart. She had also quite fancied some soda, but since that came in a can, she had to make do with a carton of black currant juice. There had been a tricky moment when the attendant had tried to give her some change and Tania had only just managed to snatch her hand away. The coins had gone clattering and rolling over the floor.

Rathina chewed a mouthful of sandwich. "It will suffice." She looked around and shook her head. "I do not know how it was that Edric Chanticleer was able to live in this world for half a year." She looked at Tania. "Did he not find it strange and harsh?"

Tania pursed her lips. "I don't know," she said sharply. "Maybe. I never got around to asking him." Her fingers moved up to fondle the teardrop of black onyx at her throat. She had considered throwing it in his face or perhaps just hurling it from her balcony in the Sunset Tower. But she hadn't been able to bring herself to part with it. Not just yet.

She was nowhere near ready to talk about Edric. She was surviving their break-up only by not thinking about it. But locked away in a miserable cellar in her mind a small voice was crying, *It's not real. It can't be real. I love him. How could this have happened?*

Change the subject. Now!

"Did you know our mother wasn't from Faerie?" Tania asked. "I found out about it only yesterday."

"The tale of our mother's coming to Faerie is known by all," said Rathina.

"Except that no one told *me* about it."

"I thought you would have remembered."

"Rathina, how many more times . . . ? I can hardly remember anything. You *know* that."

"Then listen and remember now, for it is a story we all know by heart," said Rathina, glancing around the car to make sure no one was listening. "Some fifty years before the coming of the uneasy slumber of the Great Twilight, a small ship made landfall at the coastal town of Hymnal in the Earldom of Weir. It had but one passenger: a Mortal woman who was almost dead from hunger and thirst. She was taken to Caer Liel and questioned by Lord Aldritch." Rathina's eyes shone. "She told a remarkable tale. She said that her name was Titania and that she was the daughter of the House of Fenodree in the land of Alba, which lies across the Western Ocean. She revealed that it was foretold at her birth that when she came to her twentieth birthday, she should take a ship alone and seek out the Realm of Faerie. And this was a thing that none of her race had done for a thousand years. And furthermore it was prophesied that if she came to Faerie, she would be blessed with the gift of Immortality—for the people of Alba are but Mortals and live little over five score years. It was foretold also that she would never be able to return to Alba to share the secret of life everlasting but would live out her days forever in Faerie."

Tania gazed spellbound as Rathina told the tale. These were things of which she knew nothing.

"So remarkable was Titania's story that Lord Aldritch sent her south with his only son, that she might tell her tale to the King himself. But when our father first set his eyes upon her, he was consumed with such a love that he would brook no other outcome of their meeting but that they should wed." Rathina smiled. "And such was the love that swelled for the King in Titania's heart that she full gladly accepted his hand. They were married upon Midsummer's Eve, not two moons later than her ship had first made landfall. And with the Hand-Fasting Ceremony so the doom of mortality sloughed from our dear mother's soul and thus was the prophecy fulfilled."

"So she was born Mortal?" murmured Tania.

"Aye, and for twenty summers did she bear that burden." Rathina frowned thoughtfully. "Mayhap that is how she was able to endure with such fortitude her five-hundred-year exile among Mortal folk."

Tania let out a breath and sat back, gazing blankly out of the window at the rushing blur of the countryside, hardly knowing what to make of Rathina's tale. All she knew was that she felt a new closeness to her Faerie mother. She, too, had been forced to choose between the place where she was brought up and a strange new world of which she knew almost nothing.

* * *

Rathina had trouble coping with the crowds that flooded the platform at London Victoria Station. Life as a princess in Faerie had not prepared her for rush hour at a major London terminal.

"Keep up and keep with me," Tania warned her. "It's easy to get lost otherwise."

"To what manner of place have you brought me, sister?" asked Rathina, staring around her. "Is all of London thus?"

"No, this is especially bad," said Tania, linking her arm with Rathina's to keep her by her side. "It's crazy, I know, but we'll soon be out of it. Trust me, this world isn't as bad as you think. There are things here you'd really like."

"I will have to take your word on that," Rathina said doubtfully.

As the crowds surged toward the exit, Tania realized she would not be able to go through the metal ticket barriers. She pulled Rathina to one side, letting the main rush of people sweep by them. Fortunately there was a man at the swing door who allowed them through.

The forecourt was as packed as the platform but more chaotic, with people hurrying or standing around watching the departure screen that stretched above the entrance to the platforms.

"Are you hungry at all?" Tania asked her sister.

"I think not. The sandcakes you bartered for on the train sated my appetite for the present."

Tania squeezed her sister's arm. "Sand*wiches*," she

said. "And it wasn't bartering; I paid cash."

Rathina looked confused. "Yes, you must explain this *cash* to me."

"I will but not now. We have to find a phone." She tried to head for the main exit from the station—she was pretty sure that was where the pay phones were—but Rathina wouldn't budge.

"What's wrong?" Tania asked.

"What is a 'phone'?"

"I told you. It's a thing we use to talk to people a long way away."

"Ah. Like the water-mirrors from which our mother conjures distant faces and voices, yes?"

"Kind of."

"And do all Mortals have the skills to use this *phone*?"

"Rathina, it's not a mystical thing. It's a machine. Come with me and I'll show you how it works. You'll have to help me, anyway: The keypad and receiver will be metal, so you'll have to dial."

Rathina allowed herself to be led across the forecourt, but Tania could hear her muttering to herself, "Keypad! Dial! Phone! Cash! Forsooth I shall need a tutor and an almanac if I am to understand the ways of this new world."

The sisters were on another train. Tania had managed to get Connor's cell phone number from his mum, and she had called him and arranged to meet at his student digs. It was a much shorter journey this time, but the train was considerably more crowded.

They couldn't even find seats, which proved a real problem for Tania. Everything she could have held on to was made of metal. In the end she stood Rathina in a corner by a door and leaned against her for support as the train went rattling over the River Thames and away into the southeast of London.

The train finally clattered to a halt at their stop and the doors hissed open. A number of people got off with them, and Tania went with the flow along the platform. She had never been here before. She didn't really know this part of London; everything south of the Thames was a bit of a mystery to her.

Connor Estabrook had sounded really pleased to hear from her when she had called him from Victoria Station. After some general chat about their families, she had told him that she was in need of some expert medical info for a school project she had to research and write up over the summer break. He'd been only too happy to oblige, although he had been a bit surprised that she needed to see him *immediately*.

"Yeah, why not," he'd said after a moment's pause. "I've got nothing on this evening. I'm on workplace training at King's College Hospital in Camberwell. If I can get away early, I'll meet you at Denmark Hill station. If not, my address is Top Flat, thirteen Garner Road, Peckham. Ask for directions. My flatmate Peter will be there; he'll keep you entertained till I arrive."

Now here they were, coming out of the station along with several dozen commuters. The other people peeled off in different directions, leaving Tania and Rathina standing alone on the pavement outside the brick railway station.

"Is this still London?" asked Rathina, gazing around. "It has a more wholesome air, Tania. I can breathe here, and there is much that lives and grows!"

"Yes, it's still London," Tania said. "London is a big place."

But Rathina was right. It was as if all the grime and bustle and cramped oppression of the city had been left north of the river. They were on a wide street lined with trees. A short way off Tania saw huge rhododendron bushes pressing against park railings, their deep pink flowers hanging into the street. There were still tarmac and large buildings and passing traffic, but there was also a sense of space.

Tania looked around, hoping to see Connor waiting for them.

He wasn't there.

Rathina pointed into the branches of the overhanging trees. "Birds sing," she said. "Hark!"

Tania listened. Above the drone of the traffic she could hear starlings, their shrill voices crackling like electricity in the sycamores.

"Doubtless Cordelia would know what they speak of," Rathina said. "It heartens me, Tania, to hear them. If birds live merrily in this place, then belike I shall grow accustomed to it, also . . . in time."

"I expect you're right," said Tania. "Except that we haven't *got* much time right now, not if we're going to get the medicine and get back into Faerie by dawn."

"Your friend is not here," Rathina remarked. "What now?"

"He said he might not be able to get away to meet us," said Tania. "I'll ask for directions to his flat."

She went back into the station, but the ticket office was shuttered up and there was no one about. She noticed a pay phone.

She walked over to it, thinking of her Mortal parents. *I could give Mum and Dad a call.*

And tell them what, exactly? *Hi, Mum and Dad. I'm back. How are you? Yeah? Great! How's Faerie? Hey, funny you should ask. You know that sniffle Dad had? Well, they're calling it The Plague now; about fifty people have come down with it so far and the only thing that's keeping them alive is . . . No! No! No!*

It was a stupid idea. They'd want to know what was going on. She'd either have to lie to them or let them know the truth—and who would benefit from that? They'd want to see her, and she had no time to travel right across London to Camden. They'd want to try and help, and what in the world could they do? Nothing!

No. Calling her Mum and Dad wasn't an option. It was heartbreaking to know they were so close but to be unable to go to them for advice. And if Oberon closed the ways between Faerie and the Mortal World, she might never see them again.

That was too terrible even to think about!

She turned away from the phone, fighting to control

her emotions. A woman had come into the station and was buying a ticket at the machine. Tania went up to her. "Excuse me, sorry to bother you. . . ."

She came out to where Rathina was still standing, doing her best to keep the woman's directions in her head. *Follow the road to the left. At the end take another left and carry on till you come to a right turn: It's just an alley. There's an estate at the far end. Make your way through it. At the end of the estate make another left, then it's the third turn on your right.*

"Look, I don't think there's any point in waiting for Connor," she told her sister. "Let's go straight to his place." They headed along the road, Rathina keeping to the inside of the pavement, her shoulders hunching when a bus or a truck went past.

They turned left into a quiet street of detached mock Tudor houses set back behind wide front yards. The curbs were lined with cars, but there was far less traffic. They walked under the shade of dark-leaved rowan trees, the air filled with the scents of honey-suckle and purple-tipped buddleia.

Tania heard children's voices. Ahead of them balloons floated on the ends of ribbons tied to a garden gate set between clipped privet.

"What are those colored spheres?" asked Rathina, her voice filled with wonder. She looked at Tania. "See how they dance in the air! Is it Mortal magic?"

Tania smiled. "No, it's only helium," she said. "They're balloons. I think there's some kind of kids' party going on."

An odd swishing, rattling sound came up quickly behind them. Tania turned in time to see a girl of maybe six or seven years old racing along the pavement toward them on inline skates. She was wearing a short, wide-skirted lilac dress that frothed with white lace and netting. She had a very intent look on her freckled face, and her arms were spread for balance.

"Excuse me!" she piped. "Fairy princess coming through!"

Swerving expertly and gathering speed, she passed the two sisters.

"Tania!" Rathina gasped as the little girl sped past. "Look! On your mercy, *look*! The child has *wings*!"

Rathina was right. Clipped to the back of the little girl's party dress was a pair of gauzy fairy wings.

"They're not real." Tania laughed. "It's a costume; they're attached to the dress."

The girl came to a sudden twirling halt, her fists on her hips. "They are too real," she exclaimed. "I'm Polly the Party Fairy. Don't you know *anything*?"

"Sorry," Tania said, smiling. "I didn't recognize you at first, Polly."

Rathina stared at the girl in utter confusion. "Mortal children have no wings!" she said. "And yet . . . and yet . . ."

"It's just make-believe, Rathina," Tania said under her breath. "Play along with her."

"I'm not *Mortal*!" said the girl. "I'm a fairy princess. Fairy princesses live for always."

"Indeed they do, little one," said Rathina, a smile

of understanding spreading across her face. "We, too, are Faerie princesses."

The little girl eyed her dubiously. "You don't look like fairy princesses!" she said. "You look totally ordinary."

"We're in disguise," Tania said. "We're on a secret quest. You won't give us away, will you?"

The little girl shook her head. "And fairy princesses always keep their word!" she added. "Are you coming to Rosie's party? If you're not invited, you can come with me. Rosie won't mind."

"We'd love to," Tania said. "But we don't have time. Secret quest, remember?"

The little girl shrugged. "Okay," she said. "Bye." She turned and scooted off, balancing with careless ease on her blades. She turned in at the open gateway with the balloons, where her mother was waiting for her. She gave them a final look. "Good luck with the quest," she called. With a wave she disappeared between the hedges.

Rathina's face was shining with delight. "She knew of Faerie!" she said. "You told me that Mortals did not know, did not believe—"

"Children believe all kinds of wonderful things," Tania told her. "Everything's possible when you're seven years old." She sighed. "But then you hit an age where you decide its cooler not to believe in anything at all." She slipped her hand into Rathina's and they walked together along the pavement. "It's called being grown-up."

Through the gap in the privet they saw about twenty children, most in party costume, laughing and playing games on a long lawn. The house beyond was shrouded in wisteria, the heavy clusters of white flowers hanging over the open doorway. Some women were bringing out trays of food and drink, and a clown was making balloon animals.

"They are as merry as Faerie children," murmured Rathina. "I had never thought that Mortal children would know such joy!"

"I told you, this world isn't as bad as you think."

"Indeed not," Rathina said thoughtfully.

Tania led her across the road. They were looking now for a right turn.

They came to it after about fifty yards. They turned into it and found themselves walking along a narrow alley between high wooden fences draped with russet ivy.

Beyond the alley everything was different. There were fewer trees and the houses were in terraced rows now, looking shabby and uncared for.

They crossed the road and headed into a large estate of gray housing blocks and concrete walkways.

"I like this not," said Rathina. "'Tis a sad place."

"It is a bit grim," Tania admitted, looking at the litter and the scrubby patches of struggling grass. They crossed an open space and walked into a narrow passageway between two housing blocks.

"Sister, all is not well," Rathina murmured, pausing suddenly, her dark eyes glittering.

"What?"

"Danger. Close at hand."

"The thing you sensed before, is it still with us?" Tania asked.

Rathina frowned. "I do not speak of that," she said. "Our peril is Mortal—and it lies ahead."

"What?"

"They show themselves!"

Two young men stepped from a covered doorway farther along the passageway. They both wore jackets with the hoods drawn so their faces were in shadow.

"Got the time, love?" called one of them, swaggering forward.

"We need to get out of here," Tania said, catching hold of Rathina's wrist and pulling her back the way they had come.

"Don't go, darling," called the other.

"What do they want of us?" asked Rathina. "They reek of bad intent!"

"Our money, probably," said Tania. "Come on."

Tania turned, but two more young men had emerged behind them.

Both ends of the passageway were blocked.

Grinning, the four men closed in.

"Evening, girls." The young man's mouth stretched in an evil smirk. "Glad you could join us—and I thought this was going to be a boring night."

XIII

Tania gazed into the cruel faces of the young men and forgot that she was a princess of Faerie, a warrior maiden who had fought the Gray Knights of Lyonesse, the slayer of the Sorcerer King, seventh daughter of a seventh daughter, walker between the worlds. In an instant she became a frightened, cornered sixteen-year-old girl.

"You have to pay a toll to come through here, girls," said the leader, a lad with a face like raw meat.

Rathina twisted her wrist loose from Tania's grip and drew herself up to her full height, her eyes flashing as she stared at the boy.

"I am a princess of Faerie and pay a toll to no man." She looked him up and down. "Nor neither to any passing goblin, as it would seem here."

"She's calling you names, Robbie," said the boy's sidekick, a skinny weasel whose eyes peered out from an eruption of acne.

"Watch your mouth, girlie, or you'll get a slapping," Robbie said with a scowl.

"You're making a big mistake, boys," Tania said loudly, glancing back and forth between the two pairs of lads. "Just let us go and everything will be fine."

"No can do," said Robbie, putting his hand out. "Pay the toll."

Rathina's voice sang out through the passageway. "Get you gone from here, goblin-spawn, or the wrath of the daughters of Oberon and Titania will teach you better manners."

"You talk funny!" croaked the spotty sidekick. "You mental or something?"

"I asked you girls nicely," said Robbie. "Now I'm going to have to insist."

The four boys were only a couple of yards from Tania and Rathina by now.

Suddenly Robbie had a knife in his hand.

Tania eyed the sliver of steel. *It half kills me just to touch metal,* she thought. *What's going to happen to me if I get stabbed?*

"You fool!" said Rathina. "Do you not know that I am immune to the bane of Isenmort?" She sprang forward, the side of her hand chopping down on the boy's wrist before he had the chance to pull away.

She swept her other arm low and caught the knife as it fell from his fingers. Her shoulder hammered into his chest, sending him staggering backward with a grunt.

Tania followed her sister, leaping at the skinny weasel, thrusting her elbow into his stomach, doubling him up. She heard angry shouts from behind and saw that the two other boys had also drawn knives.

"Rathina, let's get out of here!" Tania shouted.

"I have but half begun!" yelled Rathina, advancing on Robbie with his knife tight in her fist. "Look into the eyes of your nemesis, you stinking gutter filth," she snarled. "May the blood putrefy in your veins! I shall split you open like a spatchcock fowl!"

Robbie backed off, his expression showing more anger than fear.

"They get the point," Tania said. "Let's go!"

She grabbed Rathina's arm. As they ran out into the open at the far end of the passageway, Tania heard Robbie's voice.

"This ain't over! I ain't done with you!"

Rathina turned and pulled back, apparently eager to continue the confrontation.

"No," Tania said. "We've got more important things to do, remember?"

Rathina grinned at her. "The warriors of this land are weak and witless," she said. "We should have hurled them through the dark gates of Abred!"

"Those weren't warriors. They were just a bunch of thugs."

"And what is this puny thing, a peeler of fruit?" She held the knife up to her face. "A weapon to strike fear into an enemy, indeed!" She laughed.

"Get rid of it, Rathina," said Tania.

"So be it." Rathina tossed the knife casually over her shoulder. "It is a feeble tool, and I would trade a dozen so for one fine crystal Faerie sword."

Tania looked back toward the shadowy slot of the passageway. "Let's hope we won't need to," she said, certain that malevolent eyes were watching them.

They had taken Robbie and his gang by surprise. If they were to meet up with that bunch of thugs again, she had the feeling she and Rathina would not get away quite so easily.

It was early evening as Tania and Rathina mounted the three stone steps that led to the front door of 13 Garner Road, one of a row of terraced houses in a small backstreet. Tania pressed the top of five bells. A scrap of paper under the button had three names written on it: Estabrook, Diss, Novak.

A pale young man with carrot-colored hair and a skimpy ginger beard answered the door.

"You'd be Anita, yes?" he said. "I'm Peter. Come in. Connor said I should make you some tea while you wait; he'll be here soon."

"A cup of tea would be great," said Tania as she stepped cautiously over the metal threshold. "This is Rathina. I hope we're not being a nuisance."

"Not at all."

Peter led them along a dim-lit hallway and up several flights of stairs till they came to a door that opened into a square room cluttered with unmatched furniture. There was a threadbare couch, worn-out armchairs, a desk, a low table with a television set, and a sideboard; and every surface, including the carpet, seemed to be covered in magazines and crumpled, discarded clothing and old pizza boxes, forgotten coffee mugs and books and sheaves of paper and odd, solo sneakers.

"That's the communal room," Peter called from another room, obviously the kitchen. "Clear a space and make yourselves at home."

Rathina turned in a slow circle, perusing the shambles that surrounded them. "Are all households in the Mortal World thus?" she asked.

"All households shared by three lads are, pretty much," said Tania. She lifted a pile of magazines off the couch and gestured to Rathina to sit down.

A couple of minutes later Peter came back into the room with three mugs in his hands. "It's only bag, I'm afraid," he said, sitting on a pile of clothes in the armchair.

"That's fine," said Tania, handing a mug to Rathina.

Her sister sipped the tea cautiously. "Hmm," she said, quickly putting the mug down. "'Tis a most curious brew, forsooth."

Peter gave her an odd look, but before he had time to say anything a cheerful yell came echoing up the stairs. "Is she here yet?"

Tania recognized Connor's voice. "Yes, I am," she called back.

"Sorry I'm late," Connor said as he came into the living room. "Has Peter been keeping you entertained?"

"He has," said Tania, smiling. "Nice to see you." Connor was tall and broad-shouldered with fine blond hair and a quick smile. Apart from his hair being shorter, he looked no different from when their families had last met up eight months ago.

"Likewise," said Connor. He moved toward Rathina, his hand extended. "I'm Connor," he said.

"This is Rathina," Tania said. "She's a friend from school. I hope you don't mind her tagging along."

"Not at all," said Connor. "The more, the merrier."

"Merry, sirrah?" Rathina said. "I think not, by my faith." She stood up and took his hand. "We have come far to seek your wisdom and aid, Master Connor." She turned to look at Tania. "And now to business," she said. "Will you lay out our plight to this Mortal Healer, sister, or shall I?"

Connor gave Rathina a puzzled smile. "Sorry, have I walked in on the middle of a *Lord of the Rings* role-playing game?" he asked. "If so, who's who? And has Gollum been allocated yet? I'd really like to be Gollum."

"I'll make you some tea, *Gollum*," said Peter. Connor followed him into the kitchen.

"Rathina!" exclaimed Tania. "That wasn't the way to do it at all. You can't just blurt out stuff like that."

"He must be told the truth," Rathina said, unperturbed. "Or did you intend to ensnare this Connor with trickery?"

"Well, no," said Tania. "But I was going to . . ." She paused. "Okay, I'm not sure exactly *what* I was going to do, but what *you* just did, that wasn't it!"

Rathina came up to her and laid her hands on the sides of her face. "We have no time for deception or guile, sister. We must secure this man's aid and return to Faerie as swift as may be." She looked deep into Tania's eyes. "Have you given thought to how we are to return? We must enter Faerie as we left it—within the bounds of the Summer Palace—for we will not be allowed to pass the guards with a Mortal in our midst, not while the terror of the plague manifests itself."

"We'll have to go back to Beachy Head," said Tania. "We can worry about *how* later. First of all we have to get Connor to help." She pulled away. "Please, Rathina, let me do the talking, yes?"

"As you wish." Rathina sat down. "But give thought to this, sister. Something passed through from Faerie in our wake, and the more time that is wasted spinning beguiling tales to enchant yon Healer, the more likely it is that the dark thing will find us."

"I know," Tania said. "Believe me, I *know*."

The kitchen door opened. Peter emerged. He walked to an armchair, grabbing a jacket. "Gotta love you and leave you, girls," he said. "Have a nice evening." And with that he went pounding down the stairs.

They heard the hollow reverberation of the front door slamming.

Tania took a deep breath and went into the kitchen. Connor had his head in the fridge. He looked up.

"There's some stuff I have to tell you," Tania said. "And it's totally ridiculous and you're going to think I'm insane, but—"

"I'm starved," Connor said. "We've got frozen pizza." He took a carton of orange juice out of the door and unscrewed the lid. He offered it to her. She shook her head. He took a long swig. "Would you and your friend like some pizza?"

"Uh . . . yes. Thanks."

He opened the freezer compartment and pulled out a pizza box.

"'A few minutes in the oven,'" he read. "That'll do." He pointed toward a drawer. "Fetch out the knives and forks, will you?"

"I can't," Tania said.

"What? You dieting?"

"No, I mean I can't touch the knives and forks. I'm allergic to metal."

"Really? You never used to be. When did this happen?" He walked across the kitchen, ripping the box open.

"A few weeks back."

He turned around and stared at her. "Excuse me?"

Her frustration boiled up in her. "I need your help," she blurted out. "I need some antibiotics."

His face showed no reaction. "What sort?"

"I don't know. Something that you'd use to treat someone with a really bad fever."

Connor nodded. "You don't know the specific nature of the disease?"

"Only that it's like a really, really severe flu. People get feverish. Sweaty. There are headaches and sometimes they cough up blood."

He leaned back against the work surface. "Okay," he said. "You'd probably want to use some broad-spectrum antibiotics. I'd guess something like tigecycline or levofloxacin would do the trick. How many doses will you need?"

Tania couldn't believe this. Connor was willing to help; she hadn't had to talk him round at all.

"Uh . . . about . . . fifty or so . . . and . . . and—this is going to sound weird—but it needs to work really quickly, but you can't use injections; you can't use needles."

"No problem," Connor said with a smile. "You could use a gas-powered noninvasive injection device. It delivers the antibiotics without needles by blasting it through the epidermis at high speed."

"And you can get one?"

Connor lifted his shoulders. "Sure," he said. "Or you could get one yourself. Anytime. Just go to the hospital and ask for the chief medical consultant. He'll give you a big box crammed full of them if you ask him nicely. No charge and glad to be of service."

The truth finally dawned. Connor was playing her.

"What's going on with you?" he asked, and now the light, casual tone had gone from his voice. "My folks have been telling me some weird stuff about you. Like, that you had a boating accident a couple of months ago. And that you went missing from the hospital, then turned up out of the blue with some story of having gone to Wales and back. And the latest is that you and your folks were abroad somewhere on vacation—which is kind of weird in itself, seeing you're only just supposed to have come back from two weeks in Cornwall. Oh, and thank your mum and dad for the Cornish card, by the way. Nice scenery."

Tania looked at him. She could think of nothing to say.

"Listen, Anita," he said gently. "Are you okay? If you're in trouble, just tell me the truth and I'll do what I can for you. Are you feeling a bit messed up in your head, is that it? Concussion can do strange things."

"I'm not crazy, if that's what you mean," Tania said softly.

"Crazy people never think they are," said Connor. "That's the problem with being crazy. And I don't think you're crazy—but you have to admit this is all a bit off the wall, know what I mean?"

"Tania, you *must* tell him the truth."

Tania looked around. Rathina was standing in the doorway.

Connor gave her a hard look. "Who exactly are you?"

"I am *exactly* Princess Rathina Aurealis," said Rathina. "And you must prepare yourself for revelations beyond Mortal imagination." She turned to Tania. "Sister, place the yearnstone bracelet about his wrist. Reveal to him the truth; take him between the worlds."

A look of alarm flickered across Connor's face. "I think maybe I should give your folks a call, Anita," he said.

"No!" Desperately as she longed to hear her parents' voices, to pour out her wounded heart to them, she knew that it was impossible to involve them.

"Why not?"

"Because I don't want them to know about this."

"Okay, that's it," Connor said firmly. He glared at Rathina. "I don't know who you are or what you're playing at, but Anita is a friend of mine and I'm going to put a stop to this right now. Anita, I'm taking you home. Whether you like it or not. If I have to carry you downstairs and force you into my car, I will."

"You know not what is at stake!" Rathina declared. "Think you that I would allow you to abduct my sister?"

"Anita doesn't *have* a sister!" shouted Connor.

Tania didn't raise her voice. "No, she doesn't," she said. "But Tania does." There was only one sure way to convince Connor that they were telling the truth, and that was to give him the kind of proof that even his scientific mind couldn't deny.

Taking a Mortal into Faerie was a huge decision to make, but what other choice did she have? Without Connor's help the whole of Faerie could perish.

"Listen, Connor," she said. "I know what you think, but you have to give me a chance to show you something. We need to be on ground level. Is there a garden to this house?"

His voice was guarded. "Yes."

"Do you have access to it?"

He nodded.

"Take me down there please," Tania said. "If I haven't convinced you within two minutes that there's something unbelievable happening here, I promise I'll get into the car with you and you can take me wherever you like. Deal?"

For a few moments Connor's expression was skeptical, but then he shrugged. "What the hell," he said. He pointed at Rathina. "You're *definitely* looney tunes, and you . . ." He looked at Tania. "I don't know *what's* going on with you. But let's get it over with. I've had a long day. I really don't need crazy stuff like this when I get home." He walked out of the kitchen. "You know what? I was looking forward to blobbing in front of the telly with a microwave pizza before you girls turned up."

Tania ran down the stairs with Rathina right

behind her. She turned back. "Connor, come *on*; it's really urgent."

He followed them down slowly. "Yes, I'm sure it is," he said.

"It *is*! You have no idea!"

A rickety door led to a narrow side alley and a small garden overhung with dense ivy and entirely consumed by lanky weeds.

Connor pushed his hands into his pockets. "Well? What are you going to show me, your *spaceship*?"

"Not quite," said Tania. "Can anyone see us here?"

"I shouldn't think so."

Tania opened her bag and delved for the white crystal bracelet that Eden had given her.

"You think us either lunatics or liars, is it not so, Master Connor?" said Rathina.

"Not necessarily," said Connor. "I guess this could all be a big setup." He gazed around as if he was looking for hidden cameras. "You planning on filming this and putting it on YouTube? Goof of the week or something?"

Rathina smiled darkly. "Prepare yourself for marvels!"

Tania found the bracelet. "I want you to put this on," she said.

"Whatever." Connor took the bracelet and clasped it around his wrist.

"Hold hands with me."

She caught hold of his hand. Rathina took her other hand.

Tania looked at Connor, wondering how he would react to what she was about to do to him. "Okay, step forward on three, yes?"

"Fine."

"One . . . two . . . three."

The garden shimmered and they stepped into a place filled with trees.

XIV

"What just happened?" Connor sounded more amazed than scared.

"Did I not say to prepare yourself for marvels?" said Rathina. "Ahh! But it is good to smell the dulcet air of Faerie once again!"

"We just left your world and entered Faerie," Tania told him.

Connor looked at her, his face incredulous. "Anita . . . *my* world? Don't you mean *our* world?" Tania smiled as Connor gazed around himself.

They were in a dense oak forest. Evening sunshine penetrated the canopy of leaves, slanting down, splashing pools of light over the gnarled trunks and forest floor. Birds caroled in the branches. The air was rich with odors of damp earth and leaf mold, as well as the sweeter scents of leaf and shoot and bud.

"I don't think we're in Peckham anymore," Connor murmured to himself.

"You're in the Immortal Realm of Faerie," Tania

said. "I am Princess Tania and this is my sister Rathina. Our parents are King Oberon and Queen Titania and . . . and we're Immortal."

Connor lifted his hand and felt his head. "I'm just checking you haven't whacked me over the skull," he said. "Because if that's *not* the case, then I'm in real trouble."

"I know what you're going through," Tania said. "I felt exactly the same the first time I was brought here. I promise to take you back home as quickly as possible, okay? But we need your help, so we don't have time for you to adjust. This is real, okay? Really real."

Connor looked hollowly at her, shaking his head. "No . . . *way.*"

"Connor! Look around you!"

Rathina stepped forward and gave him a hard slap across the face. Connor jerked back with a yelp, his hand coming to his cheek.

"*Rathina!*" exclaimed Tania.

"Do you believe this is real now, Master Connor?" Rathina asked. "Or do you require more proof?"

"No," gasped Connor. "Please. No more proof."

"You will help us?" Rathina added. "Our need is great and there is little time."

"If you . . . if . . . I . . ." He took a deep breath. "Listen, when we get a minute, will it be okay for me to curl in a ball and do some primal screaming?"

Tania smiled. "Later, maybe." She looked closely into his face. "I have to tell you what's going on and what we need you to do," she said. "Are you in an okay state to take in what I'm going to say? It's really important."

He nodded, although he still looked shell-shocked.

"Okay," said Tania. "Brace yourself. Here's the thing. . . ."

"How much longer must we wait for him?"

"Give him a minute, Rathina. It's a lot to process."

Connor was sitting under a tree, his legs drawn up, his elbows on his knees and his head in his hands.

Tania knew how he must be feeling: like someone had reached into his skull and pulled his brain inside out.

But Rathina was right. Tania stared southward through ranks of ancient oak trees. Away beyond sight, where the land ended in high sea-lashed chalk cliffs, stood Veraglad Palace and the plague victims quarantined within its walls. For how much longer could Oberon hold the sickly Faerie folk in suspension? Days? Weeks?

Maybe only hours?

She crouched in front of Connor. "How are you doing?" she asked.

He took his hands away from his face and looked at her. His eyes were haunted and still full of disbelief. "This is actually happening?"

"Yes."

"It's not some kind of elaborate trick?"

"No."

He pulled his phone out of his pocket. "There's no

signal," he said dully.

"No, there wouldn't be." She gave him a sympathetic smile. "Different world, Connor."

He put the phone away and swore quietly. Tania rested her hand on his knee.

"You have to pull yourself together."

"Why?"

"Because we need you."

Rathina stood at Tania's back. "I hear a splashing stream close to hand," she said. "Mayhap if his head were held under the water for a while, it would aid his recovery?"

Connor eyed her uneasily. "You have a rotten bedside manner, you know that?"

"Mooncalf!" Rathina muttered.

"Come on," said Tania, dragging him to his feet. "What can we do to speed this along? You're the doctor. What would you give someone suffering from shock?"

"Shock?" said Connor. "This isn't shock; this is *devastation*. Do you really think you can lay all this on me and expect me to act like nothing's happened? I'm in another *world*, Anita!"

"Yes, you are. And people are *dying*."

Connor closed his eyes. When he opened them again, a fragile clarity seemed to have returned. "Okay," he said. "You think your dad brought the illness here? How is he now? Better or worse?"

"I don't know," said Tania, trying hard to subdue the agony that hit her every time she thought of her parents. "I haven't been in contact with my folks since I arrived in London. It hurts so bad not to be with them, Connor, but I didn't even know what to say to them."

"I can see that," said Connor. "Listen, how difficult is it for you to get me back home?"

"Not difficult at all," Tania said. "But there's something else I have to tell you. Something you really need to understand." She took a breath. He had to realize how serious this was. "We're working on a deadline," she told him. "The way I get from world to world—that's going to stop working at first light tomorrow morning."

"So we need to get back here tonight, yes?"

Tania looked anxiously at him. "That's right, but if you come with us into Faerie again and don't get out before dawn, you're going to be stuck here forever." She stared into his face. "Do you understand what I'm telling you? You won't ever be able to get back."

Taking him into Faerie was a desperate risk, but so many lives depended on it. Difficult as it was for her, how could she not ask him?

"So it's a nighttime raid," Connor said. "In and out before the sun comes up." He frowned, his face uncertain. "You're asking a lot," he said.

"I know." Part of her almost wished he would say no, so that the chance of his being stranded would be taken out of her hands.

He nodded at last. "Okay, I can handle that," he said. "Now then, the first thing to do is to find out how your dad is doing—that should help me to try and figure out what illness we're dealing with here." He frowned. "It could be something really simple, you know? A cold, mild flu. I've read stuff about tribes in the jungle who got wiped out by explorers introducing them to the common cold. They had no natural immunity to it, you see? I think that might be what's happening here." He looked at Rathina. "In a world that has no disease even a relatively minor ailment could cause havoc."

"Mum and Dad mustn't know how bad things have got," Tania said. "They'd lose their minds if they found out."

"I get that. Listen, I'll give them a call. I'll say I'm just catching up. I won't say anything about having seen you. I'll say something about a lot of people having summer colds this year and ask how they're doing. That should give me enough info to be getting on with. Then it's a case of figuring out what drugs to use."

"And remember: no needles," said Tania.

"That's not a problem. I won't be able to lay my hands on a huge amount of stuff, but I think I know how I can get hold of a single air-jet inoculator and a couple of ampoules of broad-spectrum antibiotics. That should be enough to do a test run on a single patient." He looked at her, and now his eyes were bright. "And if it works, you can just magic yourself into the hospital pharmacy and help yourself to as much as you need."

"Steal it, you mean?" asked Tania.

"Leave money, if it makes you feel better."

"I don't have any; we don't use money here."

"Diamonds, then. Whatever." He held up the wrist with the yearnstone bracelet on it. "Take me back. Let's get this show on the road!"

Connor put the phone down, his face pensive. It had been agonizing for Tania to stand by while he had spoken with her mother. Every fiber of her being cried out to her to snatch the phone out of his hand. But she knew she mustn't.

"How's my dad?" she asked.

"He's doing okay," Connor said thoughtfully.

"You're sure?"

"Mmm? Oh—yes, yes. No problem." His face cleared and he smiled. "*Wow*, but your mum is cool. If I didn't already know all that stuff you told me, I'd never have guessed there was anything weird happening with her." His eyebrows rose. "So the question is what to do next?"

"Go gather your medicaments, Master Connor," said Rathina. "And that full speedily!"

"Yes. Of course. Let me think." Tania watched him anxiously. "Okay, here's what we do," he said after a few moments. "I'll take the car back to King's College. I know where the stuff we need is kept. I'll slip in and borrow it from the emergency room dispensary. They're used to me hanging around there, so they won't be suspicious. Then I'll come back here and pick up you two, and then we drive to Beachy Head. That's where we need to be, right?"

"We should go with you," said Tania.

"And how would I explain what the two of you were doing in the emergency room?" Connor asked. "No. Believe me, this will run a lot smoother if you stay put."

"Okay." Tania nodded. *Would it really be as simple as that?*

"Give me"—he studied his watch—"half an hour to be on the safe side. Make yourselves something to eat if you're peckish. In fact, you can make us all some sandwiches. There's bread and cheese and stuff. And we'll take some drinks. It'll be quite a long journey." He stood at the door and took a last look at them.

"Wow," he said. "This is some head trip!"

"Thank you for helping us," said Tania.

"You think I'd turn down a chance like this?" he said with a breathless laugh. "No way! It's the coolest thing ever." He smiled and ran down the stairs.

"Your friend hides his fear well," said Rathina. "But it disturbs him, I think, to know he is to be taken between the worlds."

Tania nodded. "He's always been like that," she said. "You can never tell what he's really thinking." She frowned. "I hope he'll be okay with it."

"He is no coward, I deem," said Rathina. "He will be . . . *okay*."

The front door clanged.

"So, sister, we wait," said Rathina.

Tania nodded. "Hungry?"

"Indeed."

"Come on, then. Let's see what there is. You'll have

to do most of the work; the kitchens here are full of metal stuff. Do you fancy pizza?"

"Is it tasty?"

"Oh, yes. So long as there aren't any anchovies. They're disgusting."

"Then lead on, Tania. And let us hope that you are wise to put your faith in this man. All of Faerie hangs in the balance."

"No pressure, then," murmured Tania as she walked into the kitchen. "No pressure at all."

The two sisters sat at the rickety kitchen table, helping themselves to slices of pepperoni pizza and drinking milk from tall glasses.

"I am puzzled, sister," Rathina said. "I know of the love you bear for Master Clive and Mistress Mary, and I know how it tears at your soul to be apart from them, but I cannot fathom your affection for this world. When you speak of your previous life here, it is with a wistful air, as though this Mortal domain has some hold on you. And yet you have shown me little that lifts the heart, save maybe the laughter of children and the singing of birds in the trees. But how is that enough for you?"

Tania frowned, her emotions bubbling to the surface as she spoke. "I guess it's down to what you're used to," she said. "London doesn't seem like a horrible place to me. Okay, most of it is crowded and loud and kind of dirty, too, but none of that really bothers me. I was brought up in London. I'm fine with crowds.

I loved it when I used to get together with Jade and the others and we'd go on a crazy shopping spree in Camden Market." She swallowed, realizing just how much she would lose forever if the ways between the worlds were closed. "And I really like loud music. We used to go to gigs—music concerts—and we'd all crush down into the mosh pit and go mental! It was . . . exciting. Amazing. I don't know how else to explain it."

Rathina chewed reflectively. "I see," she said at last. "It is hard to comprehend, but as you say, to the bird the swaying treetops are home, to the fish it is the briny deeps. But if you revel in such things, sister, how is it that you bear any love for Faerie?"

"Wow, you go for the big questions, don't you?"

"I do not mean to confound you, Tania—but I do not understand how a person can love both the Mortal World and Faerie."

"I guess I'm just a complicated girl," Tania said, hoping a joke would deflect the question.

Rathina looked steadily at her and said nothing.

"I don't know the answer," Tania said at last. "If you'd asked me six months ago whether I could live without my cell phone and the Internet and my iPod and junk food and all that stuff, I'd have probably said no way! But when I'm in Faerie, none of those things seem to matter anymore. It's like . . . like . . . here in London you *need* all those things to survive, but in Faerie they're totally irrelevant. And maybe—"

Rathina's eyes widened, and a sudden alarm came

into her face. "Sister! Beware!" she hissed. "It is close!"

"What? *Oh!*" A chill gripped her heart. "The thing from Faerie? The thing that followed us?"

"Aye, Tania. It has found us." Rathina touched her forehead with a fingertip. "I feel it here. It burns like cold fire. And I can taste it in my mouth: bitter and sour on my tongue." She moved to the window and drew back the curtain, peering down into the street.

Tania got up, the feet of her chair scraping on the linoleum. She came to Rathina's side. Beyond the window the street was a shadowy gulf. The isolated pools of orange light from the lampposts only emphasized the gloom. She was reminded with a sudden sense of dread of the Gray Knights of Lyonesse, the undead creatures that had pursued her into the Mortal World only a few short weeks ago.

Were *they* what Rathina was sensing? Had some of them survived the death of their King—and had they come here to wreak revenge? She could almost hear the clatter of their horses' hooves on the tarmac.

Her heart pounding, she watched for some movement in the street.

"I see nothing," Rathina said. "But the thing is close. Perilously close—at the very door, mayhap."

"Trying to get into the house, do you mean?"

"Perhaps."

"We have to get out of here."

"Nay, sister, we must face it. We must fight this thing and drive it off."

Tania gasped. "Fight it with *what*? Knives and forks? And I can't even use *them*! If it knows how to use the Dark Arts, it'll be more powerful than us. If it traps us up here . . ." She didn't finish the thought. "No! We have to get out. Quickly."

"And what of Master Connor and his medicaments?"

"We'll go to the hospital. It's on the main road on the other side of the railway station; it'll be easy enough to find. We'll meet him there." She snatched up her shoulder bag and ran from the kitchen.

Flight was the only safe option. Tania hit the timer button on the stairway lights, and the two sisters ran quickly down the stairs.

At the top of the final flight that led to the hallway, Rathina let out a hiss and caught hold of Tania's arm, bringing her to a halt.

"So close!" she whispered.

As they hesitated, the timer switch turned off the lights and they were plunged into sudden gloom. But there was a light on in the porch, and through the frosted glass panels of the door Tania saw a dark shape.

She caught hold of Rathina's hand and side-stepped.

The walls and the sloping ceiling faded and the stairs dissolved away beneath her feet. She fell, still clinging to Rathina's hand. Tree limbs buffeted her and leafy branches clawed at her as she plunged through the air. The pain tore the breath out of her.

She had known they would enter Faerie above ground level, but hopefully not so far above it that they would be injured in the fall.

They had emerged among the leaves of a tall oak tree. The vicious slap of the branches ceased. They came crashing onto earth covered in leaf mold and broken twigs.

Breathlessly, Tania stumbled to her feet. Wincing, Rathina got up, stooping to run a hand over her ankle.

"Are you all right?" Tania asked.

"My ankle turned as I landed," said Rathina. "But I do not think I have done myself any harm." She eyed Tania. "Think you we have evaded our pursuer?" she said. "It followed us into the Mortal World. Mayhap it will follow us back into Faerie again." Tania hadn't thought of that. But at least they were no longer trapped in that house, vulnerable to its attack.

She stared anxiously through the trees. "We should get away from here," she said. "We have to go back into the other place to meet Connor. But I don't know which way to go."

"Do your senses not guide you?" Rathina asked. "Much of your Faerie heritage slumbers in you, Tania." She looked around as if casting for a scent. "We traveled east to get to Master Connor's home," she said. She pointed. "West will retrace our footsteps. Come, follow."

Rathina led her through the trees. Tania kept glancing over her shoulder, almost expecting to see something chasing them—like a billowing of gray smoke among the trees.

"Rathina?" she asked after a while. "Where are we now? I mean, if we went back into the Mortal World, where would we be?"

Rathina's eyes shone in the gloom. "And how would I know that, sister?" she asked. "Think you I carry a map of that place in my head?"

"Take my hand; let's find out."

Hands clasped, facing west, the sisters sidestepped back into the Mortal World.

They found themselves in a gritty, concrete development, its grim walls and shadowy alleys sinister now that night was descending. There were a couple of vandalized cars and some overturned rubbish bins. There were no people about.

Of all the places! thought Tania.

But at least they were on the way to the railway station. She ran across a bleak open area, heading for a passageway that she was certain would lead to the street. They were swallowed up by darkness. A wall light buzzed and flickered with a pale sheen. There was the stale smell of urine. Several figures stepped out to block the end of the passage.

A voice cut across the quiet. "It's them!"

Tania recognized the pinched nasal tone: the gang!

"Well, so it is," came Robbie's cruel voice. "Outstanding!"

Tania stopped and looked over her shoulder, already knowing what she would see. More figures black against the dim light, walling off the other end of the passageway. Her heart pounded and she fought the urge to run. Run where? They had walked into a trap and already the gang was moving in on them.

"I should have kept the knife, sister," Rathina murmured. "Casting it aside was a mistake, I think." There was no fear in her voice. "Stand we back to back, Tania—the better to defend ourselves against these goblins."

Gray steel glinted in the darkness. Knives. And eyes glinted, too, cruel as broken glass.

Tania struggled with her mounting terror. A simple side step would take her and Rathina into Faerie and out of danger. But Rathina was not scared of the boys, and Tania knew that she, too, had to find the strength to face down her fear. "You'll probably beat us in the end," she called. "But some of you are going to get hurt. We know how to fight!"

"Indeed we do!" howled Rathina. "Come, do not play cat-a-mouse with us, my little goblin army. Who will be the first to feel the bite of my fingernails in their eye sockets?"

Tania could see them clearly now: hooded and feral, at least seven or eight young men, and five of them had knives in their fists. But they held back, forming a ring around the two sisters—as if Rathina's threat had made them wary.

Tania prepared herself to fight for her life. She'd never been in a street fight before, but she'd led an entire army to victory. The gang would not find her an easy target!

She focused on the boy closest to her. He had a pale, nice-looking face, hair cropped to a grayish stubble. Nasty eyes, though. The knife blade that poked from his fist was about five inches long, she guessed. It could do a lot of damage if he was prepared to use it on her.

She needed to gain the advantage somehow, to make them more frightened of her than she was of them. She lowered her head and stared intently and unblinkingly up into his eyes. Then she spread her lips in a cold grin.

"I am Tania, Princess of Faerie," she hissed. "I killed the Sorcerer King of Lyonesse! Do you think I'm afraid of you?" She gave a menacing laugh. "Come on, this is what you wanted, isn't it? Don't be shy, now."

The young thug narrowed his eyes and his knuckles whitened on his knife hand. Whatever he had expected from a cornered girl, this was not it. The others were holding back, waiting silently for him to make the first move. He hesitated.

She sprang toward him with a howl, her lips drawn back, her teeth bared.

He fell back, slashing wildly at her, his face tightening in alarm. She came up under his swinging arm and used all her weight to send him staggering backward. She was aware of someone coming at her from the side. She shifted her balance and aimed a high sidekick at her assailant. She felt her foot make contact with something soft. There was a grunt as the boy doubled up and dropped to his knees.

The first boy came up hard against the wall, her shoulder in his stomach, the breath beaten out of him. She caught hold of his knife hand and twisted savagely. He gave a yell and the knife clattered to the ground.

She spun around, still keeping low. But the other two boys—the ones still standing—backed off with sneers that Tania knew were intended to hide their panic.

"That's it!" she shrieked. "Run away, you cowards! You're worse than the Gray Knights! At least they couldn't help themselves!"

She leaped forward, hissing. The boys turned and ran.

Then she remembered Rathina. She swiveled on her heel, ready to defend her sister.

But Rathina needed no such help. Of the four boys who had attacked her, three were already running. The fourth was sprawled on his back with Rathina on top of him, her knee jammed in his chest. It was Robbie. She had his knife and he was clutching her wrist with both hands as she fought to bring the blade to his throat.

Tania ran over to them. Robbie was weakening. All pretense of swagger and arrogance were gone now; he looked like a terrified little boy fighting for his life.

"Let him go, Rathina," said Tania.

Rathina didn't reply. All her energy was focused on forcing the knife closer to Robbie's neck. He was weakening. The blade made contact with his skin. Tania saw a trickle of blood.

"Rathina! No!" Tania caught hold of her sister's arm.

Rathina snarled, turning her head. "Let me loose!" Her eyes were ferocious.

But the instant she looked into Tania's face, the rage faded and she let out a gasp.

She pulled herself to her feet, dropping the knife. Robbie curled up on the ground, his knees to his chest, arms over his head.

"Sister, thanks." Rathina panted. "I almost did murder!" She looked down at the cowering thug. "Let's away from this place."

Tania smiled grimly and nodded.

They turned and headed to the mouth of the passageway. Tania's muscles were aching, and her heart was still fluttering in her chest.

A small sound behind them made the hairs on the back of Tania's neck stand up. She looked over her shoulder to see Robbie rushing at them, his knife raised, his face twisted into a snarl.

He's come back for more!

Tania was taken off balance. She tripped and fell heavily, jarring her shoulder and hip. Rathina was knocked backward by the force of the young thug's attack, staggering till she was pinned to the wall, his knife now against her throat.

"Payback's a bitch, ain't it?" he hissed.

A voice rang out, brave and strong. Singing aloud a snatch of a song that Tania almost knew.

Where are now the Warring Princesses?
Where is the heart of Faerie?
They awake and hunt amain
Through the depths of the moonless night!

"Edric . . ." she gasped as the ancient battle-song of Faerie resounded off the high concrete walls of the passageway. "Edric!"

Edric strode forward, dressed all in black, a bright crystal sword whirring in the air.

"Get you gone, carrion!" he shouted. "My blade is thirsty for blood."

Robbie swore and flung his knife, but Edric swung his sword in a shining arc, striking the knife clean and hard so that it glanced off to one side and clattered to the ground.

"I am Edric Chanticleer," announced Edric. "I hold the rank of captain at arms in the court of Lord Aldritch, great and puissant earl of Weir! Get you gone from here or I will leave of you only such scraps as worms and spiders may carry off!"

Robbie stood his ground until the shining whirl of Edric's sword was only inches from his chest. Then he turned and fled.

Tania scrambled to her feet. Edric stood in front of the two sisters, his sword resting now on his shoulder, a look of grim satisfaction on his face. "I found you in the nick of time, it would seem," he said. "And a merry chase you have led me on since I followed you into this world!"

XV

"It was *you*?" said Tania. "You all the time?"

Edric nodded. "I had to know that you would be all right," he said, looking deep into Tania's eyes. "You still have my heart, Tania, despite the things that have come between us. Don't you know that?"

Tania stepped close to him and rested her hand on his chest, too choked with emotion to speak.

Rathina's words rang in her head. *Love never dies in Faerie, Tania. Never.*

He laid a hand softly in her hair. The gesture was so familiar, so gentle, that she had to hide her face against his chest and fight back the tears.

"How did you know where I was?" she asked.

"I had something to guide me," Edric said. "The necklace I gave you—the black onyx stone—led me to you. It whispered in my ear when you came into this world. So I followed, thinking you were on your own, thinking you had made this decision alone. I wanted to help. Have you got the medicine yet?"

She looked up at him, eyes brimming. "How did you know about that?"

"I know *you*, Tania," he said. "As soon as I knew you had come here, I guessed the reason. You were going to try and find Mortal medicine to fight the plague." He smiled. "Why else would you come here when the King had forbidden it? I know you wouldn't have abandoned us."

"Oh, Edric . . ." He had crossed worlds to be with her. He had—

She stepped away from him. "How?" she asked, her voice cracking. "*How* did you follow me?"

"A pertinent question, indeed," said Rathina, speaking for the first time since Edric had appeared. "For few are they of Faerie who can thus penetrate the veil between the Realms. Tania has the gift, and our Father Oberon is mighty in the Mystic Arts, as is Eden and her husband, the Earl of Mynwy Clun. But I know of none other, Master Chanticleer."

Edric didn't answer. Tania saw a muscle in his jaw twitch.

"And . . . and why did Rathina sense a *dark* force?" Tania whispered, dreading the answer.

"I had to be with you," Edric said guardedly. "I had to use whatever power was available to me."

"Spirits of thunder!" said Rathina breathlessly. "You used the Dark Arts! 'Tis no wonder your presence leaned so heavy on my heart!"

"The Mystic Arts are all one and the same," Edric replied. "The spirits summoned are neither good nor bad. It's how the power is wielded that divides the dark from the light."

"You are a fool if you believe that," said Rathina. "How came you by the power? Who taught it to you?"

"No one did," said Edric.

Tania looked at him. "Edric, it takes years to learn to use the Mystic Arts, even I know that." Her eyes widened. "Drake!" she gasped. "Gabriel Drake taught you!"

"No, he didn't *teach* me," Edric replied. "But I was his amanuensis for five hundred years, Tania. I was with him when he made his enchantments. I saw enough to allow me to duplicate some of his work. But not for any bad purpose. You know I wouldn't do that. You know me better than that."

Tania watched him, but for the moment she couldn't speak.

"It is not the *power* that corrupts the soul, Master Chanticleer," came Rathina's clear, steady voice. "It is the manner in which the power is attained. The spirits can be befriended or they can be enslaved—there is no other course." Her voice faltered now. "Gabriel Drake chose the quick path of enslavement, harnessing the spirits to his own ends, heedless of their agonies and distress. You have followed in his footsteps and the stench of his corruption is all about you." She raised her arm and pointed a warning finger. "Beware, fool.

You know not how swift the evil can enter you and take command." Her eyes blazed and her voice broke. "Do you not know? Once on a time, even Lord Gabriel was pure of heart."

Tania saw fear flicker across Edric's face. "That won't happen to me," he said. "I'm not Drake. I used the power to help Tania, that's all." He looked at Tania. "You know I wouldn't do anything bad," he said, a note of desperation in his voice. "You *know* that!"

Her mouth was dry and she felt hollow, as though her heart had turned to ash. She looked into Edric's face but saw only the soulless glitter of Gabriel Drake's silvery eyes.

She ran her hand over her face, and when she looked again, Edric's warm brown eyes were gazing anxiously at her. Had it been fear that had shown her that brief vision—or had it been a glimpse of what was to come?

She swallowed, hardly able to hear her own voice over the insistent throbbing in her head. "Promise me, Edric," she said. "Promise me you'll never use Drake's powers again. Ever!"

"Do you think I'm so weak that I'll lose control?" Edric replied. "Don't you trust me at all?"

"It's nothing to do with *trust*," Tania said. "Don't you get it? I'm *frightened*! I'm frightened of what that power will do to you if you use it. Didn't you hear what Rathina said? Gabriel Drake was good once. Do you think you're stronger than him? Do you?"

"I know I'm *better* than him."

"The arrogance of the novice," murmured Rathina. "Thus it ever begins!"

"I have to know you'll be safe," Tania insisted. "Even if we can't be together, even if you go back to Weir and we never see each other again, I have to know that . . . that you'll be all right." Her voice faltered. "I'm sorry. . . . I can't bear the thought of you changing into . . . into someone I don't know. Someone cruel and horrible."

"That will never happen," said Edric. "But if you want, then I promise. I promise you that I'll never use the power again, not unless I have no choice."

Was that enough? What did it mean to have no choice?

Rathina stepped up to him and looked candidly into his eyes. "Listen to me, Master Chanticleer, and understand that I speak knowing of the love that my sister holds for you. The powers you have used are dangerous beyond your comprehension. If you should call on them again, they will twist your deeds and warp your soul and you will know nothing of it until all that was you has been consumed and lost." Her eyes blazed. "But know this: Before that happens I will come upon you no matter where you may go and I will run a keen blade across your throat and wash my hands in your life's blood." She almost choked as she finished. "I will not allow a second Gabriel Drake loose in Faerie, Master Chanticleer. Upon mine honor I will not!"

"It won't come to that," Edric said. "It would never come to that."

Rathina nodded. "Then all is well." She turned to Tania. "Let us fulfill the quest, sister. Let us seek for Master Connor."

King's College Hospital was not hard to find. A main road ran down a steep hill on the far side of the railway station, and as the three of them stood on the corner waiting for the traffic light to change, they could clearly see the sprawling hospital buildings built of red brick and decorated with cream-colored stonework stretching away along the roadside below them.

"It's huge," said Edric. "Do you know where Connor will be?"

"He said he'd get the stuff at the emergency room dispensary," Tania said. "But we don't need to go inside. If he's still here, his car will be in the lot. It's a dark red Ford Fiesta, and knowing Connor, it won't have been washed for months, so it should stand out."

She was right. They quickly found Connor's car in a far corner of the hospital parking lot.

"Master Connor has agreed to take us to the coast," Rathina told Edric as they made their way across the lot. "We need to be within the walls of Veraglad Castle ere dawn."

"A good bit earlier than that, I hope," said Tania. "I'm not sure what the time is." She looked into the velvety sky. Stars were just beginning to appear, twinkling palely through the nocturnal sheen of the big city. "Not later than half past nine, I don't think. That ought to give us time to get back well before Faerie is closed off to us."

"Lo! He comes!" said Rathina, pointing to a small dark shape that moved quickly from the portico entrance of the hospital and ran across the parking lot. Connor came to a halt as he saw them.

"What are you doing here?" He looked at Edric. "Who's this?"

"He's Edric," Tania said. "He's from Faerie as well. As for why we're here—well, that's a long story, and I'd rather get you up to speed on the way, if that's okay. Did you get the stuff?"

Connor nodded. He opened his jacket and briefly showed them a small plastic box. "The needle-free inoculator is in there," he said. "And I have a couple of ampoules of levofloxacin in my pocket."

"Is that the best one?" asked Tania.

"For a broad-spectrum antibiotic, it's probably the best there is right now," said Connor. "It's effective against gram-positive and gram-negative bacteria, and it's used even when the specific bacterium is unknown—like in this case. It's usually the first drug people are given when they show the symptoms of pneumonia—and right now pneumonia is my best guess for what your people have."

"Then let us make haste, sirrah," said Rathina. "My people await your skills."

Connor unlocked the car. "Did you remember the sandwiches and drinks?" he asked.

"We did not," said Rathina. "More urgent concerns distracted us." She looked at Edric. "Or so we thought."

"We'll buy something on the way," said Tania. "How long will it take to get to Beachy Head?"

"Half an hour to get out of London," said Connor. "Then another hour or so down the A twenty-two if the road's clear, which it should be at this time of night." He looked at his watch. "We should be there before midnight. I can administer the antibiotics and still have plenty of time to check out how our guinea pig is doing before the sun shows up."

Tania let out a breath of relief. They would be back in the palace hours before the dawn deadline. She looked at Edric. "We can't just stroll into Cerulean Hall with Connor," she said.

"I agree," said Edric. "In fact, I'd say it was a mistake to stroll *anywhere* in Faerie with a Mortal among us."

"Can you think of another way to fight the plague?" Tania asked. "Hopie and Sancha haven't had any luck with a cure. Connor is our only hope."

Edric looked at her. "Have you considered the fact that he may make things worse?" he asked.

"It's a chance we have to take," said Tania.

"I just want to be sure you've thought it through, that's all."

"I have," said Tania. "I've been thinking about nothing else ever since we got here! Now, like I said, we have to get into the palace secretly or the wardens will stop us. And I think we should try out the drugs on Cordelia first." She turned to Rathina. "Can we get to her rooms without being seen?"

"Indeed we can."

"And once you've given the drugs, how long then?" Edric asked Connor.

"We should start to see an improvement in a few hours," Connor said. "If everything goes according to plan, we should know whether this is going to work in plenty of time for me to get back home safe and sound."

If Tania's hopes and prayers were answered, then in just a few short hours Connor's medicine would start to work. And once they knew the plague could be cured, she would be able to insist that the portals between the worlds be kept open to allow more of the medicine through.

The plague would be defeated. All would be well. Things could return to normal in Faerie.

In just a few short hours . . .

Tania stretched her aching limbs and looked into a sky full of stars. It was a relief finally to get out of the metal shell of the car. It had given her a massive headache to be cooped up in the backseat for so long, but now the journey to Beachy Head was over.

From the pained expression on Edric's face she assumed he was feeling pretty rough as well. A few weeks ago they would have comforted each other, but now their body language was awkward and they walked separately through the lank grass.

"Does anyone know where we're going?" asked Connor. He had pulled a rubber flashlight out of the back of the car and he was swinging it around, randomly illuminating patches of long grass.

There was something eerie and disturbing about this place in the middle of the night. The dark sky was too big, the stars too distant.

"We are almost at the place where we entered this world," said Rathina. Once more Tania was astonished by her sister's built-in sense of direction. If it had been up to her, she doubted whether they would ever have found the right spot, and yet Rathina led them unerringly through the grass toward the cliff edge.

"Here!" Rathina said, spreading her arms.

"Are you sure?" asked Tania.

Rathina gave her a sharp look.

"Sorry." They were very close to the edge of the cliff. Tania didn't look down. She could hear the sea flailing the rocks below them. She could feel the immense expanse of empty air that opened out only a few short steps away.

Tania shivered and turned her back to the cliff edge, reaching out her hands. "Hold on to me," she said.

Connor took her right hand and Rathina closed

her fingers around her right wrist. Edric hesitated for a moment then put his hand in her left hand.

She sidestepped.

The stars went out like a thousand blown candles, and the air became still.

They were back in the Well Room in Veraglad Palace.

Part Three

The Road of

Faith

XVI

Edric's hand slipped out of Tania's the moment they came into Faerie. It was as if he couldn't bear to touch her. How had that happened?

"Wow!" Connor's awestruck voice was the first to break the silence. He let the flashlight beam rove over the stone walls of the small room. The various entrances and exits stood out sharp and black. "Where are we?"

"You are in the hidden heart of Veraglad Palace," said Rathina. "This chamber and the passages that lead from it were delved from solid stone by the Mystic Arts of our sister Eden." She looked at Tania. "We will be able to enter Cordelia's chamber without the need to show ourselves." She pointed to a narrow slot. "That is the way." She held out a hand to Connor. "I shall light our path," she said.

Connor handed over the flashlight. Rathina looked into the beam, her eyes narrowing against the bright white light. "A marvelous, odd thing, indeed," she said.

"Like a hundred candles without flame. Is this . . . What did you call it, sister?"

"Electricity," said Tania.

"You don't have electricity?" said Connor. "Is this whole world stuck in, like, the sixteenth century?"

"I don't think they'd appreciate the word *stuck*," Tania replied. "And trust me, it's not like any sixteenth century you've ever seen on the History Channel."

"Well, no," agreed Connor. "I got that. For a start there's that whole magical side step thing you have going for you. And I guess that's not all. Your sister mentioned Mystic Arts? Does she mean—*magic*?"

"There is no time for this foolishness," said Rathina. "Come, Master Prattler. Your lessons can wait; you have stern work to do."

Rathina stepped into the shoulder-width gap in the stonework and began to mount a flight of wedge-shaped spiral stairs. Connor followed after her, then Tania and finally Edric—keeping always a couple of steps behind her.

The stairway led to a cramped corridor and finally to a slender wooden panel set in the stonework.

"We are here," Rathina said. She pressed her hand against the panel and it slid smoothly to one side. The flashlight beam shone onto what looked to Tania like the inside of an empty wardrobe.

Rathina walked through the wall and into the wardrobe. She pushed the door open. There was a click and the sudden yellow glow of candlelight.

"Oh my god," she heard Connor murmur. "It's just

like getting into *Narnia!*"

A moment later and they stepped out of the wooden closet and into Cordelia's bedchamber.

Cordelia lay unmoving in her bed, pale as death, surrounded by watchful birds. A lump filled Tania's throat.

Please let Connor's drugs work.

Many tall candelabrums had been set up around the bed and the air was filled with a slightly sour, spicy scent.

"Sweet spirits of peace." Rathina sighed, handing Connor the flashlight and leaning over her sister's still figure as the birds edged away from her. "Look, Tania, she is no better. Master Hollin's healing stones do nothing!"

"What mischief is this?" asked a voice from the doorway. "How came you here to my wife's chamber?"

They turned. Bryn was at the part-open door, his face gray and drawn, his eyebrows knitting as he took in the strange clothing that Tania, Rathina, and Connor were wearing.

"We mean nought but good," Rathina said quickly. She gestured toward Connor. "This man is a Healer. He has medicines with him. Tania has great faith in his powers."

Bryn's eyes narrowed with distrust. He stepped quickly into the room, coming between Connor and the bed. "You are not of Faerie," he said, looking Connor up and down. "Whence come you?"

"I'm here to help," Connor said nervously. "Tania—tell him!"

Bryn glanced sharply at Tania as realization dawned in his face. "He is Mortal! You have been to the Mortal World—against the most specific commandment of the King! Lord Aldritch said it was so when you could not be found, but I did not believe him. I thought you had gone to some private place to consider your future. But now I see he was in the right! And you have brought another Mortal into Faerie!"

The look of disquiet on Bryn's face made Tania feel uncomfortable. "I had to bring Connor here secretly," she explained. "The earls are going to close the ways between the worlds in a few hours. Then it would have been too late. Connor is going to help. Trust me, Bryn."

Edric's voice was low but authoritative. "Bryn Lightfoot—if you love your wife, allow this man to do his work," he said. "For I tell you true, none other than he can lift the shadow of death from our people."

Tania looked at Edric. It was so strange to think that this was the same smiling boy she had fallen in love with in the Mortal World. Back then he had spoken like an ordinary Londoner, but now, unless he was specifically talking to her, he sounded like any other man of Faerie.

"I can help," Connor added. "If you'll let me."

Bryn stepped to the door and closed it. "Then work swift, Mortal," he said. "Master Hollin's acolytes return here betimes to sing their healing dirges over the princess—not that their ministrations have awoken her nor put the blood back into her cheeks."

"What's Hollin doing now?" asked Tania.

"He resides in Lord Aldritch's chambers," Bryn said with a growl. "No doubt playing at pitch and toss with his worthless pebbles." He glanced at Edric. "Lord Aldritch spoke against it, but the Conclave of Earls had decreed that none other shall be taken from the Gildensleep until some proof of the Healer's powers is revealed."

"I think they'll have a long wait," said Tania. "What about their plans for shutting the doorways between the worlds? Is that still going ahead?"

"It is," said Bryn. "All the enchantments have been prepared. When the sun rises, the ways between the worlds will close forever."

Tania saw alarm flicker for a moment in Connor's eyes, but he said nothing.

"Not if Connor's medicine works," said Tania. "If Cordelia gets better, I'll be able to convince them to leave the portals open, I'm sure of it."

Connor gave her a worried look. "I'd better get a move on," he said.

Tania turned to him. "Yes. Do it," she said. "Do it now."

"What about these pebbles?" Connor asked, gesturing at Hollin's healing stones. "Can I move them?"

Tania nodded. "Yes, get rid of them."

Connor picked the stones off Cordelia's body and placed them in a pile on the bedcovers. He then took the plastic box from under his jacket. He laid it on the bed and clicked it open. Cordelia's birds shuffled away to the far side of the bed and one or two fluttered to safer perches, but none left the room and all kept their black eyes on the ailing princess.

Tania leaned close, anxious to see what Connor was doing. Inside the box was an oblong green device that looked to Tania a little like an office stapler. Beside it were a small green vial and a silver-colored plastic tube with a kind of trigger device on one side.

Connor felt in his jacket pocket and took out a small clear, plastic vial filled with a pale liquid. As she watched, he inserted this into the silver tube and snapped the trigger closed.

"Have you ever used one of these things before?" Tania asked quietly.

"No. But I've seen it done." He looked at her and smiled. "I can do this, Anita—sorry—*Tania*. Don't worry. I really can."

There was a tense silence in the room as Connor lifted the oblong device out of its box and opened it. He placed the silver tube inside and closed it again.

"That's it," he said. "All ready." He moved up the bed, pulling back Cordelia's sleeve to reveal her bare arm.

A crow croaked warningly from Cordelia's pillow.

Connor glanced at it. It bobbed its head and glared at him. He took a breath, paused for a moment with the device cocked in his hand, then pressed the end against her upper arm and brought his thumb down on a button at the top.

There was a sharp rushing, hissing sound.

"What is that thing?" Bryn demanded. "What has this Mortal done to Cordelia?"

"He's helping," said Tania.

Connor lifted the device away and looked up at Bryn. There was a small reddish stain on Cordelia's skin.

"Okay," he said. "Antibiotics administered. Now all we have to do is wait."

"I must go," said Edric. "I have been already too long from my lord's side." He didn't seem to Tania to be speaking particularly to her; he didn't even look at her.

"Say nothing of this!" warned Rathina.

Deep lines appeared between Edric's eyebrows. "If the healing is successful, all shall soon know of it," he said to her. "If not, send the boy back whence he came and hope the dawn brings a miracle. I shall say nothing, my oath on it."

He turned and swept from the room.

On an impulse Tania followed him. "Edric?"

He paused at the door that led to the corridor. There was a look of such pain in his face that Tania stepped toward him, her arms reaching out.

"No!" He backed off, and Tania saw tears in his eyes. "You're only making it harder!" he said. "We can't do this."

"But you followed me . . . into the Mortal World—"

"To *protect* you, not to . . ." His voice faded. "I can't stand this anymore. I can't bear being near you and knowing we can't be together. It's tearing me apart."

"Edric, I *love* you. . . ."

But he was gone and the door had slammed on his back.

Tania stood alone in the room, her breath shuddering. She took a few moments to gather herself, then walked back into the sickroom.

Connor stared at her. "Are you sure you trust him?" he asked.

"Yes," Tania said quietly.

"Master Chanticleer has given his word," said Rathina. "He will keep silent."

Bryn was sitting on the edge of the bed holding Cordelia's hand. "I am loathe to leave her side, but it would be prudent for me to await in the outer chambers," he said, gazing down at her ashen face. "That way I will be able to prevent Master Hollin's acolytes from entering, should they seek to return." He leaned over Cordelia's face and kissed her gently on the mouth. "Wake soon, my love," he whispered. "Eternity awaits you with impatience."

The door closed behind him with a sharp click.

Tania hugged her arms, unable to tear her eyes from the pitiful sight of Cordelia's white face. Rathina was standing at the head of the bed, her back ramrod straight, her hands clasped behind her. She was pale and her lips formed a tight line.

Connor appeared at Tania's side. "How are you

doing?" he asked softly.

She shook her head but didn't reply.

"When it starts working, do I get to take a look around this place?" he asked.

She almost managed a smile. "If this works, I will personally take you on an all-expenses-paid guided tour of this entire country," she said. "And that's a promise."

The candles burned low. A few had guttered and died. Rathina had found new ones yellow as butter and had thrust them into the molten wax of the foundered ones, lighting them with a taper.

The moon moved across the sky, as large as a plate and as white as snow. Every now and then Connor would lean over Cordelia, lifting her arm, his fingers at her wrist, or he would lay the back of his hand against her forehead as though testing for a change in temperature.

At some point Tania knew she would have to take Connor back down to the Well Room and lead him to safety in the Mortal World. But not quite yet. For now the two of them were sitting side-by-side, backs against the wall, whispering softly together.

"It's so hard to tell what's happening to her," Connor said. "Back at King's, we'd have her hooked up to all kinds of equipment. She'd be wired up to an ECG monitor to check her heart rate, and there'd be display screens showing her arterial blood pressure and rate of oxygenation, and there'd be two temperature graphs. She'd have wires all over. Plus we'd have her on a saline drip and there'd be a crash cart nearby in case something went wrong."

"They don't have anything like that here," Tania said.

"Listen," Connor said, "if things don't improve in the next couple of hours, what say you do that magic trick of yours and we take her back home? She'd be far better off in a hospital."

"I can't do that. I told you. The way I get between the worlds is going to be shut down at dawn. She'd never be able to get back here again."

"At least she'd be alive."

Tania shook her head. "She'd hate it. And what about all the other people who are ill here? No, we have to wait and pray that the stuff you gave her works. Then I can go to the King and convince him not to close off the Mortal World. And *then* we can go back and get enough stuff to cure everyone."

"The 'Mortal World'?" Connor said thoughtfully. "You say that as if you're talking about the planet Mars."

"Do I?" She sighed. "Yes, I suppose I do sometimes. It's hard to explain."

"I bet it is."

There was silence between them for a little while. Connor looked at his watch. The hands showed one thirty.

The night was not yet half over.

* * *

Tania opened her eyes and for a few moments she couldn't make sense of what she was seeing. Then she recognized the flicker of yellow candlelight on the walls, and she saw the open window of Cordelia's bedroom with the moon cut in half by the frame. Lace curtains trembled in the breeze.

She was curled on the floor with her head in someone's lap. For a stupid, forgetful, blissful moment she thought it was . . .

Idiot! It's Connor.

She could feel his hand resting on her shoulder, and she could hear him breathing deep and slow. Asleep, she guessed.

She felt that she ought to move, to sit up, to check on Cordelia. But it was hard not to surrender to her drowsiness, to drift back into the warm embrace of sleep. . . .

Rathina will wake me if anything happens with Cordelia . . . and she'll keep an eye on the time . . . and I will get up in a minute . . . in just a minute. . . .

She was running. Running for her life along a deep, dark valley. All around her the hills rose like fangs against a bloodred sky. She couldn't remember how she had got here; all she knew was that she had to run. Was something chasing her? Did she have to be somewhere?

Don't know. Don't care. Keep running!

The whole world shuddered around her and the stars trembled in the bleeding sky. She stumbled, losing balance, feeling the reverberations rising through her body. It was as though, deep under the ground, some huge being was beating a vast iron gong—soundless, but as big as the moon.

And there was iron in her mouth, and her blood was burning and lightning was firing in her head. And then an impossibly deep voice intoned, the deadly words booming through the shivering air.

"The ways are shut!"

Tania awoke with a gasp, her whole body shaking. She opened her eyes to a wash of gray-blue light. She was lying on the floor, stiff and woolly-headed and with a taste in her mouth like rusty nails. Something had been draped over her shoulders. Connor's jacket.

She pushed herself up into a sitting position.

Day had come. The candles had been snuffed.

She turned in alarm and saw that Connor was leaning over the bed.

"Connor!" she gasped. "You idiot! Why did you let me sleep? It's daytime! You won't be able to get back!"

"Peace, sister," said Rathina. "It was Master Connor's choice to stay."

"No!" Tania shouted, wild with guilt. "Don't you realize? They've already shut the portals!" She scrambled to her feet. "I can't let this happen." She ran for the door. "Oberon will listen to me. He'll open the portals again."

Rathina leaped into her path, her arms spread out. "The Mortal knew what he risked," she said. "The

King cannot open the ways again, Tania. They are closed for all eternity."

Connor caught hold of her arm. "I couldn't just run away," he said. "I had to know if the antibiotics are working."

"Don't you understand?" cried Tania. "Faerie is closed off now; there's no way for you to get home!"

"I figured that one out," Connor said flatly. "I'll worry about it later, if that's okay with you."

"I should *never* have brought you here!"

"You had to!" he said sharply. "Don't blame yourself. This is not your fault. It was my decision to stop Rathina from waking you."

Trembling and torn by remorse, Tania moved to the bed and looked down at her sister. "Was it worth it?" she asked. "Is she any better?" Cordelia's face was as pale as before. In fact, to Tania's eyes, she looked exactly the same. Her birds had moved away, some now perching on the headboard, others on the top of the four-poster rail.

"An apt question, Master Healer," said Rathina. "What progress?"

"None that I can see," Connor replied, his voice shaking. "I don't get it. By now she should have . . ." His words faded away.

"Why hasn't it worked?" Tania asked.

Connor looked at her. "I don't know. The antibiotics should have had some effect." He reached down and pressed his fingers to the side of Cordelia's throat. He shook his head. "It doesn't make any sense."

"Then your vaunted medicaments are no better than the gewgaws of Master Hollin," Rathina said angrily. She glared at Tania. "What say you now, sister?"

"I don't know." Tania looked at Connor. "Did you bring the wrong stuff?"

"No. I brought exactly the right stuff. But . . . but maybe our medicine doesn't work on these people." His forehead wrinkled. "Maybe they have different body chemistry than us. I don't know the first thing about this world. Just because they look like us on the outside doesn't mean everything's the same under their skin."

"Maybe you didn't give her enough?" suggested Tania. "Could you dose her up some more?"

"I've got another ampoule with me," Connor said. "I could try it." He nodded. "Yes. Maybe you're right. Maybe she needs another shot to get her kick-started. I certainly don't have any other ideas right now."

The two sisters watched anxiously while Connor loaded the air-inoculator with his final ampoule of antibiotics.

He leaned over Cordelia, the inoculator ready in his hand.

A clamor sounded from beyond the door. There were raised voices and the dull thump of something striking against the other side of the panels.

"Hollin!" Rathina spat.

"No!" said Tania. "Not *now*!"

The door burst open. Hollin stood there, his eyes burning. Behind him Tania could see his acolytes milling in the outer chamber. Two of them were holding a struggling Bryn by the arms.

"The she-witch has returned!" Hollin howled, pointing at Tania. "It is as I foretold! She has traveled to the Mortal World and brought back death and destruction!" His voice rose to a manic shriek. "See! The succubus has enslaved a Mortal to be our ruin. Even now he works against the potency of our healing rituals. The precious stones have been removed! Our rites are disrupted! Take them and bind them before they can do any more harm."

He stepped aside as a dozen or more of his followers came pouring into the room, the white-wood staves ready in their fists, their faces full of blind fear and anger as they surged toward the bed.

"No!" shouted Tania. "It's not like that! You don't understand."

"By what authority do you dare lay hands on a princess of Faerie!" shouted Rathina. "If the King knew of this, he would banish you to Ynis Maw for all time!"

Tania heard shrill cries and the fluttering of wings behind her as Cordelia's birds took to the air in consternation. She sprang forward and caught hold of the staff of the leading man, twisting it, wrenching it out of his hands. She leaped back, brandishing the heavy, unwieldy weapon.

"Stay back!" she shouted, scything the end of the staff through the air. "Connor! Give her the shot. Now!"

"Stop him!" howled Hollin. "He will steal the princess's soul! She will rise as a banshee from her deathbed—a foul, undead thing to haunt the world!"

A moan of fear came from the men. One of them leaned back, holding his staff like a javelin. His arm snapped forward and the loosed staff came cutting through the air. It struck Connor in the stomach, sending him spinning away from the bed with a grunt of pain. The inoculator fell from his fingers and clattered to the floor. He stumbled back, hit the wall, and slumped, arms folded over his stomach.

Rathina snatched up the staff and stood over Connor, her eyes gleaming. "Where are now the Warring Princesses!" she shouted. "Come! Learn the answer, men of Alba! I will crack your heads like eggs!"

The men began to circle Tania, their staves ready. She jabbed at them, backing off slowly, trying not to let them completely surround her. One pounced, his staff whistling through the air, aimed at her head. She brought her staff up and blocked it, but the blow jarred her to the bone, sending pain shooting to her shoulders.

"Do not fear them!" howled Hollin. "Paradise awaits those who defend the world against evil!"

A second man moved in on Tania, keeping low, swinging his staff at waist height. There was a resounding crack as another staff fended the blow, and suddenly Rathina was at Tania's side, thrusting and parrying as Hollin's followers swarmed forward.

"Take them! *Destroy them!*"

Tania was vaguely aware of Hollin's voice, cracked and lunatic above the grunts and shouts of the men and the clack of wood on wood as she and Rathina held them off.

But there were so many of them. Rathina was fighting like a fury, the staff spinning in her hands, thudding against arms and legs, clashing against wood. Tania defended herself fiercely, but she found it hard to use all her strength and skills against these men. They were not the hideous undead Gray Knights of Lyonesse. Dangerous as they might be, these were *men*, not demons, and something made her hold back from using her full strength.

Tania felt a heavy blow to her thigh and almost immediately another staff struck the side of her head. She staggered, her leg throbbing and her head bursting with agony. She heard Rathina roar with rage, but a fog was coming over Tania's eyes, thick and red as blood. She fell across the bed, seeing for a moment Cordelia's ashen face. She pushed herself up again, flailing the air with her staff. A sharp crack across her knuckles jarred it out of her hands and she fell to her knees.

She heard Rathina give a cry of pain. She was aware of her crashing to the floor at her side.

She tried to get onto her feet, but three or four

staves pressed on her shoulders, holding her immobile.

She heard Hollin's voice. "And now let us rid ourselves of this pestilence ere she cast her sorceries upon us again! Lift her! Bear her to the window and cast her into the sea!"

"No!" Struggling weakly, the pain in her head blotting out all other sensations, Tania felt herself being carried across the room.

XVII

"What madness is this!" bellowed a deep voice. "Release the princess! Put her down, I say, or your heads will pay the price!"

Tania was aware of being lowered to the floor and of Hollin's acolytes moving away from her. A sturdy figure knelt at her side.

"My lady Tania, are you hurt?" It was Earl Marshal Cornelius's voice. Tania peered blearily into his broad, red-bearded face. There was concern and outrage in her uncle's blue eyes as he helped her to her feet.

"I'm okay," she murmured, pressing her hand to the side of her head. Her ears were ringing, and a dull hot pain filled her jaw on the side where the staff had struck her. "Have they hurt Rathina? Is she all right?"

"Buffeted but in one piece, sister," came Rathina's weary voice. "Had I but my sword in hand their heads would have leaped like wheat at the harvest." She turned on Hollin, who was cowering against the wall, his fingers twitching. "And as for you, Master Healer, were you not a guest in this house, I would treat you as you would have treated my sister. And the fishes would be welcome to what was left after hard rock and seawater had done with you."

Hollin's lips parted. "The she-witch has ensorcelled her also," he gibbered. "The half-thing must be destroyed ere it taint us all!"

"Silence!" boomed Cornelius. "You have no dominion here, man of Alba. Get you to your master and take your craven minions with you."

Hollin gathered his robes, his eyes fixing on Tania for a moment before he turned away. The man clearly loathed her—but there was terror there, too. "Lord Aldritch shall learn of this!" Hollin said as he strode from the chamber, his acolytes following silent and obedient.

"Don't worry," Tania shouted after him, "so will Oberon!"

She crossed the room and crouched where Connor was sitting, grimacing and clutching his stomach.

"Are you all right?"

He winced. "I've been better." He gave a weak smile. "No—I'm fine. Winded, that's all. What's a stick in the guts between friends?"

"I'm sorry you got hurt."

"Forget it. I've been beaten up worse in a rugby scrum. Who were those guys? Ninjas?"

"Come on, they're gone now." She drew him to his

feet. He flinched and clutched his stomach, but she could see that he was more shocked than injured.

She looked down for the injector. It had broken open on the floor and a foot had come down on it in the scuffle. The vial was cracked and the pale liquid had run out onto the floorboards. Cordelia would be getting no more antibiotics. Tania looked at her ailing sister. Bryn had come into the room and was at her side, holding her hand, kissing her fingers. The birds were perched all around them, even on her pillow and on his arms and shoulders.

"She is no better," Bryn said. "The Mortal medicines have failed."

"We don't know that for sure yet," said Tania.

He looked up at her and there were tears in his eyes. "Do we not?"

The earl marshal's voice drew her attention away from the sickbed. "Princess Tania, it would seem that the Lord of Weir was right when he told the Conclave of Earls that you had gone into the Mortal World. I see from the outlandish clothes that you and your sister are wearing that you have indeed acted against the King's command and crossed between the worlds."

"For the good, Uncle!" exclaimed Rathina. "For the good of all Faerie!"

"Others shall determine that." Cornelius looked grimly at Connor. "And you have brought another Mortal into Faerie with you! Who is this man?"

"He's a Healer," Tania explained, but her Uncle's

severe expression filled her with remorse. "I thought he would be able to help."

"A Mortal Healer for a Mortal disease," added Rathina.

"And has he helped?" asked Cornelius. "Princess Cordelia does not wake nor grow less pale." His eyes were piercing as he looked at Tania. "Did your peradventure in defiance of your father's edict prove worthwhile, my lady?"

Tania felt herself wilt under his gaze. He was right. She had defied Oberon to no good purpose. The only effects of her trip to London would be to turn more people against her and to rob her of her father's trust. And worst of all her actions had left poor Connor stranded here for the rest of his life.

"The antibiotics should have kicked in by now," Connor said. "I don't understand it."

Cornelius showed no sign that he'd even heard Connor. "You will come with me to the Chamber of the Conclave of Earls, my lady Princess," he said. "To answer in full to the Conclave for your misdeeds."

"No!" Tania said. "If I'm going to be condemned, I want to hear it from the King and Queen themselves. Take me to my mother and father!"

The earl marshal bowed his head. "As you wish," he said. "The King is in the Throne Room and the Queen is with him. But do not expect clemency, my lady. Your deeds have rocked the very foundations of this Realm, and even for the daughter of the King such disobedience carries with it a high penalty."

* * *

As Tania walked down the long white carpet toward the throne, it felt as though the essence of the plague had seeped into the very walls of the room; even the air that she breathed seemed sickly and stale.

The earl marshal strode at her side, and Rathina and Connor were only a pace behind.

"Wow," Connor whispered as they approached the King.

Oberon sat deep in the throne, wrapped in white furs, his face drawn, his eyes glassy. Queen Titania was at his feet, one arm resting on his knees, her hand in his lap, her fingers twined with his. Her head was bowed as though she was lost in deep thought or weighed down under a heavy burden.

Tania found herself trembling as she came close to the throne. It was not that she feared for herself, or for the King's wrath, it was the worn-down cast of Oberon's face that chilled her to the bone.

She tried to remember how many days he must have been sleepless now. When had he first conjured the Gildensleep? On the deck of the *Cloud Scudder*—and that had been in the early morning three days ago. At the very least the King had not slept for over seventy hours.

Tania paused before the throne, unspeaking.

Titania sighed and looked up, her face gray with fatigue.

"You have been to the Mortal World, Tania," she said, her voice so quiet that Tania could hardly hear it. "I sensed it when you departed and again when you returned. Did you think a daughter could use her gift without her mother's knowledge?" She turned her eyes to Connor. "And you brought a Mortal man here," she said. "That was reckless and foolhardy. You could have done great harm."

"Yes. I'm sorry. But I had to try. . . ."

"Princess Tania was discovered in Princess Cordelia's bedchamber," said the earl marshal. "The Mortal was with her, as was Princess Rathina. Had I not intervened, Master Hollin would have ordered Princess Tania thrown down the cliff face. He fears her greatly, your grace."

"Indeed?" An angry edge came into Titania's voice. "That man takes much upon himself in the shadow of Weir's patronage. Were I free to act, I would cast him out of the palace and the Realm of Faerie—but the Conclave of Earls has decreed he should be allowed to practice his skills, so I must forbear. For the moment."

"Father . . . how are you?" Tania asked the King.

"Weary, as are we all," murmured Oberon.

"I give to him such strength as I have," said Titania. "But the strain is great upon him. Sixty-three lives now lie cradled in the Gildensleep." She looked again at Connor. "And you, boy, what good have you done for us and ours?"

"I gave Cordelia some antibiotics," Connor said, stammering a little. "The result was . . . disappointing.

I can't figure out why it hasn't worked yet."

"Then I shall tell you, interloper," called a harsh voice from the far end of the long room. Lord Aldritch stood there, a black cloak swathing his body. He strode down the carpet toward them. "It is because all things that come from the Mortal Realm are a poison and a bane to the people of Faerie!"

Titania rose to her feet, her face clouded with ire. "You forget yourself, my lord," she said in a low, threatening voice. "I spent five hundred years in the Mortal Realm. Am I then a poison and a bane to my people?"

"Nay, your grace, I meant not so," said Aldritch, circling Tania as though hating to be near her, and then bowing low before the Queen. "It is to the joy and beatitude of this Realm that you passed through your ordeal untainted. But your daughter has been corrupted; she is a danger to us all." He stood erect. "The Conclave of Earls has decreed that she is to be sent forever from this Realm."

Titania's eyes flashed with anger. "This decision was made without the King and I in attendance?"

"It was," said Aldritch. "You know the ancient protocols, your grace: although the King and Queen sit at the head of the Conclave, they have no vote and once in session, the earls have the right to make judgments alone." He turned and bowed to Cornelius. "And even without you, my lord, there was a quorum."

"But how is she to be sent from Faerie?" asked the

earl marshal. "The ways between the worlds are shut. The princess cannot return to the Mortal World."

"Indeed so," cried Aldritch. "The King must banish her to Ynis Maw—there to dwell as an outcast for all time!"

"He won't do that!" Tania shouted. "He would never do that to me!"

Ynis Maw! She knew that terrible place only too well: a bleak, storm-wracked island off the northern coast of Faerie. Once Oberon had condemned you to that far-flung prison, there could be no hope of return.

"I demand that the sentence be carried out," said Aldritch. "The half-thing that was once Princess Tania must be cast from the Immortal Realm forever." He gave Connor a sneering glance. "And this Mortal must either go with her or be destroyed at once."

Tania saw the blood drain from Connor's face. "Hey, wait a minute!" he exclaimed in alarm. "I came here to *help*!"

"Hush!" The voice was a deep rumble that seemed to rise from the floor beneath them, like the distant echo of tumbling mountains.

It was the King. All eyes turned to the throne. Oberon's head moved slowly, his glazed eyes shifting from one face to another.

"Sire!" Aldritch dropped to one knee.

"Why come you here to disturb our labors, my lord?" asked the King, his voice measured and low.

"Do you not know that many lives hang in the balance?"

"I do, sire," said Aldritch. "Indeed the lives of all who dwell in your blessed Realm are at risk if the will of the Conclave of Earls is not fulfilled."

"So my daughter is to be banished," rumbled the King. "Is that the will of the earls?"

"It is, sire."

Titania grasped Oberon's hand in both of hers. "My lord, do not do this terrible thing," she said. "Not banishment. It is undeserved. Tania has done no wrong, and the Conclave of Earls acts out of fear, not justice."

"Would you have me disregard the ancient laws?" asked the King.

"No, my lord, but I would have you temper the law with mercy. Do not banish Tania. Punish her, if need be, but do not send her away from us. I yearned to have her with me for five hundred years of exile. Do not take her from me now."

"And what of the Mortal?" asked Oberon, his eyes flickering toward Connor. "Even were I to show clemency to our daughter, he could not be left to roam at will."

"An amber prison would prevent him from doing harm," said the earl marshal.

Connor stared at the King, his face confused and frightened. "A *what*?"

"No!" gasped Tania. "You can't do that! I talked him into coming here; he only wanted to help."

If the earl marshal's suggestion was followed, then Connor would be trapped motionless but alive, sleepless and aware, for all eternity in a globe of amber light, hidden away in the dungeons of the Royal Palace.

No way would she let *that* happen to him!

Rathina knelt at her father's feet. "I have been in the Mortal World, Father," she said. "It is a strange and uncanny place, but I do not think it is a threat to us."

"This is madness!" said Aldritch, rising. "The princess is bewitched! Has the coming of the plague not taught us to shun the Mortal World?"

"Indeed it has," said Cornelius. "But the plague is confined to the palace for now—and if fortune favors us, it will travel no further, even if all within are consumed by it."

Titania's head suddenly snapped up, her eyes glittering. "Something comes!" she cried, turning to face a tall clear-glass window that filled the wall behind the ermine awnings of the throne.

Tania saw a small bright shape moving bullet-fast toward the window. There was a crash, and the window turned to splintered frost as the thing burst through the glass and came hurtling down toward them.

It all happened so quickly that Tania hardly had time to register what the object was before it hit the floor in an eruption of red fire and flying sparks—but she saw a flaming comet with a white-hot human figure at its core.

They all fell back from the leaping flames, Aldritch

throwing his cloak over his face, Rathina bowled help-lessly across the floor. Tania flung herself sideways, grabbing Connor and hurling him onto his back. Cornelius and the Queen moved together to protect the King.

The flames roared, but they gave out no heat. Tania sat up, her hand shielding her eyes from the bright-ness. At the heart of the fire a female figure stood upright upon the white carpet. She stepped out of the flames, dressed in a gown of deepest purple. Her face was made ruddy by the light of the fire; flames still flickered in her snow-white hair.

"Eden!" cried Titania. "My daughter—whence come you?"

Now Tania understood: Eden had called on her Mystic Arts to travel swiftly across Faerie on the horse of air—as Oberon had done when he had transported Tania and her Mortal parents to Bonwn Tyr.

Tania got to her feet. The flames had died away at Eden's back, leaving no sign of scorching on the long white carpet.

"I bear great and terrible tidings!" Eden declared. She walked to the throne and knelt at her father's feet. "My lord King, the plague rampages throughout the Immortal Realm. I have seen it! All of Faerie suffers. The sickness is everywhere!"

"No!" gasped Titania. "By all the spirits, Eden, *no!*"

For the first time ever Tania heard real fear in the King's voice. "You say you have seen it, my daughter?"

he asked, leaning forward, his fingers gripping the arms of the throne. "What have you seen? Speak quickly, child."

"I departed this place in bird form yesterday," said Eden. "I meant to fly to the palace and seek in Sancha's library for answers to this plague."

"And did you find what you sought?" interrupted Rathina.

"Aye, I think mayhap I did!" said Eden solemnly. "But I found more. I found that the plague was rife in the palace. Some few had already died and many were ill. But worse news was to come! They told me that travelers had been arriving for several days—and that most were sick and in search of healing." Eden paused for a moment. "I reverted to bird form, this time taking on the shape of a peregrine falcon so that I could traverse the miles more swiftly. And I saw such horrors! In every town and village I visited our people were suffering."

She stood up, lifting her hand high and making a slow, sweeping gesture. Where her arm passed, the air flickered and an oval of white light opened with ragged, sparking edges.

"Behold the Mirror of the Falcon's Eye!" said Eden.

Tania gasped as a scene appeared in the floating oval disc.

It was a village of thatched cottages and stone-built houses. But something was wrong. Some of the houses were on fire, the thatched roofs burning with a pall of thick black smoke, flames gouting from windows and doors. The earthen streets were deserted save for a few people wrapped in thick cloaks, their faces masked against the smog. They were pulling handcarts along.

Rathina let out a cry of dismay, her hands coming to her face.

The carts were full of corpses.

Titania watched, horror-struck.

"How did I not know of this?" The King gasped. "What mischief has shrouded my soul from the anguish of my people?"

"They burn the plague houses in their terror," said Eden. "The dead are left alone on hilltops to make the journey to Albion without rite or ceremony. The sick are locked away or cast out of their homes. All of Faerie is in turmoil!"

"And while Faerie is ravaged by this Mortal devilry, we debate still over the fate of its progenitor!" shouted Aldritch, pointing at Tania. "Rid us of this thing, sire. Send her to Ynis Maw!"

"No!" Eden cried. "This blight is not of Tania's doing!"

"How do you know this?" asked Cornelius. "Do you have proof?"

"I do," said Eden, her eyes turning compassionately to Tania. "Your Mortal father did not bring this illness into Faerie, Tania," she said. She gestured toward the dreadful image that hung above them. "You see before you the village of Karkenmowr. It lies beyond the River Dwan in the north of Minnith Bannwg. The plague has been stalking this and many another northern village for days now. And it has taken hold in the west and the east, too." She made a flicking gesture of her hand and the vision vanished.

"This is no Mortal disease," she said. "The plague has swept over the length and breadth of this land in but a few days." Her eyes glowed like blue fire. "This sickness has not been visited upon us from some other Realm. The plague is a thing of *this* world!"

"The disease didn't come from Earth!" said Connor. He stared at Tania. "I let myself be trapped in this madhouse for *nothing*!"

Tania could hardly grasp what Eden was saying. *After everything they told me, after everything they made me believe, the disease has nothing to do with me or my parents?*

"That is not possible!" declared Lord Aldritch. "Not in ten thousand years has such sickness erupted in Faerie!"

"I said not that it came from *within* Faerie, my lord," Eden responded. "But there can be no doubt that an ill wind of *this* world has blown it to our fair shores."

"Blown on an ill wind, you say?" asked Cornelius. "But from whence?"

"That I cannot say," said Eden.

"No!" demanded Aldritch. "I will not believe such a thing!" His eyes glittered dangerously. "Princess Eden seeks to absolve her sister of blame. Had the plague been already in Weir, I would have known of it."

"You departed Caer Liel ere it struck," said Eden. "Had you remained in your stronghold but half a day longer, you would have felt its evil breath upon your neck, my lord. And had you not traveled the straight road south, doubtless you would have heard the lamentations of its victims in many a hamlet and village upon the way."

"And still I say you forswear yourself so that the escutcheon of the House of Aurealis should bear no smirch!" shouted Aldritch. "Sire, how do you countenance such falsehoods!"

The King didn't reply. Tania looked at him; he seemed stunned by Eden's fearful vision, his face pale, his eyes unseeing.

"How did I not know?" he murmured. "How *could* I not know?"

"I believe that the same dark force that brought this evil upon us has also worked to blind you to its progress, Father," said Eden.

"A dark force, indeed!" cried Aldritch. "I see the dark force." He pointed at Tania. "It stands before me. Do not be deceived, sire. The Princess Eden seeks to protect the half-thing with her lies! Mayhap they work this malevolence together. Mayhap they—"

"No more, my lord of Weir!" the King roared, half rising from his throne, his face dark with wrath. "You will cast no doubts upon the word of the Princess Eden!"

"Oberon, take care!" cried Titania, stepping forward to support the King as he stumbled. "You are weak, my lord."

"Aye, but not so weak as to suffer my own children to be malspoken thus!" said the King. "Nay, not even by so puissant a lord as Aldritch of Weir."

Lord Aldritch rose to his full height, his eyes disdainful. "Will you not proclaim the fate decreed upon the Princess Tania by the Conclave of Earls, your grace?" he said, his voice cold and haughty.

"You cannot do that, Father!" cried Rathina. "The earls did not know the truth of the matter!"

"Indeed they did not, my lord Aldritch," said Titania.

"I will not do it," said the King. "The verdict was false!"

"So be it," said Aldritch. "Then I depart this court forthwith, and all my folk with me." He turned and shouted, "Captain Chanticleer! Come forth!" He looked at Tania, and there was hatred in his eyes. "You are the wellspring of turpitude and vice," he snarled. "Choose what your sister says, I have no doubt but that you do us great harm! Were it not for you, Tania Aurealis, my son would still be alive! You are a sorcerer and a corrupter of men's hearts—and I will have nothing more to do with a court that seeks to defend you!" His voice rose. "I repudiate this court. I quit this place! Never more shall Weir show fealty to the House of Aurealis!" He glared at Oberon. "Your days as my overlord are ended!" He strode to the door, leaving a shocked silence in his wake; a silence broken only by Connor's subdued voice.

"Wow! I should have brought some tranquilizers with me," he murmured. "That guy is off his head!"

Tania stared after the lord of Weir. She had never thought of him as a friend, but to hear him blame her for Gabriel's death! How could he think such a thing? She hadn't enticed Gabriel Drake to do the things he had done; she had been his victim, not his evil seducer! And the fact that he would accuse Eden of lying to cover for her was just as bad.

She saw Edric appear at the open doorway to the Throne Room.

"My lord?"

"Get you to our quarters, Captain Chanticleer. Tell Master Hollin and his folk to prepare for immediate departure. We will board his ship ere the sun is a hand's breadth higher in the sky, and we will turn forever our backs upon this place!"

Edric stood unmoving as Aldritch stalked up to him.

"Well, captain? Are my instructions unclear?"

"No, my lord . . . but . . ." He glanced past Lord Aldritch and his eyes met Tania's. She almost ran to him, but then he bowed his head. "No, my lord," he said. He marched out of sight, leaving Tania feeling as if her heart had been clawed out of her chest.

The Throne Room door slammed on the lord of Weir.

"Your grace, what peril does this thing foreshadow?"

asked Cornelius. "Is Weir now our enemy?"

"Nay, brother," said the King, sitting wearily back into the throne, Titania's hands on his arm to help him. "We need not fear Lord Aldritch. Let him cool his wrath upon the open ocean. Wiser counsels may prevail when our present concerns are done." He turned his eyes on Eden. "And as to that, what more can you tell us, my daughter?"

Connor moved closer to Tania. "What just happened?" he said. "Tania, what kind of place have you brought me to?"

Tania looked at him. "I'm so sorry," she said, her soul weighed down with contrition for the harm she had done him. "But I need to hear what Eden has to say."

"Tania spoke to me of a dream that came to her, my lord," Eden told the King. "I believe the dream contained a riddle, the unraveling of which may reveal a possible cure to the plague. And it seemed that the answer lay in the enigma of the Lost Caer."

"Was there ever such a castle?" asked Cornelius. "I thought it but a myth."

"As did we all, my lord," said Eden. "And I concede that my search among the archives uncovered no reference to the Lost Caer." She turned again to the King. "But it seemed to me that mayhap the most ancient texts might hold a clue to our woes, hidden somewhere in the days before days."

"The days before days?" said Rathina. "Do you mean in the times before the Great Awakening? Surely no texts exist that can tell of events from before the coming of our father to Fortrenn Quay?"

"Nay, none do," agreed Eden. "Not in the Royal Library. But I discovered a brief text in the most ancient book of the Faerie Almanac. It speaks of the Helan Archaia and says that it hides a great, forbidden secret." She looked at the King. "My lord, do you know the meaning of this?"

"I do," said the King. "Although it is a thing known to few others." He took a long breath. "None now living can pierce the veil that was drawn across Faerie before the Great Awakening," he said. "But it is known to some few lords of this Realm—Earl Valentyne among them—that a place exists where it is said that such prohibited knowledge lies hidden. This place is the Hall of Archives—the Helan Archaia—a great stone tower at the heart of Caer Regnar Naal."

"I, too, have heard of this place," said Cornelius. "Although it has not been spoken of for millennia and then only in awed whispers. But the secrets within cannot be learned, if memory serves, for the chamber is protected by a great door of Isenmort, fashioned in the deeps of time and encircled with enchantments so that even black amber is no panacea to its venom."

"It is so," said Oberon. "The Isenmort Portal cannot be opened by any man or woman Faerie born."

"I have no fear of Isenmort!" Rathina declared, stepping forward. "If this room exists, then let me go there. I will open the Hall of Archives!"

"The door is too heavy for a single person to open

it," said the King. "The task is beyond you, Rathina, even were I to sanction it."

"There must be another way," said Tania. She looked from Oberon to Eden. "Can't you use your Mystic Arts to get it open?"

"Against Isenmort?" said Eden. "Nay, sister, that is not possible."

Tania stared from face to face, seeing defeat in everyone's eyes. Was a locked door of iron really going to bar their way to a knowledge that could save the whole of Faerie?

A quiet, trembling voice broke the dismal silence. "Could *two* people do it?" asked Connor.

"Aye, mayhap," said the King.

"Then I volunteer," said Connor.

Tania could see the fear in his face. "Connor, *no!*" she said. "You don't have to do this."

He gave a wan smile. "I might as well make myself useful."

The King frowned. "This would be a strange happenstance indeed," he murmured. "That a Mortal man should aid us so?"

"Can I just know one thing for certain?" Connor said. "Am I ever going to get back home?"

"The ways between the worlds have been shut," said the King. "You have my pity, Mortal, for I see now that you and your kind are innocent in this matter— but there is no power in Faerie to open the portals again."

"Thanks," Connor said heavily. "I just needed to

know for sure." He took a long breath. "So? How dangerous will it be to help with this door?"

"There is no danger to you, Master Connor," said Eden. "I will bear you and Rathina hence on the horse of air. And the bite of Isenmort will not harm you, of that I can promise."

"Connor is only here because of me," said Tania. "I have to go with him." She turned to Eden. "How soon can we leave?"

"Most soon, to be sure," said Eden. "But I must first go to my chamber and commune for a brief time with the spirits. I have demanded much from them of late, and I must give thanks." She turned and ran quickly to the door, pushing it open and disappearing into the corridor.

Connor turned and smiled bleakly at Tania. "You were always getting me into trouble even when we were kids," he said, but the crack in his voice betrayed his emotions. "I just wish I'd had time to say good-bye to my folks."

Tania swallowed hard. "I'm so sorry," she whispered.

"Don't be," he said. "My choice, remember?"

Tears burned behind her eyes, but she could think of nothing more to say.

Tania sat on a narrow window bench in the Throne Room. The plague came from *this* world! Her Mortal mother and father had been condemned and sent out of Faerie for something that had nothing to do with them—and now she would never see them again. And there was Connor, too. She'd persuaded him to come here to help, and now he was trapped in Faerie for the rest of his life.

But *had* it been pointless to bring him here?

We need him to open the Isenmort door, she thought. *Sometimes it's as if there's some kind of mind at work behind everything that happens.*

She looked toward the King. Hopie and Sancha were here, persuaded temporarily to leave Cerulean Hall now that the truth about the disease was known.

When they had arrived, Hopie had put her arms around Tania and kissed her. "I am sorry," she had said wearily. "I was too swift to seek scapegoats. I am glad Master Clive was not to blame."

Sancha had taken her hand. "You should not have gone to the Mortal World without telling us," she said. "We would have aided you."

"I didn't want you getting into trouble," Tania had told her.

Now the two sisters were by the throne with their mother. Hopie held a wooden bowl and was offering a spoon to the King's lips. Oberon was slumped in the throne, now seeming more exhausted than ever. The Queen held his hands, giving him what support and comfort she could.

But for how much longer? Tania wondered. There had to be a breaking point—even for someone as powerful as her Faerie father—and what would happen to all the people he was protecting when his strength finally ran out?

Tania turned away and gazed from the high window. She saw that several horsemen were leaving the palace, followed by a line of foot travelers. The small group was wending its way along the road that led down toward the harbor of Rhyehaven. She was in a tower high above the departing men, but she knew who they were. Lord Aldritch was on the lead horse, Edric riding at his shoulder and Aldritch's small retinue following close behind—all dressed in black.

Walking along after the horsemen was Hollin the Healer, his yellow robes easy to make out even from that distance, trailed by his green-clad acolytes. As Tania watched, Hollin turned sharply—as though sensing her eyes upon him. His head tilted toward the tower. She could not make out the details of his face, but she felt such malice coming from him that she drew back from the window, her heart thudding in her chest.

She rested her forehead against cool stone for a few moments, letting the palpitations and the unease subside. When she looked down again, the troop was farther away, and Hollin was no longer looking at her.

Lord Aldritch was making good on his threat. He was leaving the palace and leading his people to the harbor to take the ship and return to his Earldom. And he was taking Edric with him.

"Good-bye, my love," Tania whispered, her breath misting the windowpane. She looked away again, unable to bear the sight of Edric riding away from her—perhaps forever.

She closed her eyes, lifting her hands to her burning face.

"Tania? Why are you crying? You should be pleased that it wasn't your dad who brought the infection here."

Tania wiped a sleeve across her cheeks and looked up at Connor. "I am," she said. "But look what I've done to *you*!"

"I'm pretty adaptable," he said. "And who needs electricity, anyway?" He gave a fake smile. "Actually, it doesn't seem real at the moment. When the truth hits me, I'll probably want to strangle you. Will that be okay?"

"That'll be fine," Tania said. "I deserve it."

Rathina approached. "You will be made most welcome in our Realm, Master Connor," she said. "Many are the delights that Faerie can offer." She turned to Tania. "And I am glad for you, that your Mortal father did not do this harm to us. But I dread this news with all my heart." She grimaced. "If not from the Mortal World, then how has this thing come to Faerie? And how are we to defeat it?"

"Not with antibiotics, that's for sure," said Connor.

And if Eden is right and all of Faerie is infected, how will the King manage to protect everyone? And if only some can be saved, how is he going to choose?

The door to the Throne Room opened and Eden glided in. Tania noticed that she was carrying Connor's rubber flashlight in one hand and a leather satchel in the other.

Tania, Connor, and Rathina walked back to the throne.

Hopie and Sancha stood up as Eden approached the King.

Eden handed the flashlight to Connor. "I believe this Mortal tool will aid you as much where we are going as any light that I might conjure," she said.

"We're going somewhere dark, then?" said Connor.

"Aye, Mortal, that we are," said Rathina. "Dark and deep, from what I have heard of Caer Regnar Naal!"

Eden gave the satchel to Rathina. "In here is food and water," she said. "I know not how long we may need to stay in the Caer, and fresh provisions may be hard to come by."

"A wise precaution," said Rathina, hefting the bag onto her shoulder.

"All is now in readiness," said Eden. "The enchantments are cast. We must depart." She bowed to her father and mother. "With your leave I will remain in Regnar Naal with the others and see that no harm comes to them in that forsaken place."

"No, daughter," said Titania. "That you cannot do."

Tania looked sharply at her Faerie mother.

"The King would have you bring succor to our

people," Titania explained to Eden. "Once you have taken Tania and Rathina and the Mortal boy to the Caer, you must depart. We would have you use your powers to quarter the Realm as swift as you may, seeking out all the sick that you can find and swaddling them in the Gildensleep."

"Mother, I do not have such power as this would need," said Eden.

"The King and I will loan you ours," said Titania. "The strain will be great, but we cannot abandon our people."

"And I will fortify the King and Queen with such strengthening elixirs as I can brew," added Hopie. "Sancha will aid me."

"Indeed, I will," said Sancha.

"One more thing must you know before you depart," came Oberon's weak, distant voice. "The Helan Archaia is a place engorged with a knowledge of which it is forbidden to speak within the Realm of Faerie. Tread warily and with a wise fearfulness. Seek only that to which the dream has led you. And do not take anything from the Hall of Archives, for evil will come to you if you do so."

"I understand," said Tania. "We'll be careful, and I promise we won't take anything away."

"Then my blessings upon you."

Titania held her arm out to Eden. "Come, take my hand, daughter."

Eden took hold of the Queen's hand. For a moment nothing seemed to happen, but then Tania was aware of a faint golden light that surrounded all three: the King, his Queen, and their eldest daughter. And as she watched, the gold faded a little from the King and Queen and grew stronger around Eden, till she glowed like a sun.

Then the hands of Eden and her mother slipped apart and the glow faded.

The change in the King and Queen was alarming. As weary as they had both seemed before, now their faces were ash white, their bodies shrunken and eyes dull.

Hopie knelt by the throne, looking anxiously into her father's face while Sancha put an arm protectively around the Queen.

"Go . . . now . . ." breathed the King, his voice a distant whisper. "Save the people of Faerie. . . ."

Eden turned to Tania and the others, and the golden light was still visible in her eyes. She raised her arms above her head, her hands palm to palm, her fingers pointing upward, her eyes half closed so that the golden light seeped out over her cheeks. She began to speak in a silky language, words that Tania did not understand. She brought her arms circling down, her fingertips leaving an arcing trail of white fire.

Her hands came together low on her body, completing the ring of flame. It grew, blossoming out and swelling until it became a globe of white flames that entirely surrounded her.

Her voice rang out from within the fiery globe.

"Come," she called. "Come to me!"

Rathina was the first to step into the ball of fire. Connor didn't move. He was staring at the blazing sphere with his mouth half open and white flames reflecting in his eyes.

"Come on," said Tania, taking his hand. "Let's do it together."

Side-by-side they walked into the cool, flickering dance of Eden's mystical flames.

XVIII

The orb of white fire dwindled until it was no more than a circle of flickering light in the grass.

Tania blinked the dazzle out of her eyes and saw that Eden had brought them to a land of flat pastures, lush meadows, and tall, dark forests. A hill rose before them, tree-mantled and somber under the clear blue Faerie sky. Close by a small herd of wild horses stood watching them. There was no birdsong and no breeze and the shadows under the trees seemed to brood in sullen silence.

"Behold Caer Regnar Naal," said Eden.

"Wow . . ." breathed Connor. "I'm like . . . *Wow.* That side step thing you do is amazing enough, but your sister's horse of air is the coolest yet." He turned to Eden. "How do you do that?" he asked.

"I request the aid of the spirits of fire and air," Eden replied.

"Oh. Right. I see. . . ."

"Where's the castle?" asked Tania. She had looked

all around, and unless trees hid the Caer, she couldn't quite work out where it might be.

Eden pointed toward the hill. "See yonder gray stone set in the hillside?" she said. "That is the entrance to the Caer."

Tania could see the long gray slab of stone leaning deep into the hillside in a narrow area clear of the thick cloaking trees. "You mean it's actually *in* the hill?" she said. "How does that work?"

"Knock thrice upon the stone and you will see," said Eden. "I must depart now and do what I can to bring ease and comfort to the belabored people of Faerie. But these gifts shall I bestow on you ere I go." She turned to face the three of them. She reached out a forefinger and touched the base of each of their throats in turn. Connor flinched but only a little.

"I have gifted you the Arossa Charm," Eden said. She pointed to the wild horses. "When your work here is done, speak gently to them and they will do your bidding."

"That is a fine gift," said Rathina. "I had given no thought to how we might return hence. Wild horses, ho! 'Tis better by far than to foot-slog it down all the long miles of Faerie."

Eden looked at Tania. "And to you I give this." She took Tania's head between her hands and tilted it down, planting a kiss on Tania's forehead before releasing her. "It is the Kiss of Seeking. It will help to guide you to your quarry."

"Thank you," said Tania.

"And now," said Eden, stepping away from them, "I wish you good fortune in your quest. Farewell. Indeed, fare you *very* well!" She lifted her arms and spoke again those strange, sibilant words. She swung her arms down and the globe of fire appeared. For a moment Tania saw Eden standing in a ball of white flame, then there was a crack like thunder, and the globe went searing through the trees, trailing a ribbon of white fire as it arced across the sky and vanished.

Connor gaped.

Rathina looked at him. "Wow?" she suggested.

He nodded, closing his mouth.

"Okay, come on," said Tania, setting off toward the long hill. "Let's get busy." She looked at Rathina. "Who lives here?" she asked.

"Did you not know?" Rathina replied. "None live in Caer Regnar Naal. It has been deserted now for many thousands of years."

"Why's that?" asked Tania.

"I never knew until today," said Rathina. "But it is easy now to understand why this place is shunned. At the heart of the citadel stands a door of purest Isenmort, sister. None of Faerie born could long bear to be close to such an abomination." She smiled. "None but the sixth daughter of Oberon and Titania."

"So who made the Isenmort Portal?" asked Tania. "And why?"

"I do not know," said Rathina.

"Well, *why* is easy, surely?" said Connor. "It was done to make sure no one could get at the archives."

His eyes gleamed as he looked at Tania. "There must be secrets in there that no one was ever meant to know. Exciting, huh? Maybe we're about to find the formula for Immortality."

"Maybe," Tania said dubiously. She wasn't convinced that the Immortality of the Faerie folk was something that could be pinned down quite that easily.

As they came closer to the hill, Tania became aware of a heaviness all about her, as though the air was pressing in on her. The darkness under the trees was impenetrable—as if the gloom was covering something, or as if something was hiding itself in the gloom.

"This place has a strange mood," Rathina said. "Methinks it is the poison of the Isenmort Portal pervading the very ground beneath our feet."

"I don't feel anything," said Connor. "It's quiet, though, isn't it? No birds. Nothing. And it's getting hot; have you noticed that?"

"The sun stands at the zenith of the sky," said Rathina. "See how the heat rises from yon stone doorway. What was it Eden told us to do?"

"Knock three times," Tania said.

Up close the slab of gray stone was far bigger than she had expected. It lay impressed in the hillside, ten feet across and twice that high.

"It must weigh forty tons or more," Connor said, kicking a corner. "It doesn't look natural, though. How did they ever get it here?" He looked at Tania. "I'm assuming they don't have much in the way of machinery."

Tania shook her head. "No, not much." Rathina

was right: She could see the heat shimmering off the stone, quivering in the air and distorting the shapes of the trees farther up the hill.

She stooped and picked up a stone. As she leaned over the gray slab, the heat beat into her face. She pounded the stone three times on the slab then stepped back.

Nothing happened.

"Maybe it's broken?" suggested Connor.

"Wait!" said Rathina.

Slowly at first, so slowly that it was hardly perceptible, the massive slab began to rise from the ground, pivoting on one side like a vast door. Cool air seeped out of the widening black gap.

The stone lifted itself, two feet thick, ragged and rough-hewn. Blackness yawned, cold and fathomless.

"Time for your flashlight, I think," Tania said to Connor. "I don't imagine there'll be any lights in there."

Connor moved forward to the very lip of darkness. He switched on the flashlight. The beam shone onto a flight of black stone steps that plunged away into cavernous depths. He looked uneasily at Tania. "Ladies first," he said.

"Cute," she said, stepping over the grassy threshold. "Very cute." Cold air crept around her ankles as she began to descend.

Connor followed close behind, shining the light onto the steps, but Tania's own shadow went racing ahead into the black gulf, swallowed up in the cool darkness. She could hear Rathina whistling softly between her teeth.

I remember that! She does it when she's scared, to make out that everything's okay.

Somehow that tiny flash of memory warmed Tania and lifted her heart.

She came to a black arch at the foot of the stairs. Connor was at her side shining his flashlight into the darkness. Black stone glinted, reflecting the light. A cobbled roadway stretched away.

Rathina's tuneless whistling was close by Tania's ear.

Tania stepped through the arch.

She gazed around herself in surprise. The subterranean darkness seemed far less intense now—only as dark perhaps as a starless night—and she could see buildings all around her. They were uniformly black, made from a smooth stone that shone with a dusky bloom. They appeared to be ordinary houses and cottages with steep-sloping, tiled roofs and tall chimneys and mullioned windows, leading away up either side of a twisty, cobbled street. Here and there she saw squat turrets or towers attached to the buildings. Elsewhere there were sunken windows behind black bars, and curved flights of stone steps leading to raised doorways. There were deep-set doors under stone lintels. Black ivy climbed the walls and black roses overhung the windows. Everything black. It was as if a village had been dipped in oil and then left wet and shining under a night sky.

Tania looked up, expecting to see the roof of this great cavern—but all she saw was a black vault so featureless that, for all Tania could tell, it might be hanging a few feet above her head or it might be a thousand miles away—or not there at all.

It was not cold in the village, but the silence was eerie, and for some reason Tania was reminded of the sinister ruins she had flown above in her dream.

"Such a sad place," murmured Rathina. "They say that in ancient times there was light and laughter and love in Caer Regnar Naal. But I do not know who lived here nor what happened to them." She began softly to sing.

> *"The living earth founded me, I lay beneath*
> *And the flowers were as bright as stars*
> *The womb-hill surrounded me, I lay asleep*
> *Till the day I sought my birth*
> *In a tapestried room in Caer Regnar Naal . . ."*

Connor walked across the street and gingerly touched a rose head. He turned to look at Tania. "It feels real," he said. "But it can't be, can it? Down here? With no light or anything?"

"When are you going to get that this world runs on magic, Connor?" Tania asked. "Rathina? Do you have any idea where the Hall of Archives might be?"

"Nay, sister," said Rathina. "But it should not be hard to find. Do you not yet sense the presence of the Isenmort Portal?"

"No, not really."

"You shall, Tania. As we grow closer, you will feel it."

They walked together along the street. Even though there was enough dim light for them to see by, Connor still turned the beam of his flashlight this way and that to pick out the odd details of the crooked old houses.

They came to a wide paved square. A black fountain stood in the middle, its deep basin long dry. Connor lifted the beam of light onto the statue that rose from its central plinth.

Tania gasped as the fierce white light picked out the black shape of a giant owl caught wide-winged as it surged forward from a branch, every feather carved with pinpoint detail, its predatory eyes so sharp and bright that they almost seemed to be alive.

"Which way now?" asked Connor, roving the beam of light along the several streets that led from the square.

"Close your eyes, Tania," said Rathina. "Turn about; feel for the scorching of Isenmort on your mind."

Tania did as her sister suggested.

"There's nothing," she said. "It all feels— Oh! Wait!" She opened her eyes. A sensation had touched her— like the shadowy intimation of a headache behind her eyes. She pointed. "That way."

It was a street as strange and as ordinary as any other in the underground village, but at the far end a large square edifice loomed above the rooftops. As they approached, Tania saw that it was a tower, its blunt bulk windowless and unadorned. It was built of stone, but it was not smooth and black. Its face was rough and sharp-edged and uneven.

It was a tower made of flint, and in the center of its facing wall stood a huge door of gray iron.

Large bolts of iron studded the door, and to one side hung a braided hoop of iron attached to a massive iron lock.

As she came closer, Tania felt the dull pressure growing behind her eyes and now she could see that the face of the iron door was etched all over with intricate and unpleasant designs. In the light of Connor's flashlight beam the unsettling shapes of centipedes and squids and spiders and crabs and worms writhed and crawled with sinister intent over the cold gray iron.

"Horrible," muttered Rathina, shrinking away. "Most horrible!"

"I'll say," said Connor. "What total sicko came up with all this?"

"Like you said," murmured Tania, "it was put here to keep people out." She screwed up her eyes against the discomfort that was bearing down on her from the door. "Can you get it open?"

Connor looked at Rathina. "How about it?"

Rathina grimaced but nodded. She put down the leather satchel and stepped up to the door. She gripped the iron hoop with both hands and wrenched at it.

"'Tis well closed!" she said puffing. "Come, Master Connor, lend your weight to our cause!"

Connor handed Tania the rubber flashlight, and

together he and Rathina took a double-handed grip on the hoop.

"Three—two—go!" said Connor.

They fought together with the hoop, and gradually inch by slow inch it began to turn with a piercing noise that set Tania's teeth on edge.

As they managed to get the hoop to a half turn, there was a low clanking sound from deep within the door.

"The lock is free!" shouted Rathina. "Pull now, Master Connor. Pull with all your might!"

They dug their heels in and hauled back on the door—and with the terrible screeching of metal grazing stone it began to open.

Tania stepped back as the door grated toward her, the ancient iron shuddering and grinding over the threshold as it was slowly forced open.

"Ha! A hard-won struggle," said Rathina, gasping as the door finally clanked back on its hinges. She picked up the satchel and slapped Connor on the back. "'Twas well done, Master Connor! You have muscle and sinew after all, so it would seem."

"Thanks," said Connor. "Same to you. Tania? Are you okay to go inside, do you think?"

Tania nodded. Now that the iron door had been shifted, she was able to walk into the tower without too much discomfort.

She found herself in an open square vestibule. She traced the flashlight beam over a series of wooden doors that lined the four walls. A heavy wooden staircase went zigzagging up to a succession of galleries that jutted out all the way to the high roof of the tower.

Rathina strode across the floor and opened one of the doors. Tania shone the light inside. The room was large and filled with tables and lecterns and bookcases—and over every surface teemed a bewildering profusion of scrolls and books and parchments. Tomes and papers clogged every shelf, and even more spilled onto the floor.

"What a mess," remarked Connor. "Bring the light over here, Tania." He opened another door.

A similar scene of chaos met their eyes.

"I think we're going to be here a while," said Tania. She frowned. "I'd hoped we'd be able to get this done quickly. I can't bear the thought of people suffering all over Faerie."

Connor gazed into the heights of the tower. "If every room looks like this," he said, "I think we're going to be here for the next ten years!"

"Let us hope not," murmured Rathina. "For who then shall still be alive?"

"Rathina! If I felt anything, I'd tell you!"

Tania had lost all track of time. It felt as if they'd been in the flint tower for hour upon fruitless hour. For want of any other system they had worked their laborious way from the ground up, entering every room on every gallery. Connor would let the light play over the chaotic shambles of discarded books and scrolls, and Tania would stare around the crammed shelves, hoping that something would catch her eye or that there would be a tingling in her head to indicate that the Kiss of Seeking was working.

In among the manuscripts and scrolls they also came occasionally upon curious little devices and instruments, ancient-looking and inscrutable—but clearly made from metal! Rathina had no explanation for how they might have come here, and all they could assume was that in distant times, they must have been brought through from the Mortal Realm to be studied. But by whom and why they could not guess. Tania was careful to avoid touching them.

But Rathina was clearly growing impatient with the long search. And she was not the only one. Tania wished Eden had explained how the Kiss of Seeking worked. Would she feel something if she came close to the thing they were looking for? Or did she have to make physical contact with it? And what *was* it? A book? A scroll or parchment? *What?*

It was all so vague—and this whole quest had only been set in motion because of a dream. *If you would cure us all, seek the Lost Caer . . .*

But what if the words Cordelia had spoken in the dream actually meant *nothing?* What then?

Rathina pulled open another door. Dust revolved slowly in the flashlight beam. Its light was growing yellowish, as if the batteries were beginning to run out.

And what happens then? Tania wondered as she stepped into the disordered room. *How are we going to find whatever-it-is in the dark?* She stared around at the clutter of documents and books.

She was about to leave when she felt a curious sensation in her fingers: a fierce tingling like pins and needles. She stopped, her eyes widening as she looked at Connor. Rathina had already moved on to the next door.

"What?" Connor asked. "Do you feel something?"

"Yes." Tania reached out her arms and turned in a slow circle. The tingling became so sharp that she screwed up her eyes and bit her lip. She stepped toward a heaped table. An ivory-colored parchment scroll lay among others.

Her fingers prickled and buzzed as she touched it. She gasped. "This is it."

Connor came into the room. "I'll make some space so you can unroll it." With a sweep of his arm he cleared half the table, the papers and books tumbling to the floor with a flurry of dust.

Tania unrolled the scroll and gently spread it out on the table. The tingling in her fingers was gone now—as if the power in the Kiss of Seeking had done its work and faded away.

"What have you found, sister?" Rathina leaned over her shoulder. "Spirits of lore! 'Tis a marvelous ancient artifact."

The scroll was a map. It had been drawn on a length of cloth—linen or something similar—but time had stained the material to a musty brown, so that in darker brown places the depicted lands were hardly discernible in the murk.

The map showed two islands: one large and eccentrically shaped, the other smaller and more or less oval. The larger landmass was full of detail: Rivers and forests and mountains were graphically represented, and there were also many dots and small squares that Tania assumed were villages and castles. There was writing, too—presumably place names—but the script was in a language that Tania could not read. The other island was entirely blank.

"It's the British Isles," said Connor breathlessly. "What's a map of the British Isles doing *here*? And why is it lying on its side?"

"Remember?" Tania said. "Faerie is like an exact replica of the UK—well, not *exactly* exact but pretty close. And why should north always be at the top, anyway?"

Connor blinked at her. "Fair point," he said.

She leaned closer and found the curved line of the south coast. "That's Veraglad Castle," she said. "See the little building with the towers?" The palace was represented by a simple square with three narrow triangles on its top. She slid her finger along to a writhing line. "And that's the River Tamesis—the Thames to you."

"Wow," said Connor. "So that's London."

"Where you come from it is," Tania said. "But here it's the Royal Palace."

"So where are we now?"

Rathina leaned over and touched a fingertip to the map close to the center of Faerie. "We are here," she said, her finger just beneath a black square with a half-moon dome on its top. "In the Earldom of Sinadon, between Lang Fells and the Bight of Damask."

"Eden brought us quite a way in that horse-of-air thing of hers," said Connor. "I'd love to know how it works."

"That has already been explained to you," said Rathina.

"Yes, but I meant I'd like to know how to work it *myself*."

"A Mortal learn the Mystic Arts?" scoffed Rathina. "I think not!"

Connor gave her a quick, slightly irritated glance.

"It takes a long time to learn that stuff," Tania pointed out.

"If you say so." He gestured toward the top of the map. "That's Ireland, right?"

"Ireland?" said Rathina. "I know it not by that name. That is the land of Alba."

"Alba?" said Tania. "Where our mother comes from?"

"Indeed. Although this map predates her arrival on the shores of Faerie by many thousands of years." She frowned. "It is a strange place, or so the legends say, where Mortals dwell among talking salamanders and mischievous goblins and commune with water sprites who are half human and half fish."

"Have you ever been there?" asked Connor.

"Nay, Master Connor. We do not venture into the Western Ocean, not beyond sight of land, in any event."

"Why not?"

"That can wait!" Tania interrupted them. "People are ill all over Faerie. We're here to look for some mention of the Lost Caer so we can try and help them, okay?"

"Sorry," said Connor. "It's just, there's so much stuff I want to . . ." His forehead wrinkled. "Sorry."

"If the Kiss of Seeking worked right and this map is the thing we need, we should go over it really carefully," Tania said. "Rathina? You know Faerie a lot better than I do. Does anything obvious pop out at you that could help us on our quest?"

Rathina moved between Connor and Tania, leaning stiff-armed on the table, her hands on either side of the map, her head down as she studied it. "The script is in a crabbed and curious hand and much of it can no longer be read," she said after a short while. "But the map shows the ten Caers most clearly and I recognize all of them." She moved her finger over the map. "See? Cruithni in Dinsel. Eden's Caer Mynwy. Seagirt Kymry. Liel of Weir. Circinn in the north. All are here."

"But no extra one?" asked Tania.

"Give me a moment, sister," muttered Rathina. "Master Connor, hold the light steady. Why is it growing so pale?"

"The batteries are low," Connor said, slapping the side of the flashlight with his hand. "We haven't got much time." He brought the yellowing beam of light closer to the map. "That better?"

"Indeed," said Rathina. "Would that I could make out more details. Time has dealt harshly with this ancient thing."

"Can't you see *anything* unusual?" asked Tania.

"Ha!" Rathina's voice rang out sharply. "Now, *here's* a thing! Sister, I think I have it!"

"Where?" Tania and Connor leaned in close.

Rathina's finger was resting on the coastline of Faerie, some way to the northwest of Caer Regnar Naal. "See you the spit of land that pokes its tongue into the sea just beyond the southern border of Weir?" she said. "And see you moreover the steepled castle depicted at its seaward end?"

"Yes." A frisson of hope thrilled in Tania's chest. *"Yes?"*

Rathina smiled. "I know of no such promontory in that place," she said. "Nor of a castle standing at its point."

"I don't understand," said Tania. "You mean it doesn't exist?"

"She means it doesn't exist *now*," Connor said excitedly. He looked at Rathina. "You mean it's gone, right? But don't forget this map is thousands of years old. There must have been a landslide or some heavy coastal erosion at some time—and the whole lot fell into the sea." He stabbed at the map. "I'll bet you anything you like: That's our Lost Caer!"

XIX

Rathina leaned so close to the map that her hair coiled on the ancient spotted and tarnished linen. "It has a name," she murmured. "I can barely make it out." She lifted her head, her eyes triumphant. "Caer Fior!" she said. "Its name is Caer Fior!"

A curious sensation burned in Tania's heart at the sound of that name. It reminded her of the giddying, enticing terror that she had felt upon the brink of the cliffs at Beachy Head. Like the whisper of a bewitching voice luring her to her doom. Like a dangerous destiny calling from afar.

Connor let out a long breath. "Well, it looks like we've found it," he said. "Or to be more precise, we know where it *used* to be." He looked questioningly at the two sisters. "So? Now what? How does this help us with the cure?"

"I am unsure. The Lost Caer is drowned deep," said Rathina. "What possible aid can it offer us under ten fathoms of seawater?" She looked at Tania. "We must return to Veraglad and lay our discoveries before the King and Queen. Mayhap they have lore enough to understand what is to be done now."

"No," Tania said. "We must press on ourselves. Rathina? How long would it take us to get there?"

"Very long indeed, unless we are to enlist the aid of the kelpie of the deep seas," replied Rathina.

"I don't know what that means."

"Kelpie are water-horses, sister," Rathina said with a hint of humor in her voice. "We should surely need them to bear us under the waves, for the closest we will be able to come to the Lost Caer is the village that lies on the landward end of the promontory—see, it is marked here and named as Faith-in-the-Surf. A curious name, but then it lies in Weir, and in that Earldom all things are strange."

"Listen," Tania said determinedly. "Till now I've only half believed that my dream meant anything at all." She gestured toward the map. "But this changes everything. There *is* a Lost Caer, and this map shows us where it is. I don't care whether it's under the sea or not. We have to get as close as we can to it. In my dream Cordelia said, 'If you would cure us, seek the Lost Caer.' And that's exactly what I intend to do." She looked from Rathina to Connor. "Anyone coming with me?"

"You bet," said Connor. "I'm up for anything."

"I will go with you, Tania," Rathina said with a small smile. "Such ardor and purpose should not go unrewarded!"

"Good. So, like I said, how long will it take us to get there?"

"If Eden's touch proves true and the wild horses will do our bidding, we could cover the distance in two days—maybe less." Rathina eyed Connor dubiously. "If all are fit to sit bareback upon untamed steeds, that is."

Connor laughed. "You're kidding me," he said. "My parents used to run a riding stable. I could ride before I knew how to use a bicycle. Just point me in the direction of the fastest horse, and leave the rest to me."

Rathina grinned at Tania. "It seems this Mortal has some worthy skills, sister," she said. "I would feel fresh air upon my face. Need we linger anymore in this sad and desolate place?"

"No," Tania said, rolling the map. "Let's get out of here."

Rathina and Connor closed the huge iron door of the Helan Archaia, the lock clanking with a harsh sound as the Isenmort Portal slammed shut.

Connor's flashlight finally died as they approached the stairway that would take them up to daylight. "Fair exchange is no robbery," he murmured, leaving it standing on the bottom step.

Tania gave him a questioning look.

He shrugged. "It's not like we're going to be able to pop down the road and buy new batteries, is it?" he said.

"Let it stand there for all time," said Rathina. "As

proof that a Mortal man was once here to the benefit of Faerie!"

Tania nodded and began to climb the black stairs.

The sun was low in the sky as they came up out of the deep darkness of Caer Regnar Naal. They had been many hours in the colorless world of that deserted subterranean place, and Tania felt refreshed by the green of the forest and the blue of the evening sky.

The troop of horses had moved closer to the long hill, almost as though they were waiting for them to emerge.

Connor walked slowly toward them, stretching out one hand and making a clicking sound with his tongue.

One of the horses broke from the rest and ambled up to him, its hide a rich, creamy gold, its mane and tail black, its shaggy head nodding.

"There's a good boy," Connor said gently, patting the horse's neck. "Are you going to let me take a ride?" He glanced back at Tania and Rathina, then in a single nimble movement sprang onto the horse's back. He made more of the clicking noises with his tongue, patting the animal's withers and pressing in sharply with his knees. The horse broke into a trot and halted a few steps away from the two sisters.

"You sit well, Master Connor," said Rathina. "And see, two more steeds come. Eden knows her craft well."

Tania looked. A bay mare and a black stallion were trotting toward them.

"Yes, she does," said Tania with a smile. A sudden, rolling boom at her back made her jump. She spun around. The huge entrance stone to Caer Regnar Naal had slammed shut.

"Sleep well, ghosts of ghosts long departed," called Rathina. "Keep the rest of your secrets. We know now all we need to know of the ancient times."

Tania ran her hand along the shining brown flanks of the horse that had presented itself to her. It looked at her with large dark, wise eyes, then lifted its head high and neighed. She mounted up and looked at Rathina. "Which way to the Caer?"

Rathina jumped lightly onto her horse's back. She flung her arm forward, her finger pointing. "That way!" she cried. "To the north! To Weir! And to our destiny!" Her horse burst into a canter, its black mane and tail flying as it thundered through the grass. Rathina clung low to its back, her dark hair streaming.

"Wow!" said Connor, urging his own horse into movement. "Can she ride!"

Tania slapped her horse's neck. "Let's go, boy," she said. The horse surged forward. She gripped tight with her knees, leaning forward, her hands on the broad muscular neck, her head between the long ears.

The sun was warm on the left side of her face, the balmy air pulling at her long red hair. She did not know what was to come nor even what they were looking for—an enchantment, an elixir, a rare medicinal herb—but ahead of them lay new hope and the chance that she would save the ailing people of Faerie.

* * *

They rode the evening away through a flat landscape of woods and rough, tussocky grasses. At times they came across lush meadows with meandering streams and dense pillows of blue cornflowers and yellow poppies, the tall wild flower heads floating about them and sending up a rich, sweet scent. Away to their right Tania could see the rising shapes of hills black and stark against the fading light of the day.

They entered a forest, Rathina in the lead, their horses slowing to a trot as they navigated their way through a realm of broad-beamed chestnut trees. When they reemerged, it was to see an indigo sky pulsating with Faerie stars. The moon hung huge and low, full as ever, white as snow.

"We have come far," Rathina called back to them. "This is a good place to make camp for the night."

"That's fine," said Tania. "We'll stop here. But we can't sleep long. I want us to be ready to set off again at first light."

Tania lay on a mossy bank close by a rippling stream. She liked the music of the water as it danced over the stones. She was on her back, her hands behind her head, her stomach full, and her mind drowsy. A nightingale sang close by and the air was full of the scents of night flowers and the dusky fluttering of brown and cream-colored moths.

The night was warm and there had been no need to build a fire. They had sat by the stream and eaten bread and cheese and cold cuts of meat. When they had eaten and drunk enough, they stretched themselves on the ground.

But although Tania was weary, she did not immediately fall asleep. A sense of peace pervaded the place and she wanted to bask in it for a while. It was hard to believe here that a deadly plague was laying waste to the people of Faerie. But it was also an impossible thing to forget.

Connor was lying nearby. "Tania?"

"Hmm?"

"What do you expect to find when we get to Caer Fior? I mean, if Rathina is right, it's pretty much *gone*, isn't it? And even if there's anything left of it, it'll be under water." He turned onto his side, his eyes glittering in the moonlight. "I'm guessing they don't have much in the way of submarines or diving equipment here. So how would we even get to it?"

Tania turned her head. She could see the dark shape of her sister lying a little way off, curled up with her back to them. "I don't know, yes it will be, no they don't, and I don't know," she said in answer to his questions. "This whole thing started off with a dream, Connor. Do you really think I know what's coming next? I'm amazed that we've got this far."

There was a pause. "How do you cope with this?" he asked at last. "All this magic. Doesn't it do your head in?"

She smiled. "Messing with your scientific brain, is it?" she asked. "My dad had the same problem. He never said as much, but I'm sure he thought this whole place was just like some crazy computer game, you know? A nice way to pass a few idle hours but not *real*—not like London is real."

"I don't think it isn't real," said Connor. "I just can't get my head around what *kind* of real it is. I mean, I've checked out quantum mechanics and the chaos theory and all that freaky stuff, but *this* . . . ?" He shuffled a little closer. "You said that Faerie is, like, the same as the British Isles only in a different dimension, right?"

"Something like that," Tania replied. "I don't know if it's in another dimension or where it is. All I know is how to get from one to the other." She frowned. "I mean, I used to know how to do it before they closed everything down," she added regretfully. "That's all finished with now."

"Everyone I ever knew, everything I've ever done . . . it's gone. Gone forever," Connor murmured. "I still can't make sense of that. It's just too huge, know what I mean?"

"I do," Tania said softly.

"But what's puzzling me right now," he continued, "is how come the moon isn't the same as on Earth." He looked up, his eyes shimmering with silvery light. "It's bigger for a start," he said. "And there's nothing on it: no craters and shadows and stuff. How is that?"

"Don't ask me," said Tania. "For all I know it's made of green cheese."

"You are so laid-back about all this, I can't believe it," said Connor. "And you were really inquisitive when you were a kid—nosing into everything, forever asking questions. 'How does this work? What happens if I do this? What's that for?' You used to drive my mum to distraction when you came to visit."

Tania chuckled. "Did I? Poor her."

"Do you remember you wanted to be a reporter? You used to go around with a notepad and a pencil and you'd be forever writing stuff down. And you'd do interviews on me, remember? I had to pretend to be a pop star or a famous explorer, and you'd be the TV anchorgirl. You invented your own talk show: *Anita Time*. Remember that?"

That made her laugh out loud. "I had totally forgotten that. *Anita Time!* Yes!"

"You were kind of funny-looking when you were a kid," Connor said. "You always had your hair up in big bunches tied with elastic bands, and you were really skinny with long gangly arms and legs and big buckteeth."

"I know! I looked like a total geek!"

"You've improved a lot."

"Thanks."

"No. *Really.* You're amazing looking now."

There was a slight change in the tone of his voice. She looked at him and saw that he was gazing intently at her. Uneasy alarm bells rang in her mind.

"If you say so." She looked into the sky.

He reached out and slid his fingers through her hair.

"Connor, don't," she said gently.

"Sorry." He drew his hand back. "I was only check-ing to see if you had pointy ears."

"Why should I have pointy ears?"

"Well, you're Immortal and you live in a magical land. I thought maybe you were an elf."

She spluttered with laughter. "No," she said. "I'm not an *elf*. I don't actually think elves exist."

"No," Connor said softly. "And neither should beau-tiful Faerie princesses."

Tania didn't feel comfortable with the way the con-versation was going. "The stars are all different here to how they are on Earth," she said quickly. "Did you notice that?"

"I did," Connor said, his voice switching back to its regular tone. "I don't recognize any of the con-stellations up there. Do they even *have* constellations here?"

"Yes, they do," said Tania. She pointed. "Those three stars in a row with two going off at an angle— that's called the Starved Fool. And the five stars—" She stopped speaking.

"The five stars?" Connor prompted her. "They're what?"

"We should get some sleep," Tania said, her voice suddenly brittle. "Rathina wants us to get going at first light."

She turned onto her side, facing away from Connor.

"Tania? What's wrong? What just happened?"

"Nothing. Go to sleep."

She could feel him close behind her for a little while, but at last she heard him move a little way off and then become still.

She closed her eyes tightly, but still a few tears escaped, running down her face and into her hair. A vivid memory had torn through her mind like a bolt of lightning.

A memory of a similar starry night just a few short weeks ago. A night when she and Edric had lain together on a grassy hillside surrounded by the eerie blue glow of the tall standing stones of Crystalhenge. A night when he had first explained the constellations to her.

She could hear his voice in her head. *Do you see those three stars in a row with the two stars going off to the left? That's called the Starved Fool. And those five stars in the W shape is the Girl in Violet.* His arm had swung across the sky. *That's the Phoenix, and next to it is the Singing Dragon.*

How is it a dragon?

You have to use your imagination.

But the memory was so painful that Tania could hardly bear it.

It was a fine day and the morning was spent cantering through a land that gradually became more hilly as the sun climbed in the sky. A fine fresh wind blew out of the west, cooling their skin and sending skeins of white cloud scudding.

Tania had worked hard to give Connor the

impression that nothing more than tiredness had brought their nocturnal conversation to such an abrupt halt. He seemed to go along with this, except that every now and then she'd see him giving her a curious look, as if he was trying to puzzle her out.

Don't bother, Connor. It's not worth it. Trust me.

They paused at midday to rest the horses, sitting by a lakeside, eating and drinking, watching the swifts darting back and forth, listening to the drone of bees and dragonflies. Connor found a flat stone and skimmed it out over the still water so that it bounced several times, scattering glittering droplets of water and sending the ripples racing. Rathina and Tania quickly joined in, seeking out flat stones and pebbles in the thick tangled grass and then skipping them out across the wide lake. It was a brief time of carefree fun.

They kept their horses to a gentle trot in the afternoon, the three of them riding in a row as the air grew hot and still. Now they were in a landscape of green hills and valleys where shallow rivers ran between banks of white stones.

The wind changed direction during the afternoon, and by the time they stopped for the night, it was blowing cool air from the north and bringing gray clouds along with it. Tania was beginning to wonder if they would ever reach journey's end. With every hour that passed, more people were falling sick and here they were, forced to wait out another night. It was maddening!

The northern horizon had altered now; it rose

darkly into far ridges and peaks. Tania stood on a hilltop, gazing into the north. The mountains of Weir were black against the night sky. Bad memories beat their dark wings about her, but she refused to give in to them. Their journey would not take them as far as the mountains, so Rathina had said. She believed that they should reach their goal before dusk tomorrow.

And then what? Caer Fior is drowned deep. Its secrets are long gone.

There will be something there. I know there will. I was brought here on purpose—to save Faerie.

In your dreams . . .

No, it's not just dreams; it's . . . *destiny!*

"Penny for your thoughts."

Tania turned, startled by Connor's voice. She had not heard him approach. "You'd be short changed," Tania said.

Connor pointed toward the mountains. "That's Weir, right?"

"Yes."

"Where Lord Aldritch hangs out?"

"You got it."

"Is it safe?" Connor asked. "I mean, the guy did kind of sound off at the King. Is he going to be happy to have a couple of Oberon's daughters wandering about in his Earldom? I don't want to end up in some dank dungeon chained to the wall and fed on bread and water for the rest of my life."

"We're only going a few miles into Weir," Tania said. "Caer Liel—the place where he lives—is way past those mountains. Miles and miles away. We won't be going anywhere near it. Besides, he wouldn't even be back there yet."

"Here's hoping."

They stood quietly together for a few moments, looking into the north.

"It was Edric, wasn't it?" Connor said in a low voice, breaking the silence that had grown between them. "Last night. Something made you think of Edric. That's why you went all silent on me."

"It was nothing," Tania said. "I remembered something. It hurt. I'm over it now."

Connor's voice was soft in the darkness. "Over *him?*"

She let out a bleak breath of laughter. "Do you ever get over it the first time your heart is broken?" She sighed. "Yes. I guess you do. Eventually."

She felt his hand on her shoulder. "I could help," he said.

"No," she said, shrugging his hand off and stepping away from him. "Thanks, but no." She wrapped her arms around herself. "I'm going down now," she said. "I'm tired. We should sleep." She walked carefully down the steep grassy slope of the hill.

She glanced back once and saw that Connor was still standing on the hilltop, his silhouette stark and black against the starry night.

The second day was cooler than the first, the sky banked up with clumps of gray clouds. The mountains of Weir were strangely threatening, even though it seemed to Tania that they drew no nearer as the three of them rode on through the day.

Sometime in midafternoon Rathina turned and looked at them. "We are in Weir," she said. "We should come to the coast soon. We will reach our destination ere the sun is two hands' breadths above the sea." She narrowed her eyes. "I have a chill in my bones. I like it not."

Tania shivered. "We have to go on," she said. "There's no other choice."

Dark gray smoke was drifting over the hills ahead of them.

A village was burning.

They watched it from a hilltop, a quarter of a mile distant. Tania peered into the haze, searching for any sign of movement among the blazing buildings.

There was none.

"It's like the village Eden showed us; they're trying to burn the plague out. The poor people!" She turned to Rathina and Connor. "And this must be happening all over Faerie!" She dug her heels into her horse's sides and it sprang forward.

"We have to find a cure!" she shouted as they began to gallop along the hilltop. "I won't let this happen! I won't!"

The three horses cantered along the sand, their hooves leaving a trail of crescent shapes in the long sweep of the beach. Their shadows stretched away into the east, undulating over a line of dunes spiked with tufted grass. The orange sun glowered in a web of clouds, wallowing low on the sea's far horizon, like a stab wound in the sky dripping blood into the ocean.

The tide moved in and out, leaving a scum of yellowish foam behind. Gulls and curlews scuttled as the shallow waves came and went. Occasionally one would rise in an explosion of wings and fly away, dark against the ruddy clouds.

Tania breathed in the sea air. The pungent scent made her feel restless and on edge as she stared out over the ocean. Somewhere, beyond sight, across that wide stretch of green-blue water, lay the island of Alba. The island where her Faerie mother had been born.

And somewhere, far nearer but no less remote, the ruins of Caer Fior rotted under the rolling waves.

They were riding the curve of a long sandy bay. Beyond the approaching headland, they would come to journey's end.

The sun was fading as Rathina led them through a narrow, rising defile in the grass-covered dunes.

"Behold the village of Faith-in-the-Surf," she said. "I had half expected it to have sunk into the sea."

The dunes dropped away abruptly, held back by long rows of decayed wooden stakes hammered into the ground to prevent the sandy hills from creeping inland and swamping the small cluster of houses that lay beyond.

"It's very quiet," said Connor. "Are you sure anyone still lives here?"

"I can't tell," said Tania, peering out over the thatched and shingled roofs. "It looks deserted. It might have been abandoned years ago when the Caer fell into the sea."

"Or they may have left but a few days past," said Rathina. "Fleeing the plague." She nudged her heels into the stallion's flanks. "Come," she said. "Let us see what welcome awaits!"

There was a sharp, whining sound in the air and the thud of something burying itself deep in the sandy pathway. The stallion reared in panic and Rathina went crashing to the ground.

Startled and confused, Tania saw that the thing was an arrow—its feathered end still protruding from the sand. She looked down at the village, trying to work out where the arrow had come from. A second and a third bolt came zipping through the air, one making Connor's horse stumble to the side, the other only just missing her left thigh. Her horse rose on its hind legs, whinnying in fear. She felt herself slipping, and as she fought vainly to stay mounted, she heard a harsh voice crying out.

"Get you gone! We have plague enough. You will find no welcome here. Get you gone or you shall surely die!"

XX

Tania crashed heavily into the sand, her left shoulder and right knee taking the worst of the impact.

"Connor? Are you okay?" she called out as she lay recovering from the fall. There was no reply. She pressed herself deeper into the side of the dune, fearful that more arrows would come flying from the village.

She lifted her head. There was no sign of whoever had attacked them. All three horses had bolted. *"Connor?"*

"I'm fine."

Rathina's voice sounded out. "He is with me, Tania. We must get to cover. Are you hurt?"

"No." Tania squirmed around in the sand and dragged herself up and over the rise. She slid over the top then rolled a little way down and turned onto her back, panting from the effort. A few moments later there was a flurry of movement and a spatter of sand as Rathina and Connor came over the crest of the dune and scrabbled to safety close to where she was lying.

"A fine welcome indeed," remarked Rathina, sitting up and knocking sand off her clothes. "'Tis well said that a sharpened bolt in Weir is as a handshake in Udwold. So, sister, what now?"

"How should I know?" exclaimed Tania, the adrenaline surge of the unexpected attack making her temper flare.

Rathina raised her eyebrows but said nothing.

"Maybe we should wave a white flag at them," Connor suggested. "Get a truce organized."

Tania looked at him. "You *have* a white flag?"

"No. Not as such."

"We should have come armed," said Rathina. "Then we would surely have been able to answer their welcome more fittingly. But alas, we knew not where our travels would lead us. But need we disturb these people any further, Tania? They will have no knowledge of Caer Fior; that much is certain."

"They might have some useful local info," Tania said. She got onto her hands and knees and crawled up the ridge. She lifted her eyes over the crest. She saw the rooftops of the town. "We need to convince them we're not carrying the plague. Then they might be prepared to talk to us."

"Or fill us as full of arrows as a porpentine is with quills!" Rathina remarked. "The folk of Weir are dangerous and morose at the best of times, Tania."

"Bryn comes from Weir, don't forget," said Tania. "You can't generalize like that about people. They're just scared that we're going to infect them." She chewed her lip, trying to decide what to do next. There were three options: go around the village, go back, or make contact.

"I'm going to try something," she said. She took a few long, calming breaths and then stood, rising into the clear view of anyone in the village, her arms outspread, her hands open.

"Tania—you're crazy!" hissed Connor. "Get down."

"Hey!" Tania called down to the village. "Listen to me. Please. We don't have the plague. There's nothing to be afraid of. We just want to talk."

Her heart was beating like a hammer in her chest and she felt dizzy with fear—but she held her ground, waiting for a response.

"Why come you here?" called a wheezing voice. "None are upon the roads in these dark times lest they have been cast out of their homes." The speech was interrupted by coughing. The man was clearly ill.

She heard two or three subdued voices speaking together, then a second voice called up from the village. "You are not of Weir, we deem," it said. "Whence come you, that your speech is so outlandish?"

"I come from the south," Tania called back, trying to make her voice sound less alien. "We are looking for the Lost Caer. We think it is near your village."

"Then you are the more fooled, mistress," called a third voice, rough-edged but less aggressive than the first two. "There is no Caer in Weir save Caer Liel, where our lord holds court." And now, for the first time, Tania saw a shadow move out of the cover of the walls and come into plain view. A man dressed in simple peasant garb but large-framed and bearded and with the bearing of someone in authority. His face was flushed and there was sickness and fear in his eyes.

Tania lowered her arms, taking a step down toward the village. The man's hand came up. "Come no closer, mistress," he said, his voice ragged and husky. "Twenty arrows are aimed at your heart even as we speak."

"Then fire and be done!" shouted Rathina. "If it be not to your shame to shoot down folk who bear no weapons and seek to do you no hurt but have come here only to seek a cure for the illness that plagues all of Faerie."

Tania glanced around. Rathina was standing on the top of the dune just behind her, both feet planted firmly, a proud glint in her eyes. A moment later Connor's head bobbed up above the ridge, and he clambered cautiously into view and stood at her side.

"We do not kill without purpose," said the man. "If it were so, none of you would yet be drawing breath, of that be most certain." He peered up at them. "A cure, you say? Can this evil be purged from the land?"

"We hope so," said Tania. "We have seen a map—a really old map—and it shows that there used to be a long headland here." She pointed away over her shoulder toward the sea. "It must have sunk into the sea ages and ages ago, but the map shows there was a Caer at the end of it."

"Nay, mistress, 'tis no Caer that lies under the

waves," said the man. He paused, coughing. "'Tis but Muinin Tur."

"Speak on, sirrah," said Rathina. "What is Muinin Tur?"

"The Tower of Faith," croaked the man. "It was lost to the sea in the deeps of time. On stormy nights it is said that the crystal bells can be heard ringing out from under the waves—although I have never heard them, and I have dwelt in Faith-in-the-Surf for nigh on eight hundred years."

"Is there anyone alive now who saw the tower before it sank?" called Connor, his voice shaking a little.

"There is not," replied the man. "It sank in the time before time was."

Connor looked at Tania. "It's the same place," he said to her. "Caer Fior and that *Muinin* thingy are the *same place!*"

Tania thought he was probably right—and at the very least, the people here told tales that proved *something* was down there.

"Why do you seek this place?" called the man.

Tania paused a moment before replying. "I think . . . I hope . . . it will lead us to a cure for the plague," she called down. "You said people say bells can be heard under the water. But are there any other legends about Muinin Tur?"

"'Tis said that it can be reached by those who dare to walk the Road of Faith, and that any who come safe to the tower will find their heart's desire," called the man. "But none have walked that road for many thousands of years, and those who did found not their heart's desire but only a watery death and their bodies spat out to roll in the surf and to be mourned by their loved ones."

"Where is this Road of Faith?" asked Rathina.

"It lies beyond the dunes to the north," said the man. "It is marked by two lines of sea green stones set deep in the sand, leading into the sea. But do not go that way, strangers, lest you be witless and fey, for there is only one reward for those who are foolhardy enough to walk the Road of Faith." His voice rang out loudly through the evening air. "And that reward is death!"

Princess Tania Aurealis of Faerie stood in one of the in-between places of the world. Her feet were planted where land and sea melted and merged into each other. The rising tide lapped over her shoes as she gazed into the west, the salt wind troubling her hair and smarting in her eyes.

Her sister Rathina stood on her right, Connor on her left.

A dream had brought them here.

But who had sent the dream?

They had come to this place on foot; Eden's enchantment had proven less strong than fear, and the wild horses had vanished into the south, heading for home and safety.

The setting sun was hidden now behind clouds as heavy and dark as mountains. A distant haze spoke of rain falling like spears into the sea.

It was dark. An unpleasant, yellowy dark. A dangerous dark.

They stood on a road to nowhere, marked out to their left and to their right by the low humps of ancient stones. Behind them the double row of stones marched up the beach, dwindling and becoming scattered until they petered out in high dunes. Ahead of them the stones led into the sea, their water-smoothed heads slimed with green algae and studded with barnacles and limpets.

"The Road of Faith," murmured Rathina. "'Tis well named." She began to whistle softly between her teeth.

"How is this supposed to work?" asked Connor. "Do we just swim out there and see what happens or what?"

"I don't know." Tania felt curiously at peace. She turned to him. "Why would you think I know?" she asked mildly.

"Well, you did bring us here, Tania," Connor said.

"A dream brought us here," Tania said.

"Yes . . . well . . ."

She watched a rolling wave break into white foam and come surging toward them. It flooded around their ankles, cold but not chilling. It eddied and faltered and then drew away, enticing them to follow.

All across the sea the waves were rising and curling and tumbling. All along the beach the surf was hissing.

"Do we await some sign?" asked Rathina.

"No." Tania filled her lungs with sea air. "No." She stepped into the tide.

Rathina kept pace with her as she walked into the sea. Connor hesitated then splashed along after them.

The water rose to Tania's calves. She had expected it to be colder. The larger waves lifted the sea to her knees then let it fall again—but with every step she was offering more of herself to the foaming tide.

"You don't have to come with me," she said, "Neither of you."

"I come with you?" said Rathina. "Nay, sister, I thought you were coming with me."

"Connor? Go back. This has nothing to do with you."

"What? And miss all the fun. Not likely."

Suddenly they were holding hands and the moving water was up to their waists.

Step by slow step.

The sand was firm under Tania's feet. The water swirled around her ribs. Beneath the surface her fingers gripped the hands of her companions.

It was not cold. Why was it not cold?

"Know what's strange?" said Connor. "The water should be lifting us off our feet by now—but it isn't. Don't you think that's strange?"

He was right. Tania hadn't even thought about it, but they were almost shoulder deep in the sea now, and still she was able to plant her feet as firmly as ever on the seabed and walk forward without any difficulty.

"Now it's getting scary," muttered Connor. She felt

his grip tighten on her hand. The seawater was up to their necks. A big wave was coming.

The surface of the sea rose and there was saltiness in Tania's mouth and water in her eyes. But still the sea didn't lift them off their feet. It was as if there was no buoyancy to it. It was as if they were walking down a gently sloping hillside into a valley filled with cool, opaque fog.

Connor coughed out some seawater. "Tania? I've had a nasty thought. What if the *faith* part of the Road of Faith only works if you have faith in it working? See what I mean?"

"You think too much," Tania said. "Does this feel like a normal sea to you?"

"Anything but."

Rathina's whistling stopped abruptly. She was a fraction shorter than Tania. The water was up to her mouth.

Well, I don't know who you are, but you sent me the dream and you brought me here, so I hope you have a really good plan for what happens next.

"Have no fear, sweetheart. All is well."

A gentle voice whispering in her ear. A female voice—but not Rathina. Not a voice she recognized at all. But a comforting one, all the same, a trustworthy one.

The seabed took a sudden dip; she just had time to fill her lungs before a big wave rolled the sea in over her head.

Patterns of green and gray and silver wove in front

of her eyes. The seabed fell away under her feet, sloping sharply downward—and yet still she was able to walk quite normally She looked to her left and right. Connor and Rathina were still walking with her; their hands were still in hers, their grips tight.

For a few seconds the colors danced confusingly in her eyes, then it was as if a veil had been drawn away and she could see quite clearly. The seabed plunged into a deep trough, the standing stones that marked the sides of the road descending with it. And now Tania saw that the stones were no longer tide-smoothed nubs; they were tall and graceful stone pillars carved into the shapes of men and women, all of them facing inward, all of them with their hands pressed together at their chests as though in prayer—all of them winged.

Tania's chest began to ache. She squeezed tightly the hands of her companions, and they squeezed just as tightly back. How long could this go on? How long before their lungs would need oxygen?

"Where's the faith, Tania?"

Faith in what? *Faith in* whom?

Her chest was hurting badly now. She needed to breathe. Soon.

Connor ripped his hand out of hers, lifting his arms and bringing them down, jumping a little, as though trying to swim for the surface. Tania saw panic in his eyes. His cheeks bulged out. A feathery spray of bubbles escaped his nostrils.

But the sea would not lift him. He fell onto his knees, his face contorted by terror and pain.

"Connor!" Her voice was clear and lucid in her ears. She sucked in a startled breath, and the pain faded beneath her rib cage. She put her hand to her mouth. "Oh!"

Connor was sprawled on the sloping ground, panting, his eyes round in his astonished face. He looked up at her. "How is this working?" he said, gasping.

"Faith," said Rathina. "What else?"

Tania helped him to his feet.

"We're under water," Connor said. "And we're breathing and we're not floating away. This is not possible." He looked from Tania to Rathina. "I just want it clearly understood by everyone that *this* is not possible." He stared down the road into the murky depths, then turned to Tania, his eyes alight with amazement. "We're breathing underwater! Don't you get it? We're actually standing here breathing under *water*!" He dug the heels of his hands into his eyes. "If I could have taken back home just a tiny fraction of the stuff that makes this place tick, I'd have been world-famous!"

"Do you see shapes in the depths, sister?" Rathina was staring into the dusky valley into which the road plunged.

Tania followed the line of her eyes. "Maybe," she said. "I think so." Vague, lumpen darknesses that could have been boulders or clumps of seaweed. Or the ruins of a drowned Caer, lost since before time was. "But look at these statues, Rathina," she said, gesturing toward the rows of stately men and women who lined the road. "They're all adult men and women—and they have wings! Don't you see? They all have *wings!*"

They followed the road down the hillside and out onto a flat, gloomy valley floor

The light down there was strange and a little eerie: a kind of heavy, metallic blue-gray light that tinted everything with its dull luster.

It's the same kind of light as in my dream.

Tania looked up. Far above them, she could see the surface of the sea rippling slowly, like a vast sheet of blue-gray silk moving in a gentle night breeze.

"It is as you say, Tania. All are winged," said Rathina, gazing around herself at the elegant statues that lined the road. "How curious."

"Is it significant?" asked Connor.

"Only the children of Faerie are winged, Master Connor," said Rathina.

"And the Lios Foltaigg," added Tania. "But Rathina is right: We lose our wings when we hit ten or twelve."

Connor tilted his head. *"We?"*

"We. *They.* Don't confuse the issue," Tania said. "The point is that adults don't have wings—except that apparently here they do. Did, rather." She wrinkled her forehead, trying to make sense of it. "Caer Fior fell into the sea about the time of the Great Awakening, right?"

"It seems likely," agreed Connor.

"So maybe *before* the Great Awakening, all the

people of Faerie had wings."

"Or maybe only the people who lived *here* had wings," said Connor.

"But if that was the case, then why would all Faerie children still have wings. No, there has to be more to it than that."

"Sister, our quest is to find a cure for the plague," Rathina reminded her. "All else is devoid of purpose."

"Yes, I *know*!" Tania said in exasperation. "But what if the two things are linked somehow?"

"How so?" asked Rathina.

"I don't know." She stared ahead into the swirling, metallic gloom. "Perhaps we'll find out when we reach Caer Fior."

"If there's anything left to find," said Connor.

As they walked on, they began to see shapes lifting all around them. Cracked walls. Broken buildings. Ruined towers. Rubble. Fish glided in and out among the wreck and debris, and seaweed grew between the stones, lifting green fronds and ribbons and filigree fingers to the fading light that filtered down from above.

Crabs scuttled away and half-seen shapes flicked out of sight as they moved through the ruins, their steps sending up clouds of fine dust so that soon the water was misty with floating motes and scraps.

Tania paused in the middle of all the ruination, looking to the left and the right. As far as she could see in every direction, they were surrounded by desolation and destruction. Not a single building of the Lost Caer had survived intact, and most were just heaps of tumbled stone, overgrown and half-sunken in the mud.

Rathina picked her way off to one side. Tania saw what had drawn her: two pillars with a high curved lintel stood intact among all the decay. Rathina stood staring up at the lintel, her arms hanging at her sides, her hair falling like a black banner down her back.

Tania and Connor made their way to where she was standing.

There were words on the arch of the lintel. Tania could make nothing of the script, but it seemed similar to the writing on the map.

"Can you read it?" she asked Rathina.

"I can, but it has no meaning," she replied. "Or none that I can understand."

"So what does it say?" asked Connor.

"*Sorai . . . cordai . . . balai . . .*" Rathina intoned. "Endless . . . sleep . . . village . . ." She looked at them. "But here the words run together, as though to make a single word. I cannot comprehend what such a thing may mean. The village of endless sleep?"

Tania walked under the arch. She came into a wide flat area of mud and silt, out of which lifted rows and rows of flat stone slabs, each of them more or less waist-height and maybe a couple of feet across. She narrowed her eyes, trying to think what this reminded her of.

Something. Something so very familiar . . .

Connor stood at her side. "It's a cemetery," he said. "Those are gravestones."

"Cemetery? Gravestones?" said Rathina. "I know these words not."

Tania shivered, a bleak coldness rising up through her veins.

Someone is walking on my grave. . . .

"It's where dead people are put," she said. "It's what we do in the Mortal World, Rathina. We have special places where people are laid to rest when they die. We dig a hole and put the body of the dead person in it."

"And we mark the place with a gravestone," said Connor, moving in among the close-packed stones, running his fingers over the rough, time-eaten surfaces.

"I do not understand," said Rathina.

"Don't you?" Tania sighed. "I think I do." She turned to her sister. "The people of Faerie used to be Mortal," she said. "This is where they were buried when they died."

"No!" Rathina cried. "Such a thing is not possible."

"Take a look at this." Connor had moved some way into the landscape of gravestones and was crouching by a particular stone. "Most of the writing on these stones has eroded away, but this one has something readable on it." He looked over to where they were standing. "Rathina? Come and read it for us."

"No!" Rathina's eyes blazed. "This is some trick—some illusion conjured to fuddle our wits. We were ever Immortal. *Ever!* I will not believe otherwise." She turned, as if meaning to run from the desolate place.

Tania caught hold of her wrist. "You have to read it!" she declared. "You must!"

Rathina narrowed her eyes in angry defiance, but she did not try to fight back as Tania drew her through the stones to where Connor was crouching.

Rathina turned her head away, refusing to look at the stone.

"Rathina!" Tania said sharply. "Read it! Tell us what it says."

Slowly, reluctantly, Rathina lowered her gaze and focused her eyes on the stone. She licked her lips, her whole body trembling. "No! No!" she murmured, covering her eyes. "Never! Never! *Never* . . ."

Tania stepped in front of her, pulling her hands away from her face. Rathina looked as pale as death.

"Read it out loud, Rathina," Tania said. "We need to know."

Rathina gathered herself, her voice faltering and cracked, as though every word came into her throat like a shard of broken glass.

"'Here lie the Mortal remains of Androvar Ernial, son of Faerie,'" she read. "'Beloved husband and father, one of many brought to death before their allotted time by the Dark Plague of Nargostrond, cursed be his name. May our loved one's wings take his dear, sweet soul to timeless sleep in the blessed land of Avalon.'" Rathina dropped to her knees, her face in her hands again, weeping helplessly.

Tania and Connor stared at each other.

"So there was *another* plague," said Connor.

"Thousands of years ago, before Oberon was made King."

Tania felt as though everything she knew, everything she understood about Faerie, was crumbling away beneath her feet.

"They were Mortal," she said. "And they all had wings. So what happened? How did everything change? And why does no one *know* about this?"

"Because it is forbidden," said a soft, gentle voice.

Tania glanced down at her sister. Rathina was still crouched on the ground, but her face was turned upward now, her eyes silvery and vacant, her arms hanging loose.

"Rathina?"

It wasn't Rathina's voice, but it was coming from Rathina's moving lips. "It was agreed in the Ancient Covenant," said the voice as Rathina's lips moved. "That none should ever know, that none should ever remember the time before time."

"Who are you?" Tania asked.

"Do you not know me? Ahh, then mayhap it is better so," said the voice. "Call me Dream Weaver. I have guided your footsteps to this place—and I will guide you farther, if you have the heart. I will guide you all the long miles to journey's end. Will you be led by me?"

"You sent the dream?"

"I sent the dream."

"Is that your sister or not?" hissed Connor.

Tania shook her head. "I need to understand what's going on," she said to the presence that had taken over

Rathina's body. "Can you explain it to me?"

"Winged we were, before time was," said the Dream Weaver. "Winged throughout our merry Mortal lives. But a great enemy came to these shores from the uttermost north. Nargostrond was his name, and a terrible plague he brought with him, breathing out evil all across this fair land. Many are those who died, from the lowliest to the most high, and not even the family Royal was spared. The King and Queen died, and also died all their children save two—save their youngest son, Cornelius, and his older brother Oberon Aurealis.

"And Cornelius was sick and like to die, and in his grief Oberon prayed to the great spirits to show him the way to save his brother and his land. And he was told to take ship and to travel into the west, over Alba, over Erin, over Hy Brasseil, and even to Tirnanog. And there he would find the Divine Harper, and there would he learn how Faerie might be saved.

"But the Divine Harper gives not lest he receive something in return. This was the Covenant struck: that all sickness would be banished forever from the land of Faerie and that the people would become Immortal so that nevermore could Nargostrond do them harm. But the price of this Covenant was that the power of flight should be taken from them. And so it was."

"Yes, yes, I understand," said Tania. "They gave up wings for Immortality. But the plague has come back. What went wrong?"

"Two conditions did the Divine Harper attach to the Covenant," said the Dream Weaver. "That the people of Faerie should remember nothing of their old world, their old lives, and that the Covenant would hold true only so long as Oberon ruled in Faerie. Were his rule ever broken, then the Covenant would fail and the ancient enemy would be free to return once more."

"I don't understand," said Tania. "Oberon is still King."

"His rule was broken," said the Dream Weaver. "For thirteen days did the Sorcerer King of Lyonesse hold him close prisoner. For thirteen days did the Sorcerer King sit upon the throne of Faerie. The Rule of Oberon was sundered for that time, and thus did the Covenant fail."

"So what can we do—what can *I* do to put things right?"

"Travel the road that Oberon Aurealis once traveled," said the Dream Weaver. "Go into the west and seek out the Divine Harper. Renew the Covenant."

"Can I really *do* that?"

"I do not foretell," said the Dream Weaver. "I speak only of what is needed. I cannot say whether you will succeed or fail in the quest. But beware, Tania, the Divine Harper will ask a price for his help. He will ask a heavy price. Are you prepared to pay that price?" Her voice became ominous. "Even if it means losing that which is dearest to your heart?"

"Yes, of course." She looked into Rathina's vacant

face. "But why didn't you tell me all this before? Why wait till now?"

"Because it was forbidden to speak of it within the Realm of Faerie," said the Dream Weaver. "Caer Fior lies no longer in Faerie, and so here am I able to tell you the truth." Rathina's mouth smiled. "What would you do with this truth, Tania?"

"Whatever I must. But you have to help me. You have to tell me what to do next."

"Find you a ship and sail across the Western Ocean—and fare you well, Tania, fare you well." The voice faded and suddenly Rathina jerked and blinked and gave a gasp and was herself again.

She scrambled to her feet, grasping hold of Tania's arms. She gasped. "What creature was that? I was turned to stone! I could hear her voice in my head, but I could do nothing to fight her. Her power came not from the Mystic Arts, of that I would swear."

"I don't care who she is," Tania said. "She's given us the information we needed." She turned to Connor, who was staring at her with round eyes.

"I have to go," she said.

"Yes. I heard," he said. "Across the Western Ocean. I want to come with you."

"And I," said Rathina. "You cannot go on this quest alone, Tania; indeed you cannot!"

Tania let out a gasp of relief. "Thank you," she said, looking from one to the other. "I don't think I could have done it on my own." She turned, looking back the way they had come. "We have to get back to land," she said. "We have to find a ship that will take us to Tirnanog. All of Faerie is depending on us!"

"Then let us not keep Faerie waiting," said Rathina, linking arms with Tania and with Connor. "Let us be gone."

They walked together out of the drowned graveyard of ruined Caer Fior and began the long climb that would take them out of the sea and onto the dry land of the Earldom of Weir.

And then?

A ship—a ship to take them across the Western Ocean to journey's end.

Epilogue

The slender white-hulled sloop crested the waves, skimming like a flat stone, running fast before the strong east wind. The triangular sails belled, straining against the single mast; the fine rigging hummed.

Rathina was at the tiller, singing lustily, her hair whipping about her face, her cheeks red and her eyes bright.

Connor was sitting up against the mast, coiling rope and practicing knots.

Tania stood at the prow, their speed driving her hair like fire into her eyes, the spray spangling her face, the morning sun already hot on her back.

She stared out over the fretful sea, away and away to the clear blue horizon. She thought sadly of her Mortal mother and father, lost to her for all time behind impenetrable barriers. And she thought also of the King and Queen and her other sisters in Veraglad Palace, struggling against the dark tide of a disease that threatened utterly to overwhelm them.

I will save them! I will! Nothing is going to stop me! I won't rest until Nargostrond's plague is driven from Faerie forever!

At her back the dark coast of Weir was falling away. Ahead of her lay new lands where lay the answers to all riddles: a cure for the plague.

Over the shimmering horizon . . .

She recalled her mother's words, spoken to her long ago and far away. She had not realized at the time how those words would resound in her mind and in her heart.

Beyond the flaxen coasts and heathered glens of Alba, beyond the emerald hills of Erin of the enchanted waters, beyond even dragon-haunted Hy Brassail, far, far away to the land of Tirnanog, where the Divine Harper spins his songs at the absolute end of the world.

And now she was in a ship, racing headlong toward those half-remembered islands of Faerie lore. In her hands she held the fate of every soul who dwelled in the Immortal Realm.

She would not fail them!

Follow Tania's quest to save Faerie in

The
ENCHANTED
QUEST

Book Five *of The* FAERIE PATH

The Faerie Realm is no longer under its safe cloak of Immortality. Tania is determined to find a way to save her people. With the guidance of the Dream Weaver, she, Rathina, and Connor must search for the only one who can help them renew the Faerie Covenant of Immortality. Their quest will take them outside the borders of Faerie to hostile and unwelcoming lands beyond. . . .

As tensions and dangers rise, Tania is forced to question everything and everyone around her in order to decide if she is prepared to make the ultimate sacrifice to save her loved ones.